Ian H. James was born in 1948 in the town of Cheshunt in Hertfordshire, England. He met and married Béatrice, a French student spending a year in England as an au pair. They settled down to married life in Shrewsbury and had two daughters, Chloé and Lucie. Ian became a teacher of science and mathematics at several schools in Shropshire before retiring and moving to France where he now resides.

Ian H. James

20A LORDSHIP ROAD

AUSTIN MACAULEY PUBLISHERS™

LONDON • CAMBRIDGE • NEW YORK • SHARJAH

A CIP catalogue record for this title is available from the British Library.

ISBN 9781528964579 (Paperback)
ISBN 9781528965163 (ePub e-book)

www.austinmacauley.com

First Published 2022
Austin Macauley Publishers Ltd®
1 Canada Square
Canary Wharf
London
E14 5AA

Preface

My mother gave birth to her fourth child on Saturday, 27 November 1948; it was 2.00 p.m. I was born at home, under the supervision and support of a midwife.

We were four siblings; two born before the war and two after, and I was the youngest. By the time I was able to understand and communicate, my eldest brother, Derek, had left the house and had been conscripted to the RAF to complete his remaining 18 months of National Service in Singapore.

The house in which I was born (20A Lordship Road) had only been occupied by my future family for a few months before my birth. Coming from the London suburbs, they settled in the green-belt area of Cheshunt in Hertfordshire. Unlike the other two-storey houses in our street which were parallel to the road, ours, at three storeys, was not only bigger than all the others, it also faced at right angles to them and was parallel with Cheshunt Great House.

It was many years later that I began to understand more about our house through comments and research carried out by my fellow post-war brother, Colin. Though this story is fictional, the events that I experienced in the house are real, as is the outcome of Cheshunt Great House.

In the stained-glass window on our front door was a picture of Oliver Cromwell. Why Oliver Cromwell should be depicted, as he had no known attachments to Cheshunt unlike his son, Richard Cromwell who resided in Cheshunt around 1680, using a hidden identity in the form of John Clarke, until his death in 1712, remains a mystery? Though recorded as being buried at Hursley, in Winchester, there was rumour that his real resting place was, in fact, in an unmarked tomb in the grounds of St Mary's Church, in Cheshunt. Adding weight to this possibility, outside and inside St Mary's Church, there are monuments and family vaults dedicated to the *Cromwell Family of Cheshunt Park*.

St Mary's Church was close to, or in part of, the former grounds of Cheshunt Great House, which was gifted to Cardinal Thomas Wolsey by Henry VIII, and, as the crow flies, St Mary's Church was less than two minutes' walk from our house. In fact, Cheshunt Great House was only ten minutes away. Our road was a cul-de-sac; its name was '*Lordship Road*.' The lands at the end of the road, were formerly called '*The Lordship*' before becoming open ground and finally a playing field. Lordship Road, had not been constructed at the time of Cromwell, but had been built over an existing track leading up to *The Lordship*. One can only speculate at this strange name; perhaps, it is more than a just coincidence that one terminology for an Archbishop is *Your Lordship*? So, perhaps the association of the ground being part of the Cheshunt Great House estate is more than a myth?

Our road, which extended for about three-hundred yards ended at a right-angled junction to another road named *Cromwell Avenue*; again, lending itself to speculation about the involvement of the Cromwell family with Cheshunt. Not too far away from Cheshunt Great House, another significantly named road was *Wolsey Avenue*.

Our house was constructed in 1893 and the garden, which stretched for about 80 yards was, supposedly, recorded as previously having a small lake. However, the hunting lodge or gate house to Cheshunt Great House may have been formerly positioned exactly where our house was built, as not only did we have a cellar under the kitchen…we also had a tunnel. Well, we reputedly had a tunnel. Though my dad and brother Derek spent time down in the cellar, they never discovered an open tunnel; however, evidence of older masonry work, dissimilar to the surrounding stone work was apparent; as were the rumours from older neighbours regarding Richard Cromwell and a tunnel connecting St Mary's Church to our house. At the time of Wolsey's occupancy, England was about to undergo the biggest religious purge and persecution in its history; the replacement of Catholicism to Protestantism. Tunnels were needed.

Our next-door neighbours, were Mr and Mrs Palmer, who lived at 20B. Considering the size of our house and the age, I think it highly unlikely that it was constructed as a semi-detached; especially with numbers 20A and 20B. I believe, therefore, that it was originally constructed as 20 Lordship Road. The dividing wall between our two properties was by the kitchen and the stairway leading up to the first-floor bedrooms. Though I never went inside the Palmer's house, did their stairway rest alongside ours; the dividing wall separating a more grandiose stairway? The Palmer's garden ended after about 20 yards and our garden then formed a right-angled attachment to the end of theirs and continued down past a brook to an alley leading into Ripley Way and the small council estate.

Another interesting feature about Cheshunt was London's *Temple Bar*, occasionally used to display the heads of traitors on its iron spikes. The last heads being displayed were those of Townley and Fletcher. Believed to have been constructed by Sir Christopher Wren, its location in Fleet Street was deemed inappropriate because of its restriction to the rapidly increasing traffic entering London. So, on 2 January 1878, just 200 years after it had been built, Temple Bar was dismantled. The corporation of London, however, had a strong attachment to the Bar, and consequently, rather than demolish it, it was taken down brick by brick, beam by beam, numbered stone by stone and stored in a yard off Farringdon Road. Ten years later, Lady Meux, a lowly barmaid marrying the son of a wealthy family of London brewers, decided, with view to impressing Victorian high society of her new position in the social order, to buy it and re-erect it at the entrance to her estate, at Theobalds Park, Cheshunt.

Temple Bar, just after it was rebuilt in 1889.The road to the left leads to the A10 and to the right to Enfield Chase.

The house in 1960 as I remember it. The road in front is Goff's Lane. Facing the house are the playing fields and behind me is Dark Lane.

The banqueting hall in the 19th century

The banqueting hall in 1910. The caretaker is sitting on a chair to the right.
Hertfordshire Archives and Local Studies

St Mary's Church, 1915

St Mary's Church, Cheshunt

20A Lordship Road

Chapter 1

I stood in my cot and looked out at the dark world from my bedroom window. At less than two years old, I knew there was something sinister, something strange about this house. The tree on the horizon swayed near the street lamp and then, as though it knew I was gazing up, uprooted itself and bound towards me—roots and branches crushing all underneath its enormous weight. I was mesmerised, but then I became frightened—it was coming for me! I screamed! I screamed!

"What's wrong, baby?"

"The tree! It's coming for me!"

"What tree, baby?"

Shaking and through tear-stained eyes, I pointed my finger out of the window as mother lifted me from the confines of my bedding. Holding me close, she peered out of the window.

"What tree? The are no trees outside—see, look…"

I slowly uncovered my fingers from my eyes and looked through them and out into the dark. She was right, there was no tree…now, but there was a minute before!

"You've just had a bad dream, baby. Hush and go to sleep, all will be well."

With that, she laid me back down in my cot, pulled the covers over my young body, kissed me on my cheek and left.

In the dark, I lay trembling. I knew what I had seen, I hadn't been sleeping; it had been real.

Well, that was over seventy years ago, but I still vividly recall that moment; the moment that I became aware of unknown, unseen forces that were greater and more powerful than I could see with my everyday senses.

"But you were young…much too young to remember such an event?"

"Why? When are we supposed to recall events…or dreams; at what age, then? Six…seven…?"

"I don't know that anyone can put a definition on which age such traumas that you recount can be relied upon. I believe that you hallucinated and…"

"I was actually lying down in my cot and felt a need to stand up and look out of the window. Hallucination…possibly? But it was no bad dream; it felt real, I tell you."

"That was the first time that I remember that I was frightened, though on reflection, that was not the first occurrence that I found strange. That was when I was just over one-year old…"

"Hold on, hold on! No one can remember when they were one-year old!"

"I was born in November…late November and the occasion that I remember was Christmas Eve. Now, either I was one-month old, or I was one-year old; well, thirteen-months old to be exact. Now, I don't think a one-month-old baby would be able to recall events such as I recall…and be able to sit up and play with simple toys."

"Surely, you must have been two-years old, then?"

"No, one-year old; I had not yet experienced the tree drama…and I did not know how to be frightened, as I was with the tree."

"Well, what was this *first* occurrence, then?"

"I was laying in my cot and a figure stood at the end of my bedding; it was an adult and its clothing was not clothing that I was used to seeing. I did not see the face, only the torso and legs…stockinged and dark red, but within a few seconds, it turned and left the room. At the end of my bedding was a large sock and inside the sock were wrapped presents."

"That was one of your parents pretending to be Santa!"

"Perhaps, but the strange thing was, the door remained closed as the figure left; it had not been opened. I was not at all worried, just curious about the contents of this stocking. Inside, amongst other things, were some toy, plastic cars. Two of the colours have left a lasting impression on me—red and green. It was the intensity of the colours that absorbed my interest."

"One-year old, you say!"

"Yes, one-year old…absolutely!

After the tree experience, I was afraid to go upstairs—we had a three-storey house. The second-level was ok, as this was the level that I slept at, as did my parents. It was the top floor that really frightened me."

"Most children are frightened of going upstairs."

"Are they? Well, perhaps not as I was. I really felt as though once at the top floor, I would be imprisoned and held against my will."

At the very top, there was a door with a latch that led into my sister's bedroom. In fact, this was an old attic and stretched the length of the house. I managed from time to time to climb the second staircase up to the door, but dare not push down on the latch and look into the room beyond.

A few years later, my parents were both out and I was alone. Dad, well, he was working and mum, she had gone out to complete her shopping. In those days, women mainly stayed at home to look after the house and raise the family. I'm not sure of my age, but I guess I was nearly five. Yes, I know; who would leave their four-year old child at home! But that's the way things were. After all, mum couldn't drive and had to rely on public transport and, I suppose, dragging a reluctant four-year old, would have added to the pressure of needing to get back home to complete the daily domestic chores. As I wasn't very well at this time, and with the onset of winter, mum probably decided that this was the wisest and safest option, especially with a previous experience…perhaps I was three, mum and I were waiting for the bus at the *Old Pond* to take us home. Though she was holding my hand, she let go as she got on and, with the bustling, the crowded bus left with me still at the bus stop. I was terrified and didn't know what to do. Realising that I was not on, the bus came to a sudden halt, some 100 yards away. Standing on the platform, she yelled to me to run and I did, much to the relief of both me and mum.

I think that I was too young to go to primary school, though I did attend a nursery school from time to time. Despite being off-colour, curiosity grew and I needed an adventure; an outlet for my querying mind. The kitchen door that led to the stairs was shut. It was mostly shut, I suppose, to prevent heat from rising and cooling the living area. I was now tall enough to reach the latch and needed no adult to assist me. Tentatively, I pressed on the latch and tugged on the door. It opened with a grating noise. I looked up the stairs, these same stairs that I climbed every night to go to bed-but then there would be others in the house; others to keep me safe…safe from prying, unseen eyes. I put my foot on the first step and left the door to the kitchen open. Looking upwards, the stair carpet, held down with solid, brass stair rods, looked threadbare.

On either side, the painted stair boards were no longer white, but stained yellow and the paint cracking. I moved to the second stair, holding onto the handrail, more for security, than balance. As the third step creaked under my weight, I stood still and looked down at the latched door below me. There below, was warmth and safety; no harm down there. But here, I felt more vulnerable. From here, though, I could dash down the stairs and shut the door on any unwelcome visitor chasing after me.

I looked up at the landing. Daylight shone from the small window and highlighted the red cushion on the chair underneath. Holding tight onto the handrail, I pushed myself up another step. Whether I could dash and escape now, was less certain. By the fifth step, I could see the chair completely, but not yet make out the landing. On the sixth step, I could see the landing carpet in its mixture of patterns-greys, blues and reds. The light suddenly darkened, as the sun became obscured by some passing clouds. I grew frightened as the light diminished and the colours of the carpet blended into one colourless and soulless fabric. But this was momentary and the sun shone again. With this new intensity of light, my courage returned and I lifted myself onto the landing. This was where all our bedrooms were located-except for my sister's; hers was at the very top.

Stealthily, I made my way into the bedroom that I shared with Colin. Normally, a safe, comfortable place, but not today; not on my own. I had a toy gun, which lay on the floor by my bed and felt it prudent to take this with me. Creeping out of our bedroom, I hesitantly pushed my head around mum and dad's bedroom door, which was ajar. This room felt safe; but this wasn't the reason that I had climbed the stairs—that reason still had to be faced. Circling around the landing, I stood by the bathroom door which was adjacent to the next set of stairs and looked up. There was no stair carpet here; just plain, wooden steps. Unlike with the first stairway, these stairs were divided into two and separated by a small landing, just wide enough for two people to pass and about three yards long. On this small landing, was also a window, but smaller than the one below. It let in enough light to see without the need for an electric lamp, or torch. The final stairs, towards my sister's bedroom, were at 180^0 to those that I had just climbed. As with the first stairway, I took hold of the painted banister and started to climb. Another cloud passed and I was in almost complete darkness. I panicked, turned and fled down the stairs to the safety of the kitchen."

16

Chapter 2

I ran into the wooden shed and panicked. I needed to hide…hide, but where? I could hear the running steps on the gravel outside and the pounding on the door. There was not much choice and I tried to duck under the bench, but my movements were sluggish and despite every effort, I could not slide under the bench and flee from my pursuers.

"There is no room here…you must hide."

The small girl looked at me with a face that looked both kind and yet hid an underlying secret.

"Let me under…let me under…"

But she had gone and I grappled to clamber under the bench. As I did so, a soldier burst in through the door as I lay on the ground and I could feel the heat from the shots as they pierced my flesh and penetrated into my body. The thudding of the bullets as the machine gun continued to fire was relentless and I just prayed for it to stop and cried out:

"STOP! STOP! Please stop!"

The hand shook me as my body reverberated to the thudding gunshots.

"STOP!"

"IAN!"

I looked up; my mum was shaking me awake.

"IAN! Another nightmare?"

My bed and my pyjamas were soaked in sweat.

"Mum…I don't like this house."

Luckily, it was not a school day and I didn't have to leap out of bed and get dressed, but the bedding was drenched and my mum needed to change the sheets, so I, thankfully, got up and changed into some dry clothes. The frequency of my nightmares had started to increase and I had begun to dread going to bed.

Chapter 3

"What was your next recollection?"

"Did I tell you about the tunnel?"

"Tunnel? No; is that relevant?"

"Well, not at the time, no; but later, much later, I wondered whether there was any connection?"

"Go on."

"In our kitchen, we had a cellar. The entrance to the cellar was through a trap-door in the floor. This cellar was not used by us; I mean it was filthy down there and the floor was only rubble and dried mud. Consequently, dad covered the kitchen floor in lino, as we had no need to go down."

"How did you know what it was like if you couldn't go down?"

"Dad told me."

"Ok."

"When mum came back from her shopping, after I had been ill, she found the place as she had left it and I had behaved myself. So, when she needed to pop out, she felt more confident to leave me at home—especially as she only was out for a short while. As I mentioned, we only had the one car, which dad had to use to get to work and she had to use the London buses."

"London buses! I thought that you lived in the *Green Belt*?"

"Cheshunt *was* in the Green Belt. In fact, Cheshunt had a plethora of greenhouses growing food; recovering from the war, I guess. The North London suburbs ended at Enfield, but London Transport provided services out as far as South Mimms and our house was near the bus route."

"Hm, hm…"

"I am not sure how long it was after my scare of going up to my sister's room, but I was older, albeit it only a few weeks, but older, braver, not ill…and inquisitive."

"A few weeks doesn't make you *older*!"

"When you are very young, a few weeks makes a lot of difference."

"Well, I beg to differ…so, carry on."

"Feeling bolder, I climbed the stairs to my sister's bedroom and stood outside. I placed my hand on the latch and as I did so, felt that same apprehension that I had those weeks before. I wanted to press down on the latch but, whether it was fear or something else, it wouldn't press."

"Wouldn't press?"

"No, wrong word, I couldn't press it. I had the strength to press it, but the will to do so was lacking; it was as though I shouldn't press it…as if to do so would unleash all kinds of terror, like a Pandora's Box, from which there would be no escape. I hesitated, and as I did so, was certain that I could hear movement and voices inside. My sister was at school, well, she was a teenager now and being at Grammar School, did not have the luxury that I had of being at home. So, who could be inside? I wanted to find out; my curiosity was begging me to find out, but my fear…my foreboding of what harm may be behind that door, was preventing the simple task of pushing down on the latch. Then I heard it! Clear as day…"

"Come in then! Don't dally, come in!"

It was not a voice I recognised; it was like a whisper and had an air of menace in its tone; like a threat, not an invitation. Though my hand was on the latch, it was not I who pushed it down, but down it went. At this instant, I didn't push on the door, I pulled; pulled so hard to stop this pandemic from leaving the room to spread its cadaverous filth throughout the house.

"I said, COME IN!"

And with that, the door was wrenched from my grasp and I stood facing a blazing room. The heat was unbearable as I watched the wardrobe, bed, curtains and furniture being enveloped in flames. The roar and crackling of that inferno was overpowering. I put my hands up to my face to shield the heat, turned and fled down the stairs. I reached the safety of the kitchen, but as I did so, heard the unmistakeable sounds of other feet running down the stairs. In an instant, they were there; it happened so fast it became a blur, but the torso and legs entered the kitchen and disappeared through the trap-door. Terrified, I opened the kitchen door and leapt out into the garden…and safety. Mum arrived shortly after.

"Playing outside, Ian?"

"Yes, mum, because of the fire."

"Fire! What fire…where?"

"Upstairs in Maureen's room."

"Maureen's room!"

"Don't go, mum, it's too hot; you'll get burnt."

But my mum sped into the kitchen, dropped her shopping on the table and ran up the stairs. I cautiously followed and when I got to the top, mum was inside Maureen's room.

"Ian, don't make up stories like that; I was really scared. I thought that there really was a fire."

I peered into the same room that had been blazing a few moments before, but everything was normal; well, unburned; I didn't really know what normal was like in my sister's bedroom, but there was nothing to suggest that any fire had taken place.

"Mum, honestly, there was a fire…and a man told me to come in…and…"

"IAN! Enough! No more lies."

I was upset because mum didn't believe me and she had scolded me, even though I had told her the truth. But there was nothing to support what I had witnessed; nothing to show the inferno I vividly stood in front of; nothing to suggest still remotely that any catastrophe had taken place. I had forgotten, in that moment with the injustice of not being believed, the feet following me downstairs and disappearing below the kitchen floor.

Chapter 4

I'd like to say that I remember the date, but I was too young. I had to rely on my older brother, Colin to recall the exact date. It was 2 February, 1954. I had now been going to Burleigh Primary School in Blindman's Lane, since September 1953. I wasn't yet old enough to wash myself, and showers, for the large part, were not an everyday feature of the old houses of Lordship Road. My nightly routine would be to sit on the kitchen table, whilst my mum gave me a flannel wash. It was dark and I waited for her to come in from the garden with the washing that had been hanging outside on the line.

As I sat on the table pushing a small plastic car, I heard a commotion upstairs, together with the sound of running feet. My sister, Maureen was out at the pictures with a German student, Wilhelm Hürner, who was staying with us whilst he studied English. Colin and dad were in the room next-door and so I was at a bit of a loss as to who was upstairs; and why the commotion. It didn't bother me; I was just curious. Then feet tumbled down the stairs and the same voice that I had heard a few months back, when I had gone up to my sister's bedroom, shouted 'Fire, fire…get out, get out!' and with that fled into the cellar beneath the kitchen floor. As before, the form was unclear and only the legs and lower torso were apparent; but also, the lino over the kitchen floor prevented easy access into the cellar. I was frightened, but I was also worried that having been chastised previously about the 'fire-that-never-was,' if I told my mum when she came back in, I would be in for more scolding.

With a big smile on her face when she came in, she placed all the shirts on the table beside me and they were rigid with frost. In fact, they were so frozen, they could be smacked against the wall and produce a dull thud. My attention was now on the stiff and rigid shirts. I took a sleeve and tried to bend it, but it would not give; it was solid.

"Shall we use this as the flannel, Ian," she said with a smile.

Touching me on the face with the icy shirt, I cowered quickly as I felt the cold and pushed my arms around my face. She then proceeded to wash me. There was a knock at the front door and I heard two male voices, one being my dad's. Suddenly, he dashed into the kitchen, and opening the latch to the stairway, raced upstairs. Within seconds, he almost fell down the stairs as he panicked, shouting, "Fire, fire…get out, get out!"

The very same words that I had heard, but a few minutes ago, but this time, it was my dad's voice. My mum, wrapped me in a blanket and we all dashed outside and looked up at the blazing chimney and roof. I was still far too young to appreciate the seriousness of what was before us and within a few minutes, fire-engines were outside our house trying to put out the inferno. Mr Atkinson, who had, I found out afterwards been the other voice talking to my dad informing him of the catastrophe in our home, and his wife, put us up for the night in their house, which was at the bend on Lordship Road.

I walked to school the next day, as if nothing had happened. After all, I really was still too young to appreciate the momentousness of what had taken place. When I got back home later that day, dad took me upstairs to the burned-out shell of the attic and my sister's bedroom; the same room that I had witnessed ablaze but a few months ago. I smelled the damp, burned wood. It is a smell that has remained with me for all my life; if I smell burned, damp wood, I am immediately drawn to that scene as a five-year old, holding my dad's hand. I gazed out from a roof that had no tiles. The late afternoon sun, with a clear sky, heralding another cold, frosty night ahead, reflected in the puddles on the charred flooring. Here was the reality, and yet I knew that I had been warned about this fire several months before. My mum had not believed me, though she had every right, as there was nothing to suggest that what I, a four-year old, had told her, was anything other than a fantasy; a made-up story; or was this a re-enactment of something that had happened in the past? Or was it a portent of something still to come?

Steven Parker was a little boy, aged about eighteen-months; he had an older brother, Albert, who was about the same age as Colin. He lived three-doors down from our house and was nicknamed '*Pappy*' by Colin because of his appearance. These were the days of cotton nappies and Pappy always stood by the gate at the end of his small garden, with a nappy fully of poo and pee. He must have been uncomfortable carrying this around. With sore thighs and bottom, he was always crying, clinging to the gate, with his dummy on the ground. I was too young to appreciate Pappy's situation; it was only later I realised what he must have been going through.

At the side of the Parker's Garden was a narrow path, separating their house from their neighbour's. This path was just wide enough for one person to walk down. Snivelling, Pappy, watched me as I passed him and went down the path to his back garden. At the back, this path joined another path, which led past the rear of all the houses on this side of Lordship Road. With overhanging trees, it was dark and did not feel very welcoming. The path was beside a slope leading down to the bank of a brook. I did not know it then, but found out when I was older that this brook, which flowed past our house was the same brook which flowed past Cheshunt Great House. It made sense, therefore, that this brook would have supplied the water that fed the lake that was supposedly where our garden now was. I don't know why I went down to the brook, but when I looked back, Pappy was there watching me. I started to walk alongside the water's edge and turned to look again at Pappy; but he was not watching me. His gaze was directed along the path, which eventually stopped at the front of the Palmer's house, alongside the brook. He pointed and following his gaze, I thought that I could make out a turbulent scene before me, but remained unsure. The turbulence became a hazy outline of a bare-headed man, running, as though being pursued. I awoke from my reverie as Pappy let out a scream and I ran from the brook and back of the houses to the lighter and safer road at the front.

When I was a bit older, without realising its significance, I went into the playing fields, right in front of Cheshunt Great House. The area was divided into two large fields, one, on the left of the house contained the changing rooms and rugby pitch, whist the other one, directly in front of the house, held two football pitches and a cricket pitch. The two fields were separated by the brook and joined by a small bridge. This vast landscape was totally flat, and I wondered, at times, whether this may not have also supported a shallow lake, as the land was about four-metres lower than Cheshunt Great House. The other end of the field, facing the house, contained raised land and was surrounded by a stagnant moat. In the middle of it, in mediaeval times stood a manor house, though this may have been part of the strategy of the mediaeval aristocracy, as a place of fun, like a tree house, rather than as a habitable dwelling. Once, when I had been collecting tadpoles and newts from this moat, I saw the rigid corpse of a dead dog. It looked like a Terrier, but its hair was matted and decaying, as was the mouth, displaying protruding teeth. I was horrified and ran away, leaving my newts and tadpoles behind.

I arrived home from school one afternoon. It was late October, and though there was some intermittent sun, the weather was cold and very windy. I remember looking up at the great beech tree that we had at the border of our garden with the road and watching the leaves blowing and dropping with the wind. I didn't know it at the time, but this was going to be my last October here. I opened the back door, which was always unlocked and went inside. I knew my mum wasn't going to be in, so put my satchel on the table and went into the front room. Even now, I don't why, but I was scared; scared to go in the house. Was it intuition; was it a premonition; or was it just childish fantasy, I don't know? I didn't want to be seen-I wanted to hide. So, by the dining-room table, I placed all the dining chairs, making a tunnel. I crawled under these and made my way from one end to the other. As I got to the end, they were there! Legs! I was frozen with fear! The legs were not of this era, they were stockinged and dark-red, with strange shoes that I had not seen before. Did they know that I was there under the table? Had they come searching for me? Was there a torso attached to those legs? I remained as still as my fear would let me, but the legs did not move; they remained stationary. I couldn't stay; I had to run. I clambered out of the tunnel, grabbed my coat and scarf and ran out of the back door. I did not attempt to see whether those legs had a body attached, I was too frightened. Shutting the back door, I thought I saw eyes peering at me from the glass in the door as I ran for my swing. I leapt on and swung as hard and as high as I could. Any entity would be unable to catch me now, I thought, and though cold, felt the safety of my swing was preferable to the warmer comfort of a haunted house.

I started to understand fear more; trips to the dentist later taught me that. In those days, drillings were given without any numbing injections and the drills used were the old-fashioned mechanical type, with a grinding vibration on the jaw as the dentist attempted to find the tooth nerve…always successfully. However, fear of the unknown was also increasingly manifesting itself.

Prior to my experience above, I was about four and my mother put me in the bath, leaving me to idle away a few minutes with my toy boats, whilst she went downstairs. I had been washed and this gave us both the opportunity to relax independently. Our house was not modern and the ceiling had been set using plaster coated onto wooden laths. Some of the plaster had broken away and left a gaping hole in the ceiling, which was the base of the flooring to my sister's bedroom above the bath. Not only this, but the laths were left exposed like skeletal fingers. I looked up and felt a slight trepidation. I continued to push the boats around the bath, but kept looking up, with an increasing feeling of unease. As I kneeled on the bath, by the taps, a small portion of the plaster fell into the bath and I looked up. There, staring at me, were two menacing eyes. I could not make out the face as the cavity was totally black, the eyes, though, were sufficient for me to leap out of the bath and run downstairs to the safety of the kitchen and my mother.

Sometime after my sixth birthday, my dad's elderly aunt Mabel came to stay with us. She was severe and totally committed to her Victorian and religious upbringing. Never having had the joy of parenthood, my dad's spinster aunt possessed all the worst virtues of that epoch. Our house became her house and she controlled me with the venom of her upbringing. Later in life, I wondered why my parents did not stand up to her when she scolded me; perhaps, the Victorian hierarchy forbad it and we were all subjected to her harsh wrath. I only remember how she treated me and it made me miserable. I didn't wish her any harm, vengeance hadn't yet become part of my personality, but I did want her gone. At that same time, my parents had recently bought our very first television; a black and white small screened device, which took several minutes to warm up. One of the early soaps of the day was '*The Grove Family*' and *Granny Groves* was one of the key actors, resembling an authoritative old lady. I saw very little difference between her and my dad's aunt and when she appeared on the screen exclaimed:

"Oh, look Aunty, there's you!"

Her rebuff was a surprise, as I was merely pointing out, that to a six-year-old, the resemblance was uncanny.

"You nasty little boy. Go to your room!"

And with sadness, I made my way upstairs. Why my parents did not stand up to her was no surprise as I was now used to being reprimanded for any minor triviality. Merely as curiosity, not as a wish, as though there was a pre-ordained date, I asked her as we were eating one day, "Aunty, when are you going to die?"

I think that if she had had a cane, I would have had the belting of my life, but luckily for me she didn't.

"How dare you! Stan, how do you tolerate his impertinent behaviour?"

Shortly after this, she, as though by power of thought, fulfilled my wishes and conveniently passed into the Great Beyond. I had never seen a dead body before and asked my mother to be shown her corpse. My mother walked into the darkened room and drew back the shroud. Lifeless and white, she was not what I had imagined; she was not the phantoms that I had witnessed since my birth. She lay motionless, and though I could not see her legs, I imagined that these would be motionless too.

Not knowing that this was going to happen, a few weeks later, Colin, my brother and I were put into the very room that my dad's aunt had used and died in. It didn't bother me, in terms of fearing her phantom form would continue to chastise me from beyond the grave and initially, I felt comfortable in this room. However, this was soon to change with more wild and vivid nightmares, some of which, like being shot underneath the bench mentioned earlier, I remember to this day.

I was in a swamp, dark, dank and cold, with vines dangling from overhanging trees. This was not a forest; this was a jungle. I needed to cross this swamp and started to wade into the water. As I got deeper, I saw something monstrous moving swiftly towards me. I ran as best as I could in this murky waterlogged place and as the unknown, submerged creature approached me, grabbed hold of an overhanging vine and pulled myself up from the water. With legs bended to stop contact with the water beneath, a crocodile reared its savage head and started to snap at my feet, inches from its jaws. The vine started to creak and dropped me lower to the gapping open mouth of this reptile. I screamed and screamed and awoke, as my mother ran into our room and comforted me.

"Another nightmare, Ian?"

"Yes, mum…Mum, I'm scared, can I sleep with you, please?"

Trembling and afraid to stay in this room, she took me to her bed and I snuggled up in the care and safety of my mother. However, worse was to come.

My brother and I slept in two separate, single beds, separated by a small set of draws. I was restless as another troubled nightmare took me into the land of fear and dread. I peeped out from under the covers at Colin, who was fast asleep. He could not feel the draught of cold air swirling about the room. Even under the cover of my bedding the cold was penetrating me like an ice-pack. For my sixth birthday, mum and dad had given me a Hornby 00 electric train-set, which relatives could donate to at Christmas with additional accessories. One of the things I really liked about this train-set was the smell of the electric motor, especially if I overloaded the current from the transformer. Despite the penetrating cold, I could now smell the electric motor that my train-set gave.

Faintly, at first, but then the smell became stronger, until it began to absorb onto my tongue and down into my throat. Colin still remained oblivious to the changes occurring in our room as I started to shiver. I blew into the room and the vapour drifted across the expanse between our beds, then dissipated. I peeked out and saw his form rise and fall slowly under his quilt. The door at the end of our room was ajar, as it was every night and opened onto the landing with the bathroom opposite. Mum and dad's bedroom was adjacent and then a spare room next to the bathroom. I turned onto my back, pursed my lips and exhaled more vapour, watching it blow about in the breeze. I pulled the covers back as far as my chin and blew again. This time, the vapour was directed towards the open door, as though it was being channelled by some unseen force. I saw it swirl by the door and remain in turbulence by the floor. I blew again, but as the vapour left my lips, the turbulence began to take on the form of a torso. The added vapour formed below the torso into legs. I was petrified! As I spoke to my brother, to awaken him, the vapour from my mouth joined the already forming shape into the shroud that I had witnessed in this very room a few weeks earlier. I dived under the bedclothes, shivering; both from the cold and fear. The atmosphere was static and I was numb. I wanted to call out to Colin, but the words would not come. I was rigid!

Later, in life, as I took an interest in the occult, ghost stories often involved some menacing form reaching out with skeletal fingers; this was not the case here. The shrouded form remained in the misty vapour from my breath at the doorway, like a sentinel guarding the way to freedom. If there was God, then surely, He would protect me from this monstrosity. As staunch Methodists, we believed fervently in the Almighty and His protection from any evil menace. But my lips could not move to ask for His help. I was spellbound and started sweating profusely. In my mind, I spoke to this Deity, pleading for help and with the sweating, lost all sense of the biting cold. I needed to breathe and the covers of my bedding were stopping this. In desperation, I threw the top of the quilt down and stared at the door…but there was nothing but the dark landing. I was still trembling and too frightened to get out of bed and investigate. I have never mentioned this before; sceptics are always too ready to refute the macabre and things that cannot be logically explained away. I knew what I had seen, and it stays with me to this day.

Cardinal Wolsey

Chapter 5

The Palace of Placentia at Greenwich represented the grandeur and wealth of the monarchy at the potential expense of bankruptcy of the country. Its magnificence and splendour may well have been influential in the building of the Palace of Versailles nearly one hundred and fifty years later. With lawns, gently sloping towards the Thames and gardens that exemplified the horticulturists of the times, this man-made citadel demonstrated the proximity of the ruling dynasty to Paradise…and God. The affluential nobility of the land, themselves, could only marvel with envious eyes at the murals, tapestries, exotica and wealth before them in the fifteen hundred rooms of this temple to the king. Though pewter was the easiest of the manageable metals, only silver was used for the more exclusive guests; and gold for the aristocracy, foreign nobility and royalties. The original abode built in 1443 by Humphrey, Duke of Gloucester now appeared humble and insignificant compared to this royal shrine in which, probably, the greatest Tudor monarch of all times, the future Queen Elizabeth 1, would be born. Words were futile to attempt to describe its opulence.

"Wolsey!"

"Your Majesty?"

"A moment, if you please."

"To what do I owe the privilege, Sire?"

"Come, take a walk with me in these fine gardens."

The monarch and his Lord High Chancellor strolled out onto the glorious lawns sloping gently towards the mighty river below them. Henry, in the magnificence and splendour of his younger years and Wolsey, in his cardinal's robes of scarlet, watched as the setting sun lowered towards the left of the palace. The solace and gentle breezes in the fading light inspired both men.

"What could befit a monarch, man, woman or child to behold such splendour! Even if the world should be devoured today, no finer land was there in this world existed, than England!"

"Indeed, Your Majesty, and if I may say so, by no finer a king."

"Thomas, you have served my father and me faithfully and restored England's rights as the capital of the world. No monarch could have had a more devoted and trusted ally, such as you. The *Treaty of London*-a masterpiece of wielding and diplomacy warrants no less a reward than I offer to you now. My father had built a small country house in the county of Hertfordshire. A modest manor house with some acres of unspoilt land. The deeds are here and I give them to you with unreserved blessing and gratitude."

"My Lord…I am honoured…truly honoured. How could a servant, such as I, be a beneficiary to such generosity? I cannot accept such a bounteous gift."

"Thomas, are you refusing a directive from your king?"

"Directive?"

"Cannot a king be allowed to bestow on those that he holds dear, the occasional gift? Here take these deeds."

Your Majesty…words fail me…"

"Fail you! Damned good they didn't fail you last week at the *Treaty*!"

"Hertfordshire, you say?"

"Yes, Cestrehunt; the locals call themselves Cestrians; but I believe it is now being called '*Cheshunt*' by the modernists in our society. Unspoilt land – good for game, I might even visit there myself once you are settled in."

"An honour and privilege, Sire. But at the moment, I cannot make myself available to this dwelling; why the journey would take the best part of the day and there is much still to do here. I shall, for the moment maintain residence at Hampton; however, the deeds I shall accept with humility. Thank you."

"Good, good…well done, my friend. Thomas, there is an affair afoot, to which I will draw your attention and trust that it will be administered without much delay."

"Your Majesty?"

"You have in your employ, I believe, a young noble cheapskate by the name of *Percy*?"

"Indeed, Sire, *Henry* Percy as befits a good, honest name!"

"I believe that he has intentions with Anne, the teenage daughter of Sir Thomas Boleyn?"

"Of that I am unaware, Sire."

"Hm…so, of this I have heard, though, that may be merely court gossip. That tempestuous teenager has quite an ability for being easy on the eye."

"In all honesty, Sire, the Boleyn's are no more to me than just nobles of the land and their offspring even less so. I cannot say that I am acquainted with the daughter, Anne."

"As I say, easy on the eye. Perhaps this betrothal be best delayed for an indefinite period? I think Catherine has her eyes set upon a younger maid and Anne would suit her nicely. As wedded, she would be less suitable for court duties. Besides, the betrothal needs your agreement, does it not, as master of the household?"

"And yours too, Your Majesty."

"Be that as it may, I think my influence should not be brought into the matter?"

"If this be the case, perhaps, we could soften the blow with, perhaps, a royal favour?"

"A knighthood, you mean?"

"The way to a man's heart is not necessarily through the stomach, Sire. Such a bestowal would incur unwavering loyalty and not impeach you in any way."

"Hm…done! It was good fortune that my father discovered your attributes…England owes you a lot."

"As it does to you, Your Majesty."

The two men disappeared in the fading light as the sun surrendered its hold on the daylight and, with a moonless night, the God of the Underworld took the world into its tortuous grip of fear and superstition.

'*Easy on the eye, easy on the eye*'; Mary Boleyn, Henry's mistress and Anne's sister were easy on the eye, as far as the king was concerned. Wolsey puzzled over the situation that the king had set before him. Jousting, sport, hunting and humping were the king's main outlets for his pleasure, though not necessarily in that specific order. The bastards that Mary conceived were never acknowledged by Henry, the convenience of marriage shielding their illegitimacy; but *Henry Fitzroy* was. What if no male heir could be conceived in marriage, would Fitzroy become the next king? But *easy on the eye* left Wolsey in no doubt of the king's intentions. Another mistress, another bed-partner…another bastard?

As godfather to Henry Fitzroy, Wolsey was a little perturbed concerning his commitment to the boy. Believing the role of *godfather* to be a sacred obligation, he needed to tread diplomatically and carefully in order to satisfy both his secular beliefs and maintain his position as Henry's right-hand man. But that could wait until later, at the moment, the king had given him a command that he had to endorse.

"Percy…"

"Your Eminence?"

"I have it on good authority that you have intentions regarding Lady Anne Boleyn?"

"We are pledged, Your Eminence…"

"Pledged…PLEDGED! Who has given you reason to think that you have the right to *pledge* yourself to anyone without prior sequestering that permission from your employer, father or king?"

"You do not approve, then, Your Eminence?"

"Approve…approve! No, I damn well do not approve. Nor does your father! Do have any idea how many hours and tactful negotiations have been involved in ensuring that the very foundations of England remain firmly in place, and your pledge is nothing more than a hollow and meaningless fantasy!"

"But we are in love…"

"LOVE…LOVE, what the hell's love got to do with it! Serfs, peasants, even yeomen may marry for love, but *love* is not a concern for the nobility of our land…it is not even in the vocabulary of the aristocracy! If love happens to develop after the commitment has been made…well, that is in everybody's good interests; it is the icing on the cake. But love is not the prime reason for unions between the noble families of our land!"

"But we are committed, before witnesses, that I know not how to avoid myself, nor to discharge my conscience."

"Conscience be damned! First, you had absolutely no right whatsoever to commit yourself either verbally or officially to any woman of this land without consultation and approval from both your father and myself. Second, the position of the girl is woe beneath your status…why not marry a servant girl or a harlot, if you wish to denigrate yourself and your dignity so much. Third, the organisation of this country is based on the selections of those privileged few, to ensure continuity of the values that we cherish…"

"But I…"

"DO NOT INTERUPT ME! The backbone of this land is out there right now, striving, working, starving, to keep the likes of you and this blessed country safe and secure and *you* wish to disrupt and condemn this very stalwart regime that has made this land the envy of every nation on God's good Earth! If we were to succumb to every man's whim and spontaneity, this land, of which you have done well by, this land would become like that of the heathen savages of old…unkempt, chaotic, dangerous and constantly warring within its insignificant factions. Centuries of history, invasions, defence, retaliation, organisation and order have, at last, created the very land that we call proudly, England; and you wish to destroy that very order that has made you one of the privileged few! How dare you!"

Wolsey's Usher walked into the room.

"Your Eminence…?"

"Edmund?"

"Sir Henry Percy, 5th Earl of Northumberland…"

"Sir Henry…an opportune moment! I was at this very moment berating your son, Henry Percy, for his unsolicitous declaration of betrothal to Lady Anne Boleyn."

"The very reason that I am here, Your Eminence."

"Father, I…"

"Be quiet! How dare you dishonour me and our good family name with this preposterous annunciation of betrothal to that line of Boleyn's! You will, when the time is right, marry into the family and the woman that I have chosen for you! Your ostentatious behaviour appals me! You will not humiliate the line of the Percy's ever again…failure to attune yourself to my wishes may well see you cast into the realms of obscurity; portraits will be removed as well as acknowledgement of your existence. As my heir, your inheritance is your right by birth, but mark my words, the solicitors are even now awaiting my instructions to amend my will to name your brother as my successor! Do you understand me?"

"Yes father, I do."

"…And wipe your face, boy; no son of mine shows the disgrace of tears in the public rooms and corridors of power! Now, get out, damn you before I whip you to within an inch of your life!"

The tearful Henry Percy left the room, as Wolsey and the 5th Earl of Northumberland fumed over the events that had just taken place.

"Sir Henry, will you join me for lunch…I believe that there is much at hand to discuss."

"Indeed, Your Eminence, and now seems to be as good a time as any."

With tempers in abeyance, the two men strolled out into the grounds of Hampton Court as the servants prepared the table for lunch.

"The king is not in any favour of this union between the Boleyn's and the Percy's."

"Nor am I. The Percy family didn't climb the ranks of the nobility, to merely have one of their lines diminish the status of our name to the level of that of the Boleyn's!"

"He does, however, see an advantage to the union of Lady Anne and James Butler. The issue with the Earldom of Ormond would, at last, be sorted and that has been a thorn in the flesh of Henry and his father before him."

"Indeed, but that is of little consequence to me, Your Eminence, my concern is for that insolent young toe-rag of mine and the Earl of Shrewsbury to combine. Our two earldoms would form one of the greatest nobilities in the land...and he has a daughter, Mary...Mary Talbot. Methinks that an arranged union twixt our two houses would suit the king, grandly. What say you?"

"It would resolve the issue with Lady Anne, and that would please the king grandly. Yes, that would do well."

"Then, may I count upon your support and input into an arrangement twixt the Shrewsbury's and Northumberland's, Your Eminence?"

"Absolutely...and I believe luncheon beckons, Sir Henry..."

Chapter 6

The despatch rider arrived at the manor in the morning dew. Tethering his horse to the stone balustrade, he strode up the steps to the large oak door and knocked loudly with the hilt of his dagger. A second knocking brought a lowly maid to the door.

"Sir?"

"I have correspondence for Lady Anne…"

"I'll see that she gets it, Sir."

"It is for her eyes only…"

"Only her eyes will see it, Sir."

"No, I mean that I will deliver it to her directly…no one else."

"Please wait here, Sir… I will fetch the butler."

After a few moments, before the grand oak door stood the manor's butler, impeccably dressed and with an aloof air, surveyed the unkempt man before him.

"You have correspondence for Lady Anne, I understand?"

"Indeed, I do… but it is for her eyes only."

"I will see that she receives it without delay."

"As I explained to the wench…It must be delivered directly…by me."

"May I be informed of the reason for the correspondence?"

The butler retained an air of arrogance, regarding the man before him as beneath his dignity and offered him no courtesy of a title, such as 'sir.'

"You may not! I have correspondence from His Majesty to be delivered directly to Lady Anne…here, you may recognise his seal!"

The butler, now somewhat flustered having regarded the rider before him as no more than a vagabond, realised that the man was entrusted with confidences from the king and must be accepted within the court. The rider reached within his knapsack and brought out a scroll, with the red stamp of Henry Tudor.

"…Or, perhaps I should return to his Majesty and say that I was denied permission to deliver his personal dispatch by…what is your name…?"

"Very well; please enter and I shall inform my Lady of your arrival."

Anne was at her toilet, with her maid attending her. She gazed out of the window, and despite the brightness of the day, felt morose. Those recent, terrible events had set her heart and mind into dark thoughts and the morning songs from the birds only made her sadder. There, before her, was the advent of hope and new life, but hers was at its terminus. The brush met with tangled hair and pulled at the roots.

"Alice!"

"Sorry, my Lady. There are knots and I fear that more discomfort may be necessary…"

The knock at the door stopped the conversation.

"Yes?"

The butler entered.

"My Lady, there is a rider in the hall with a message from the king."

"What…the king? Where is this message?"

"The rider refuses to part with the correspondence. He said that he has to deliver it to you directly, my Lady."

"Who is this courier with such personal and secretive documents?"

"He did not give his name, my Lady."

"You did not think to ask, then? Am I to give audience to every vagrant that deems it his right to address me directly? Demand it of the man this instant!"

"My lady…"

With a courteous bow, the butler left her room and descended the stairs. Still with the brush stuck firmly in her hair, Anne threw the chair to one side and strode out to the balustrade, watching her servant address the man below. There was something familiar about the man that made Anne decide that she wished to meet with him and read the correspondence that he had brought.

Returning to her boudoir, the maid completed dressing and attending to Anne. Knocking again at her door, the butler returned.

"Sir Henry Norris, my Lady."

"Henry Norris…? Never heard of the man. Ask for his weaponry and show him into the library…I shall attend him in due course."

Now, Anne was intrigued. Sir Henry Norris, Groom of the Stool to Henry Tudor…as a despatch rider!

Sword and dagger were placed on the mahogany table in the hall as the butler led the rider into the library. Looking about him, he noticed an array of books and literature akin to that he himself had back home. Like Anne, awhile before, he stood gazing out at the bright morning, but unlike Anne, the songs of the birds filled his heart with gladness. The door opened and there before him stood Anne, in her gracefulness and elegance. His heart pounded at the sight of the woman before him. Anne, however, saw before her a traveller with the filth of the journey that he had endured and her heart beat as one under duress; but at the same time, her curiosity as to why the Groom of the Stool would travel through the night to bring correspondence from Henry Tudor, sent her mind into a turmoil.

"My Lady Anne."

"Sir Henry…?"

"The freshness of the spring morning brings joy to the heart, does it not?"

"You have ridden through the night to bring me news of the thrill of the morning dew, Sir Henry?"

"Indeed, I have not…but such rapture as befits the very first morning Adam gazed upon Eve could no grander an occasion be such as this."

"Then what, may I ask, requires such secrecy as you have in your possession…correspondence from the king, I understand?"

Sir Henry turned towards Anne, and with a telling smile, reached into his knapsack for the enclosed document. As he gazed at Anne, holding before him the scroll, she felt that knew this man; of that, she was sure. Yes, he was unkempt and dishevelled from the long ride, but there was something in his eyes that she was familiar with; but she had never set her sight upon Sir Henry Norris before, so what was so similar about this man…and his voice.

"This is not the king's seal!"

"No, it is the seal of Wolsey, but the content comes from the highest admirer in the land."

Anne broke the seal, unwrapped the parchment and read the transcript:

Could the water of the mountain stream taste like the kiss you gave to me,
Then I will be that mountain stream flowing, flowing, flowing, onward to the sea.
Onward and over, gliding and rolling, as the ripples of the flow
Hold thy kiss as a memory of that time so long ago.
Yet as a butterfly lifts its wing to the gentle breeze that blows,
The drop of rain on that butterfly falls to the stream that flows
Onward, onward, ever onward with that embrace you gave to me

Your Loving Henry...now and always.

"Did the king really write this?"

"No, Anne...I did."

Anne looked up immediately...the voice! She knew the voice and her heart beat wildly.

"Henry! How? How? I did not recognise you...how did you manage to get here...we are banned? Wait!"

Taking her skirt, she let the water from the jug on the table absorb into the cloth and then lifting the hem up to Henry's face, wiped the dirt and grime away. Removing his hood and with face free from the dust of the journey, she now gazed into the eyes of Henry Percy.

"Henry! Henry...where is your beard...?"

"Gone...for the moment. I could not chance being discovered and the smooth skin kept my true identity well hidden...even you did not recognise me?"

"I recognised...no, I sensed something about you...even from the balustrade I felt that I knew you...somehow, but did not for the life of me think that it was you."

"Anne, hold me, embrace me...as we did at our commitment."

The couple held each other with a passion and fervour akin to that first embrace. Her mind in turmoil, first the sadness of the day and now the excitement of the chase, Anne held her head back and gazed at Henry.

"You do not realise just how fortuitous is your timing to come here, Henry. Mother is visiting family at Arundel, father is in London and I am a prisoner here, in my home."

"...And Wolsey is in Paris with the French king... No, Anne, it was not fortuitous, I knew the arrangements, that is why I chose to come now."

"...And the risk of showing Stowell the king's seal..."

"I feared not...the servants will have no knowledge of the king's seal...nor that of Wolsey's, for that matter. Why, I believe that I could have even used my own?"

"Henry...you mad, mad, adorable fool!"

For the first time since she could remember, Anne smiled. Weeks of isolation, weeks of desolation, weeks of loneliness; and now the man that she loved was in her arms. The reality of her life was now but a bad dream for a few moments, as she absorbed the caress and comfort of her lover.

"Henry, where will you stay…what will you do now?"

"My love, I had not planned beyond holding you again…my thoughts had not dared venture into a scheme that could prolong our union."

"Henry, you will stay here…with me. I shall inform Stowell that the king awaits my reply and that I need time to consider; and you will stay to await my reply, to take to the king!"

"Anne, can we really be together? I knew only that I had to get here…to you. But how long can I stay?"

"Mother said that she would be with the Howard's for several weeks and father's work could keep him at bay for a while…and Wolsey?"

"Wolsey will be gone for the best part of the month. I feel that we could guarantee at least until the solstice to remain undiscovered. But my beard, my clothing…"

"I will tell Alice that you had not realised the duration of your stay and will get her to fetch some of father's clothes. She will attend to you every morning, your skin will remain smooth…though I prefer the beard, I have to confess."

With that, a joyful Anne Boleyn, rang the bell for the butler, Stowell.

"My lady?"

"Stowell, Sir Henry Norris will be staying for several days. Please arrange for the maids to prepare a room for him."

"My lady…"

Alice, Stowell and the remainder of the household staff noticed a change, a vibrancy, about the teenager. From being the morose, unpleasant girl of the past few weeks, she possessed the manner of someone to whom the world had been offered…and they couldn't help but notice that it seemed to revolve around the king's messenger. Though bound to the house by her father's instructions, she used the pretext of riding the estate in the company of her 'chaperone' Sir Henry Norris. Even when the weather prevented jaunts on the saddle, she could be heard laughing and giggling like a child at play, and the atmosphere in the house responded with an air of gaiety.

"Henry, what will become of our lives?"

"I know not; but these days with you, should I live a thousand years, will be the most joyous always. These shall I keep and treasure until the Good Shepherd calls me home."

"As will be mine…Henry, should we see Wolsey again?"

"His mind is set against our union, Anne; though I know not why; I do mean to contest his decision though. But, my father…that is a burden too strong to contest. Should he die tomorrow, Wolsey, or no Wolsey, I would take you as wife…my fortune would be mine and no Lord Chancellor or cardinal could take that from me. We would be as two lovers in Eden, with only the embrace of nature to enfold us in our naked forms, in the beauty of paradise."

"And if your father does not die tomorrow…? Henry, are we doomed to live those lives that will be forced upon us? Lives that we will be obliged to follow because of our rank and nobility? To be apart and sworn to another…Henry, I think that I would rather die…"

"Let us not venture into what may, or may not, be. Let us enjoy today…this moment, this now, together. Tomorrow, the tide may turn, but today…today is our day."

Under the great oak, Henry and Anne embraced in the afternoon sun. Anne, eased her lover to one side and gazed into his eyes.

"Do you know, Henry, I could get to like the smooth skin; there is a gentleness when our lips meet. …Henry…will you lay with me tonight…? If the will of the world is that we must lay with others, then I want you to be the first…"

"Anne, my love, why wait until tonight…? I want you also to be my first, perhaps my only, if the good Lord permits, but why wait until the moon lightens the dark woods? Why wait for a time that may never be? *Now* is the time that we have; the night…the morrow, the plan is already afoot and no wishing, or hoping will change the fate of what is to be. But *now* is ours, for this, the briefest of moments, we can be as one."

Gazing into each other's eyes, Anne slid her arms around Henry's neck and pulled him towards her waiting lips. The gentle kiss, gave way to a more ardent passion as Henry caressed the hands of the woman before him. In their naked forms, the union of Henry Percy and Anne Boleyn was completed amidst the songs of the birds and the breeze rustling the leaves of the trees.

"If our time together should last a thousand years, there was, and never will be, a more wonderful moment than this. Henry, kiss me one more time and then we must away to the house."

The late afternoon sun shone through the trees as Henry Percy steadied Anne Boleyn's hand as she mounted her Georgian Grande horse. Leaning forward, she stroked the face of the man before her and, with one last kiss, they ambled through the remainder of the woods, until in the open expanse, the grand castle of Hever stood before them in the distance.

The horses strolled down the slope, as the sun's rays lit up the castle's turrets like flaming beacons. Anne pulled her horse to a halt and stared at the driveway a mere 100 yards away.

"Henry…stop!"

Pulling on the reins, Henry turned towards Anne and smiled.

"Another jaunt back to the woods, then Anne?"

"Henry…it's mother's carriage!"

"What…your mother?"

"I…I didn't expect her back so soon! She cannot see you! Does she know you?"

"I have never met your mother as Henry Percy, but whether she knows of, or has met Sir Henry Norris, of that I have no idea."

"Then you must leave…go immediately! Our lives are finished if she so much as has an inkling of your presence here."

"Anne! Is this the last time we are to be together?"

"Henry, if there is a way, I will move every stone to find it. Alice, is a simple girl, but trustworthy. I will use her, if I can…but you must away…now!"

"The gods of fortune were with us this day, then…should we have waited until the night, then there would have been no union…no bond."

"Henry…I love you, this I know; but go now my love, before the gods of fate find us…and you!"

With no farewell kiss, Henry Percy turned his own Andalusian horse back towards the woods and with a brisk gallop disappeared into the slowly fading light. Anne dismounted and, leading her horse to the care of the stable grooms, quietly entered the house and made for her bedroom.

"Alice…"

"My Lady?"

"Dinner will be served shortly and I need to be correctly dressed."

"The pink gown, my Lady?"

"Yes, that will do nicely…and my hair can be left as it is…I quite like the wild, rustic look; see how the wind curls the hair"

"And sweeps it over the shoulder, my Lady; very becoming. Your mother has returned from Arundel, I believe."

"Then make haste, Alice, we must not keep mother waiting."

The dinner gong sounded throughout the chambers and Anne descended into the dining room, where her mother was already sat.

"Mama, what a lovely surprise; you have returned earlier than I had expected."

"Indeed, Anne. Family is all very well and I do like to see my sister Margaret, but there is only so much trivia one can absorb before saturation point."

The butler lit the candles as the light started to dwindle outside.

"You may serve us now, Stowell."

"My Lady…are we not to await Sir Henry…?"

"Sir Henry…?"

Elizabeth Boleyn surveyed the table and noticed an empty place that had been laid.

"Sir Henry Norris, my Lady."

"Sir Henry Norris…what in the name of heaven is he doing here?"

"You know him, mama…?"

"Know of the man, but never met him; your father knows him well enough, though. So, what is Sir Henry doing here?"

"He came here with a message from the king for me, mama."

"A message from the king! But the man has no reason to bring messages from the king, that is not his position. There are other, lower ranks that carry out Henry Tudor's biddings, but not Sir Henry Norris. What was this message that required such hierarchy to deliver?"

"That I cannot divulge, mama. Sir Henry emphasised that, on the king's instructions, it was for my eyes only…and bid me to secrecy."

"From your own mother!"

"From anyone's mother, mama."

"Anne this is intolerable! Where is Sir Henry Norris…I wish to speak with the man."

"He has departed, mama…"

"Departed?"

"Yes, mama…"

"Why…when?"

"Within the last hour, mama. A rider from court arrived with instructions that he was to return to court immediately…and not delay. He departed and I returned here alone."

"Returned here alone. What…you have been out riding with Sir Henry Norris; you are housebound, young lady, may I remind you of that!"

"Sir Henry was my chaperone…he ensured that I did not venture beyond the grounds, mama…surely you cannot deny me to take the air; do you expect me to stay confined in my room for the duration of my penance? I have kept to father's orders, have I not?"

"Be that as it may, Anne…I am not altogether comfortable with this cloak and dagger situation…secrecies; Groom of the Stool; sudden departures…not comfortable at all."

Chapter 7

The entourage arrived at the Great Manor in Cheshunt. Lord Chancellor stepped out of the carriage and surveyed the scene before him. The wooded grounds cast a sombre scene around the house and prevented the true beauty and tranquillity of the place. This was not quite as grand as the palace at Hampton, but as a country retreat, it had potential, and with the right imagination… He needed a gardener; a visionary; someone who could see beyond the woods, swamps and hills; someone who could transform this isolated manor house into a demesne of opulence with flowering gardens rolling into the distance; someone who could take his own dreams and make them a reality.

Despite his need to be at court, Wolsey found great pleasure and comfort at his Cestrian home, each time returning to see further improvement in the grounds of his estate. The darkened manor had become bright with the removal of the woods in front of the house and the wet flatland was being absorbed by those thirsty plants searching for water. The bushy black chokeberry and the snowy blooms of the arrow-wood viburnum gave the ground much of the drainage needed, whilst the marsh marigold gave colour to the once dark swamp. His favourite, though, were the Lobelia Cardinalis, their delicate white blooms giving a feeling of purity within this fertile land; perhaps their common name of the '*cardinal flower*' influencing his preference?

"Enchanting, absolutely enchanting…a true place to be nearer to God," he told his gardener James Burton.

"Thank you, Your Lordship, but with an additional small manor on the horizon, there, you could create the Keep for the estate. Perhaps, a modest fifteen rooms, with guards for the Manor House's protection?"

"Splendid, splendid…and I know just the man to complete the work…William Talman. His father, Richard Talman, carried out work for Henry's father and the son has the same skill and imagination as taught to him by Richard."

With the infrequency of his stays, the changes that Wolsey witnessed were dramatic as ideas became realities from one visit to the next. As he descended from his carriage and turned to admire his now glorious house and gardens, there, not two-hundred yards away, was the Keep, complete with moat, drawbridge and a small garrison to maintain the security and safety of his home in Cheshunt.

"William, a triumph! I could not have pictured such splendour as this here. You have transformed this barren marshland into this glorious estate."

"Your Lordship is too kind…But, without your fiscal input, I would not have been able to create this dream come true."

"Come, dine with me. This glorious summer day gives display to the richness before us and we must profit from its magnificence!"

After a voracious meal of roast pork, the two men strolled before the house and down into the sculptured gardens below. The skylark darted and the woodpecker knocked tirelessly, as the two men absorbed the sun's rays. Free from the burdens of office for this brief moment, Wolsey felt relaxed and content.

"What is beyond the woods to our left, William?"

"There is the former church of St John, the Baptist, now renamed St Mary the Virgin, Your Lordship. After that, there are a few farm houses and a small Cestrian hamlet."

"There is still much wooded ground, then?"

"Oh, indeed. It has been said that before the Conqueror, a squirrel could traverse from the forest of Epping to here without touching the ground."

"How far does the woodland go then after the Keep?"

"All the way, past Theobalds to Enfeld, Your Lordship…are you keen on the hunt?"

"When my sovereign permits, I want to pursue a little game, I must admit."

"Then, may I be so bold as to suggest a lodge the other side of the Keep?"

"A hunting-lodge?"

"Yes, Your Lordship, a hunting-lodge…away from prying eyes. There is an old shack, made of timbers beside the stream and facing a small lake. Interestingly, the woods end by this shack…as though the Gods of the waters wished for there to be no shadow cast over the lake."

"I thought that you said the woodland continues to Enfeld?"

"Yes, after the small lake, the treeline continues. It would take but a few weeks to remove the old rotting timbers and create a small lodge…which could also serve as the entrance to your estate from the south, following the small track beside the stream."

Thomas Wolsey returned to Hampton court and then onto Italy as he made his way to visit the Pontiff. He knew that Henry still had his eye on the French throne and that the king wished that his Lord Chancellor keep good relations with Charles, the Holy Emperor, and Catherine's nephew, with view to a diplomatic, if not a military, coup. His savour for recognition as a memorable, just and formidable king, though, favoured the military option, as with Henry V.

Despite all his political and wily manipulations, Wolsey could feel that the French throne would be out of Henry's reach unless the king united with Catherine in a wedded, or better still, a bedded bliss. Upon his return from Italy, Lord Chancellor could feel the pressures of diplomacy weighing heavily on his shoulders and he was becoming an exhausted man. Bidding his leave from court for rest, he made his way back to his home in Cheshunt.

"Eminence, William Talman awaits an audience."

"Please show him in."

"William! Splendid…thank you, Bosley."

"William, welcome. What news?"

"The lodge, Your Lordship, is complete…but there were some interesting developments during the renovation."

"Interesting developments…please tell me more; you have wetted my appetite already."

"We removed the old flooring; the timbers disintegrated upon touch. Underneath, there was a trench, which led outside into the ground. The overgrown foliage had concealed this trench when we arrived, but was easily cut out. I arranged for one of my men, a local Cestrian, to continue clearing the trench, as I was intrigued. The ground became deeper as he worked his way on, until he could almost no longer reach the overhanging brambles. The trench became a tunnel, until he reached the end and could go no farther."

"A trench leading to a dead-end, from there?"

"It seemed strange to me, but I thought no more about it until the next day, when the local lad who had cleared the trench told his father what he had seen. His father told him of an ancient folk tale repeated through the generations of the locals here of an eremite who lived in a cave during the time of King Ethelred. He had been a monk and was devout in his beliefs of Christ, but sought isolation from the sins of the world. He was seen by many as inspired by God and there had been occasions when he had healed the sick. Every morning, he would walk this trench and wash himself in the lake, as naked as Adam. But he also had visions and people would come to him for guidance; some say he predicted the coming of the Conqueror; he remembered being taught as a child:

The ships will traverse the waters and England will be lost.
The arrow destined for the false prince, will come at such a cost.
Don't look up, don't look up, your kingdom will fall
To the hand of he who was destined to rule over us all.

This shack was then built by some of his followers as a shrine and they left food and small gifts."

"Well, as you say, folklore, but I am not really taken with old superstitions and wives' tales. Besides, where is this cave now?"

"Well, that's it, the man just disappeared from the face of the earth, but, where he had lived in the cave, the locals built a small chapel dedicated to John, the Baptist, another eremite himself, and after that, the church was rebuilt and…there it was, but 100 yards away."

"You could see it then?"

"No, the foliage and trees were too dense, but the track led directly to…the church of St Mary's."

"St Mary's…John, the Baptist; I am a little confused?"

"No one appears to know why, but the church as it is now, was rebuilt nearly 100 years ago and dedicated to the Virgin; but why the change of dedication remains a mystery."

"Intriguing! I am certainly not into old wives' tales, nor folklore, but there is no smoke without fire, it is said! Perhaps there is more to this hermit, than meets the eye."

"You will away to the lodge, Your Lordship?"

"Yes, upon the morrow we will venture there, but for the moment, I need to rest; I am spent…the king's tasks have proved somewhat telling!"

The morning was bright as the two men faced the day. With his carriage ready, Thomas Wolsey, strode down the steps, a reinvigorated man after a good night's rest.

"William, what say you to a stroll to the lodge?"

"As you wish, Your Lordship…the day sees you in good form."

"Indeed, and re-energised! Let us go forth!"

Dismissing the carriage, the cardinal and William Talman strode towards the Keep, with the stream to their left. The small garrison collected and presented arms, as Lord Chancellor marched across the drawbridge and through the open archway. The inspection, though brief, was not paramount upon Wolsey's mind at this moment. Satisfied that all was good, he descended and made his way across the small wooden bridge that straddled the stream and towards the track that led into the grounds of St Mary's. The gothic church represented God in His glory…and the decor, the humility of the crucifixion. With the need for rest, Wolsey had not worn his scarlet robes of office and was not recognised as the ultimate authority of the Catholic church's representative in England. Accepting the blessing of the local priest, he moved on towards the cemetery and out through the small wicket gate at the end.

"I have created this track to *the lodge*, Your Lordship, to gain quick and easy access."

Wolsey looked ahead and could see, through the branches before him, his magnificent manor house in the distance. Following William's instructions, the two men turned to the left and followed the newly constructed path. Turning left again, Wolsey, for the first time saw the rather pleasant lodge created from the renovation of a former shrine to an unknown eremite many generations before. The trees had been cleared up to the end of the lake and gave an open expanse to the last building on his estate.

"Rather pleasant…how many rooms?"

"Eight, Your Lordship."

"It has a feeling of…of intimacy, does it not?"

"That was the intent…and as you can see, accessed from the manor by either foot, or horse."

The two men stepped inside.

"A small kitchen, with larder, for the day's successful hunt, Your Lordship and a wine cellar below to keep out the heat of the day."

"And the trench; I did not notice it?"

"It has been covered, to prevent accidents and falls; 'tis below within the cellar."

"Hm…most pleasant. Perhaps, I need to employ a gamekeeper for the estate; this will make good his residence. Wine, venison, boar…good, good; you have done well, William…most pleasant."

Two days later, the rider arrived with the message he had hoped would be delayed a bit longer; he was to return to court…the king had business to discuss. It was the last time that cardinal Thomas Wolsey would ever see Cheshunt.

Chapter 8

The knock at the door was answered by the parlour-maid.

"Mr Wellstone, sir…"

"Good be the day to you, Mary."

"And you, sir. I will fetch Mr Bosley. Do you wish to wait in the kitchen, sir?"

Leading the gamekeeper into the kitchen, Mary left to find the butler.

"Sarah…how goes the day?"

"Mr Wellstone, sir, the day goes fine, thank you…and for you?"

"Grand, grand…here, for your labours, I believe?"

Laying the two large pheasants on the table, the gamekeeper sat himself at the large kitchen table as the cook poured mead into a pewter tankard.

"There…to keep out the winter's chill, Mr Wellstone."

"Thank you kindly, Sarah."

"Them's two fine birds that you have there, Mr Wellstone."

"Just to prevent you getting too idle, Sarah…"

"Ooh, Mr Wellstone, sir…away with your cheek; rushed off my feet, I am."

The two employees of Thomas Wolsey sat for a few moments enjoying a short break, as Bosley walked in.

"Mr Wellstone, sir…"

"Ah, Mr Bosley…I have just delivered these two fine birds for the household and on yonder mule, there, you will find two hogs…"

"I'll get the groom to bring them in, thank you…will you stay for lunch, Mr Wellstone?

"A grand offer, Mr Bosley, indeed, I will if it not be too inconvenient…though, I understand Sarah is rushed off her feet, someone did say…!"

"Oh, you cheeky scoundrel, Mr Wellstone…"

The conviviality continued through lunch as the household enjoyed game from the estate, caught and brought by the Lordship's gamekeeper. Bidding his leave, Bosley accompanied Wellstone back to the servants outside door.

"The game is abundant, then, Mr Wellstone...and how do you find the lodge?"

"The lodge is grand, thank you, Mr Bosley. The lake, though, does not support fish; I am at a bit of a loss to understand why?"

"Of that, I have no knowledge. I will ask of the Cestrian servants here of what they understand of the lake, Mr Wellstone and give you a reply when we next meet...and Mrs Wellstone, she is well?"

"Fit as a fiddle, thank you, Mr Bosley...though she hounds me for some fish, I must say!"

Game was plentiful, throughout the season and partridge, pheasant, boar and venison were regularly brought to the attention of Sarah, the manor's head cook. Becoming well-known for his pleasant disposition and an efficient provider for the household, Edward Wellstone was often found within the walls of the manor, and despite their difference in position, became on good terms with Mr Bosley, butler and overseer of the staff.

"Mr Wellstone..."

"Mr Bosley, sir...a grand day again, is it not...?"

"Indeed, indeed...welcome. Please, pray, come into the scullery. I have some information that may be of interest to you since we last spoke."

The two men walked through the corridors and passed into the kitchen.

"Mr Wellstone..."

"Sarah, good day to you...Three rabbits to keep you out of mischief..."

"I'll give you mischief, Mr Wellstone...Something for the dryness...?"

"A small cider would be most welcome, Sarah, thank you."

Bosley disappeared into the adjoining scullery and brought back with him a young maid.

"Mr Bosley, sir, will you join Mr Wellstone in a small tankard?"

"I think not, thank you, Sarah...Mr Wellstone, this is Estrilda, our scullery maid. She is Cestrian and may provide some light for the fishless lake."

"Thank you, Mr Bosley...Estrilda, you are local, then?"

"Yes, sir."

"What do you know of the lake by the *lodge*?"

Well, sir…my grandfather, he was very knowing about our history hereabouts and would tell us of tales when we were young of wonderous times, when we were here but a few houses."

"We?"

"Oh, my sister and two brothers, sir. Well, grandfather would sit us all around the fire and tell us stories of long ago…"

"Please go on."

"Well, the lake was full to the brim with every sort of fish that swam upon God's good earth, but Erasiculdus was evil and when he saw the good people enjoying the spoils of the waters, he flew down below and destroyed all the fish in the lake with his breath."

"Erasiculdus? What exactly is Erasiculdus?"

"He was a dragon, sir, with breath of fire…"

"Dragons, hm…well, thank you, Estrilda, perhaps, you need to return to your duties…"

"But the dragon was destroyed by the Iceni Queen…"

"Iceni Queen! What do you know of the Iceni Queen?"

"Well, she was a warrior, sir…queen of all the Britons and she, with her army, destroyed Erasiculdus who was leading the invading army to conquer this land."

"What was the name of this Iceni Queen?"

"Ooh, I don't know that, sir. Grandfather kept talking about *Buddug*, but I didn't understand what *Buddug* was. Well, this invading army was ten thousand strong, sir, but the Iceni Queen, she was not afraid and took to battle with but a small army of faithful and loyal followers and in her chariot of gold, her horses breathed fire at the army before her and they fled…afraid of the Iceni Queen, who they called the Great Witch."

Does the name Boadicea mean anything to you?"

"Boadicea? No, that name means nothing to me, sir…but she chased the fleeing army in her gold chariot and killed every one of them up by the Bury, sir…cut their throats and put them to the sword; not one was spared, sir…and the priests, they took their women and gave thanks to the Gods on their alters, sir."

"And what of the lake…afterwards?"

"Once Erasiculdus had breathed on the lake, all life died. Grandfather, he said that Erasiculdus fell into the lake when he was destroyed and stays buried underneath, but his body stops all fish living there…told me to never go beyond the Bury, sir."

"Thank you, Estrilda…most informative."

With a curtsey, the scullery maid returned to her duties in the room beyond. Bosley escorted Wellstone to the servant's door.

"Well, I believe that you may have heard a fantasy tale, there, Mr Wellstone…I am sorry for the inconvenience…"

"Not at all, Mr Bosley. In fact, dragons aside, the history of the Iceni Queen is fascinating. I have heard it told before about this mythical queen of the Iceni…and her tale may have some degree of truth. Tell me, pray, where can I obtain books with information about this area.?"

"Why, the church of St Mary's has a small collection, but if you do not find what you want, there is a larger collection at the abbey of Waltham…with the monks there are some learned men charged with recording information that may not necessarily be only about the Gospels, Mr Wellstone. But the abbey from here, will take the best part of half-a-day."

Edward Wellstone toured around the small lake outside the *lodge*. Bizarrely, he observed, there were no trees from behind the lodge up to beyond the lake. Crouching, he dipped his finger into the water and let the end of his hand taste the liquid. It had a sharp taste and he was not surprised that fish were absent. Any species would struggle to survive in such waters…but why was the water as this? Dragon breath and dragon bodies… "I think not," he muttered.

With the manor well-stocked, Wellstone made his way slowly to Waltham Abbey. The scullery maid, Estrilda, hade excited his imagination about the Iceni. Though not a well-read man, he did not lack interest in affairs of the state and the history of this beautiful land. What he lacked in education, he more than made up for in his thirst for knowledge. Had opportunity been his way, he may well have been of a higher disposition than his current status; *the law* being an area that interested him enormously.

Arriving at the abbey, the abbot greeted him amiably and directed him to the significant library, where two friars and a theological scholar were at work. The encryptions and writings were a marvel to behold as Edward Wellstone withdrew several volumes, each of which, needed both of his hands to hold. The beautiful wordings were frequently accompanied with the most delicate of designs and paintings and it pained Edward Wellstone that he was unable to decipher what faced him on the table, save that of the sketches. Though he could read the

English language, he was unable to read Latin. Browsing for well into the hour, he came across two books somewhat less dense than the others, *De Excidio et Conquestu Britanniae per Gildas Albanius* and *Et Conquest of Britannia in ruinam, per Gildas Albanius*. What drew his attention to the second book was the inside cover depicting a female warrior, on a chariot. The one word that he could understand, though was *Iceni*! The two holy men had removed themselves from the library for prayers, but the scholar remained at his work, making notes from the books in front of him. Edward Wellstone moved up to him and placed the book before the man,

"Excuse me, sir…I am at a loss to understand the Latin language, but I wondered if I may trouble you for a moment to translate this chapter here…that is, I have presumed that you read Latin?"

"Indeed, I do, sir. May I enquire as to the purpose of your interest in the Iceni Queen…a pagan?"

His heart began to beat fast…had he really found the answer to his search?

"I am from Cheshunt, sir…an employee of the cardinal and have reason to believe that this queen may have been influential in the region around here?"

"Wolsey…the cardinal?"

"Indeed, the very same."

"An honour, sir…I allow me to assist in any way that I can. I know some details of the Iceni Queen, but I shall read from the chapter that you refer to…"

"No, pray, tell me of what you know first, then refer to the book, if you will be so kind."

"Well, the Iceni Queen was married to the King *Prasutagus* and they had two daughters, both princesses. In these barbaric times, the value of a princess was considered worthy of any prince, as the high priests could sacrifice these most highly-valued royal children as the ultimate offering from any tribe. They had to be given to the Gods before maturity, to ensure their purity. However, after the death of *Prasutagus*, they were violated by the Roman forces to prevent any such sacrifice that may have sent favour of the Gods to the way of the Iceni. The Iceni was a proud and fearsome Celtic tribe and joined forces with their neighbouring tribe, the Trinovantes, to extract revenge for their brutality and to drive the Romans from the land of the Britons."

"That is fascinating…I had heard of this fearsome warrior queen, but believed her to be but a myth…"

"Oh, no; she is no myth…she is, I mean was, very real. It was during this time that England started to change from a heathen, divided, tribal country into this united Christian nation that we so proudly call Britain. But those barbaric times were fraught with danger, both from internal fighting and foreign conflicts. In fact, it was only by the conquering Roman army defeating Boadicea, that we became the civilised, Christian nation of today…"

"Boadicea…that was her name, then…?"

"The Welsh call her *Buddug* and sometimes she is referred to by her other Celtic name, *Boudica*…"

"*Buddug*… Estrilda used that name…"

"Estrilda…?"

"Oh, another employee of the cardinal…in fact, it was she that started my search and ultimately led to my journey here. Was the Iceni Queen from here, then?"

"No, she was from Anglia, but then from the revolts and battles that followed, there was much involvement here…that is my knowledge of the Iceni warrior queen…shall I read the chapter now?"

Boudica, queen of all Britons, rampaged from Mona, Camulodunum and Londinium to avenge the despoilation of her daughters and the invasion of her lands. No Roman was spared, neither he nor his household. The destruction of Londinium, heralded the retreat and re-grouping of all Roman forces near Wroxeter, but many Roman soldiers were caught as she harried them on, putting to the sword all men and crucifying the women.

Her journey after the sacking of Londinium, carried her towards Verulamium where her army captured many fleeing soldiers. They were collected in a wooded area north of Ēana where they were tortured and their manhood removed. The land surrounding this sacrificial site was known to the Druid priests, who selected this for their warrior queen as a place of worship. Sacrifices were made using both the children and unmarried women to appease their Gods and grant victory over the invader in this, their holy land.

At Wroxeter, the Romans in only small numbers, marched east and met the mighty Iceni warrior queen at Etocetum. The Druid priests, believing that victory was guaranteed by the Gods, persuaded Boudica, after she invoked Andraste to defeat the Romans, to let her army run amok amongst the small Roman garrison and destroy totally their army but, under the command of Suetonius, she was met with defeat and her priests brutally murdered. Dying at the hand of her enemy, she consolidated the prophecy of the priests of her forefathers, who presaged of her creating the united tribes of this holy land.

"Her defeat was, as you bear witness to, the creation of the United Kingdoms of England under one symbolic flag."

"Indeed. As you read the chapter, I could almost feel the presence of this warrior queen. I am interested in this place, *Ēana*…Where is this location…it is not a name that I recognise?"

"*Ēana* is not far from here…perhaps, an hour's horse-ride away. You may know it as it was *Enefelde*; or as it has become, Enfeld."

Returning to the *lodge*, Edward Wellstone's mind was awash with imaginations of Druids, Celts, warrior queens and the destiny of England's history being upon his own doorstep. Was it possible that the very brutality carried out on the fleeing soldiers and their wives was here, in front of him? It made him shudder. Perhaps, the 'dragon' was, in fact, the Roman emblem which was laid to rest in the waters before him. Were the sacrifices beneath this very lake? What made the waters bitter?

As gamekeeper to the manor, provided he supplied the household with well-stocked larders, his time was very much as he chose; though poachers were not uncommon and he had regularly to check the nearby woods. The *law*, he thought, though appealing, could not have created such an excitement, surely? Beyond the lake, he took his horse into the woodlands, with which he was familiar, and journeyed further through the dense thicket, until he entered ground that he did not know. The land was dark from the dense woods and he started to notch the trees so that he could retrace his path; though the trodden bracken, temporarily left a track that he could follow. As a man used to the surroundings of the outdoors, he was not prone to inexplicable nervousness; indeed, he was a practical man who felt that all unusual happenings had a cause…a natural cause. However, he could not explain the apprehension that he felt, as he pushed further on into what was now becoming a forest.

Looking back, he could make out the marks that he had made in the trees, though the trodden undergrowth, helped him see his markers. With a squeal that startled him, a hog ran through the dark woods, and though well beyond his normal hunting-ground, he decided to lay some animal traps. Another screech and he saw a stoat end the life of one of the forest's numerous rodents. Edward

Wellstone, dismounted and withdrew both snares and animal traps that had enough force to terminate any known local animal. He knew that bears once roamed through these lands, but it was now man who represented the dominant two-legged species that controlled the woods and flatlands.

With the night starting to draw in, the forest quickly became dark. Edward Wellstone decided to turn back, but was unable to see his tree markers. The trodden ground had already sprung back to life and he had no way of knowing which direction he should follow. With no celestial markings to guide him, he could only ascertain his approximate direction by using the brightest part of the gloomy sky as a means to direct him homeward. Relying on his mount to find her way home, he sat listlessly as the horse made her way through the brush, until they arrived back at land, he could at last identify. Relieved, he finally dismounted outside the lake and walked his steed into the pasture land beside the lodge, before retiring inside to the warmth and comfort of a blazing fire and a good night's rest. The next day saw Edward up even before the sun had risen.

"Off to the manor, Edward?"

"Aye, then I shall recheck on the snares and traps that I set yesterday, Elena. Do you know, there's an uncanniness south of those woods? Towards Enfeld, the land takes on an air of mystery...it has a strange sensation...a feeling of...of...I'm not sure of *what* exactly, to be able to describe it, but it surely feels as though...well, it is not a land that welcomes with open arms."

"Edward, when you see Mr Bosley, please remind him of the butter that he promised."

"Oh, Sarah, will have saved us some churns...she is a good one, that Sarah."

"You keep your mind on them traps, Edward, never mind about that Sarah!"

"Oh, you know that I only have eyes for you, my love...but a little friendly chatter does help with the odd token gesture."

"Mind that it stays only as friendly chatter, then!"

With that, Edward Wellstone left his wife at the lodge and made his way to the manor, before retracing his steps and beyond, to his markers from yesterday. With the day early, he decided to check his traps and then to proceed further into the forest to ascertain how far the woods went, again marking the trees along the way. Though the day was bright, there was a chill in the air...though not a chill he had felt earlier. The morning had been warm, but with the sun's heat unable to penetrate the forest, the warmth by the lodge and in the open land, was not felt here. But also, it was not a chill that he was familiar with. Winter's chills...well, one could feel…the hands, the face; these were the chills that nature threw at us to force us to seek protection and shelter. This was a chill deep inside…not one due to the winds, or the winter's cold.

Finally, he entered some open land, and though the sun was shining, there was no warmth. He put his hand to his face and, to his surprise, this felt warm, but inside he felt as though the winter's ice had stabbed his very soul. He meandered slowly into this open expanse and could see that tracks led towards what looked like an old fort, but knew that he was now well beyond his own jurisdiction and, hesitatingly, turned his horse around to return back into the gloom. Though he had left his markers on the trees, he had not recorded where he had left the forest into the open ground and within a matter of a few minutes, became disorientated. One emotion that Edward had never experienced, now possessed him…panic! He wanted to kick his horse at the sides, say 'Yah,' and dash away as fast as his steed would let him. But this was impossible within these dark, clammy and forbidding woods. He decided to turn around and make his way back to the open land, but even after nearly half-an-hour, he was still firmly within the confines of the forest. In other words, Edward Wellstone was lost…and he knew it!

Dismounting, he led his horse through the bracken and overhanging branches, with the cold inside biting him like a knife. He heard the scream before he heard the shouting, but there was no doubt that what was approaching him in this forest sounded like an army. The trees swayed to the mighty force as all the branches began cracking under the relentless sound of war-cries and the neighing of frightened horses. His own steed reared up and tried to dash, but with his fingers tightly around the reins, his frightened mount could only remain where Edward stood. Leaping up onto its back, Edward let the animal run its course, believing that the natural instinct for its own survival would bring them to safety. Speeding past mutilated bodies on the ground, the now terrified gamekeeper watched in horror as a multitude of men rushed towards him as he flew onwards, coming from all sides with faces painted in the colours of war and with hatred in their eyes. Before him, almost hidden amongst the trees stood an Iceni warrior…a queen in her chariot, not of gold, but of wood and iron, with iron-shod wooden wheels.

In one hand, she held a spear of wood and bronze, the other held the arch of her chariot with her driver at the reins. She glared with a loathing that he had never felt before. Her eyes bore pure malice as he heard her yell in a language that Edward Wellstone did not understand. Her arms were scared in wounds of old and her robe was of hessian sack. Her hair, long and fair, was matted with the gore of battle. With the crack of his whip, the driver drove the chariot's horses on into the heart of the battle, but the Iceni Queen kept her gaze on the lone, terrified horseman. His speeding horse stumbled and Edward's head hit an overhanging branch. Falling from his mount, he tumbled onto the damp ground and became entangled with the briars and thorns of the forest's many timorous inhabitants of the undergrowth. Cut and grazed, he limped on manically, not knowing which way to go. His horse, like its rider, limped also, but Edward managed to seize the reins of his injured mount and tried to hurry on, but though both rider and steed were able to move, it was painful and slow. Wellstone, suddenly became aware of an uncanny noise…silence! There was no noise of battle; no war-cries…nothing to suggest that this was anything other than a forest; an enchanted…or perhaps, even, a damned one, but just a forest, nevertheless. In an instant, he looked behind him and with a yell that made the very trees quiver, the Iceni Queen called in her own language as she launched her spear at the quaking gamekeeper. With a searing pain, the javelin pierced his ankle, as she uttered one word that he understood: 'Go!'

Looking down at his wound, he saw no spear, but one of his animal traps that he had laid. Looking feebly up, there was no other living thing around, save himself and his mount. Pain was now paramount in Edward Wellstone's mind as he fell on the ground and tried to remove the animal trap. Even though a fit man, it took every ounce of strength for Edward to finally open the jaws of this dangerous device. With bone protruding through the flesh, he knew that his ankle had been severed. Alone and in agony, he realised that he had either witnessed British history in the happening, or had hallucinated; a damned forest, one way or another. Using his scarf as a tourniquet, he squeezed the knot around his thigh until his leg started to turn white and become numb. With only one useable leg, he knew that walking was out of question and with both hands on the saddle, hoisted himself up and lay across the animal's back. Injured itself, the steed limped slowly back as Edward passed out.

With his ankle and foot now amputated, Edward Wellstone continued his duties as best he could. Climbing stairs was increasingly painful and Elena suggested that they set the bed on the ground floor. Very much limited in what he could physically do, he was still able to perform his duties as the manor's gamekeeper, as setting traps and snares did not require an agile man; only a capable one. Some days were better than others, but most days, he had a feeling of pain from the wound that he had incurred on that formidable day. One feeling he did have though, was a fear of the woodlands beyond the lake. He still traversed the woods, but remained within his markers and did not venture beyond. The small hamlet of the Bury had been established and fell in line with the last of his markers. Apart from making the occasional acquaintance with the inhabitants, a family of woodcutters, his life was a solitary one; that fearful day had really changed his life forever.

The night of that February brought a cold so intense that the fire, itself, could barely keep the lodge warm. With a multitude of draughts, the biting wind permeated around the house. Edward, stacked the fire as high as was possible and with the cold air blowing through the room, the fire roared, but its warmth could be barely felt. Luckily, with the bed next door, there was no need to mount the stairs up into the cold floor above. In a drowsy state, husband and wife decided to make their way slowly to bed.

"A nightcap, Elena?"

"Something to keep the chill out, Edward, that would be nice."

"I have a little rum…Mr Bosley felt that we may need some sustenance with this severely cold weather."

"A little rum would go down well, Edward, thank you."

Edward Wellstone got up and with his cane for support, made his way into the kitchen. Taking out two small cups, poured the rum into both. Making his way back and handing his wife her cup, there was a loud crack and thud from the floor above.

"What the…!"

"Edward! What is that?"

"I have no idea…no idea at all!"

Forgetting the need for his cane, he thumped his way up the stairwell and onto the first floor above. Thinking that he could see a faint light, Edward hobbled towards the glow, and upon opening the door, found the room was ablaze. The fire below, that Edward had stacked to keep out the cold, had proved too fierce and the heat had penetrated the wooden flooring above and set the room alight. With a room full of black, penetrating smoke, filling his lungs, Edward turned and fled, gasping for breath. With the door open, the air currents played their part and fuelled the fire into an inferno. Edward ran to the stairs, but already the smoke had filled the flooring and he could scarcely see his hand before him.

"Fire, fire…get out, get out!"

But, unable to see before him, with eyes smarting from the smoke, his stump fell into a small hole in a floor plank; Edward was incapable to free himself…an unjust end to such an honest, fair and gentle man.

Chapter 9

"Sir Henry Percy and Lady Anne Boleyn, Your Eminence."

"Enter; please seat yourselves."

"We shall stand, Your Eminence! How dare you stop this union between Sir Henry and myself. We were betrothed…and in love!"

"Love…hm, love. That fickle emotion of mankind; the downfall of nearly every man since time immemorial."

"You have no reason; no right, other than erstwhile, ulterior motives for preventing our marriage. I shall talk to the king."

"I believe His Royal Highness has already conferred upon *Sir* Henry his own favours. Why would he wish him ill? Besides, it would be beneath the dignity of the king to discuss matrimony with every common…or noble servant of this land. An audience with the king may well see you disgraced and without influence in court, or at home; which is where you will be returning, if you continue with this domestic tragedy; and don't forget that Sir Henry's father was aghast at the suggestion of such a union. You forget your place in our society, madam and your lower rank, of which Sir Henry's father, Sir Henry himself, was so aware; he would not and could not allow such a tie as this."

"You talk of lower rank…why you are nothing more than a butcher's son…a commoner! So, tell me, Your Eminence, what is it to you that I should not marry the man beside me?"

"Well, as you so graciously ask, there are plans afoot, to which you have neither the details, nor the privy, to know, that Sir Henry has been bequeathed to another fair lady of our land."

"What! Henry, do you know of this?"

"I…I…am totally unaware. Your Eminence, to whom have I been promised?"

"The 4th Earl of Shrewsbury, Sir George Talbot, has a daughter, Mary. It is she to whom you will be committed."

"Mary Talbot! But I have never met the girl."

"May I remind you, Sir Henry, that you have privilege and rank, and with that goes commitment."

"Commitment? A commitment to whom, may I ask-you…my father?"

"To your king and country, damn it! The indolent aristocratic rich think that their birth-right is to idle away the daylight hours in trivia, demeaning the very backbone of this land…the peasantry stalwarts, that have made, kept and will create the very greatness to which your heritage deems it owes little, but owes so much."

"So, you from your lower-rank birth, defend the peasants and serfs of this land because they are the same ilk as you! Did they battle, did they ride with victory and gloriousness at Calais; at Agincourt; at Crécy and every naval battle since, to create the greatness of this OUR noble land. This is what WE earned with our blood, tears and sweat. It IS our birth-right!"

"Did they battle…did they ride. They did not ride, they were not so blessed; they ran, they feared, they pursued; but did they battle…oh yes, they battled, fought, won…and died so that you may now marry Mary talbot, daughter of the 4th Earl of Shrewsbury! And if you wish to pursue my rank, it outweighs yours through shear skill, talent, determination and hard work. I have strived for my God, king and country, for this land IS my birth-right, not by rank, nobility, or privilege, but by being born, living and one day dying here; THIS is my birth-right, as it is of every serf and peasant who declares himself to be an Englishman! And you, my Lady, may control the interest in his loin, I control the interest in his finances…and I think we both know which of the two, sways Henry Tudor the most."

"You…you…, we shall elope; France, Scotland…"

"Hell, more like. How would you survive? Your father will disown you, as yours will you, snappy wench. Will you still ardently love each other on the streets of Paris, begging for a soup, or bowl just to keep your bellies from pleading for sustenance? I think not; you have known home comforts for too long and been spoilt beyond recognition. Don't talk to me of fantasy alternatives; you will conform, obey and be grateful that a king, country…and Lord Chancellor have only your best intentions at heart. Love…hm, what idle twaddle."

"You deceitful, artful, ambitious upstart, you have decided this for your own gain that we cannot be joined as one! I will have your head; do not doubt me on that score!"

"I believe, Sir Henry, that this conversation is at an end. The door is immediately behind you."

Chapter 10

"Mary, what is it like to lie with Henry?"

"Not as enthralling as it was to lie with King Francis, in Paris. Henry grunted, fumbled and ejaculated no sooner than the bedcovers fell over us. But Francis, had a more endearing manner. His wooing technique was to parade around the bed chamber, as in a masquerade, and we would pretend to be different people. Henry lacked etiquette…and his breath smelled. I had to insist that he consumed some wine beforehand."

"Will he acknowledge your children?"

"No, he arranged for me to marry William Carey and hide behind the façade that they were William's."

"And William agreed to this?"

"Henry made William's life quite content; he…we will want for nothing; the king has ensured a comfortable lifestyle."

"A life at the king's expense, then?"

"Yes…a convenient arrangement. William and I…well it is a suitable match; we do very much as we want, though not necessarily together."

"You have other lovers, then?"

"Of course, as does William…though his are not specifically confined to the female gender. As I said, it is a suitable match…and we are fond of one another. What of you, will you succumb to Henry's lustful eye?"

"Henry expects…and will get a virgin queen; I will not succumb to his eye."

"Queen! Henry, my dear Anne, is well and truly married…you will never become queen!"

"Be not so sure, Mary. He has used you for his own lustful means, as he has used others, but I will not allow Henry between my thighs until the ring of marriage displays on my finger."

"Anne, you will lose Henry's interest sooner than you think if you do not allow him the perusal of the cuckoo's nest; and as for queen…Anne do you intend to murder the queen and expect Henry to conform to your designation for the throne?"

"Henry has already told me of his intent to rid of the Spaniard! His lust is only part of his attention towards me…he needs an heir…a son and the Spaniard cannot give him that; only girls and stillbirths. I have guaranteed Henry an heir, but only in wedlock. He has observed our lineage and can see so easily that sons are rampant within our family."

"But Henry, as you have said, expects a virgin queen! He will not accept your time in the French court with king Francis was without incident!"

"Francis was your bed partner, not mine…"

"Not Francis, but the courtier…what was his name…?"

"Charles…"

"Yes, Charles, I believe that there were several moments of indiscretion…and if I noticed, so would others."

"Charles was pretty, that is true, and he did have an amusing and charismatic charm. As a courtier, he would have befitted many of the ladies there…"

"But he had eyes for you, did he not and that indiscretion in itself would be sufficient to cast doubt into anyone's mind, particularly Henry's…and court gossip will seal the knot."

"There really is nothing for me to hide, sister, so worry not. My ambition lies beyond the French nobles and aristocracy…"

"Yes, into the realms of fantasy, Anne. The queen is young, she is pretty, she is healthy and no dreaming, or false promises made by Henry will change that. However, as his mistress, he will see you cared for: as with me, Elizabeth Blount, Anne Stafford…it is the profession of our gender."

"Mary, if truth be known, Henry is not what I would call an answer to a maiden's prayer…at least not this maiden and if I should let him dishonour me, what will the future hold…no man worthy of his status would consider me as wife! I trust him no further than he can be thrown; and unless the ring of marriage rests upon this finger, then no bed with king awaits me…except a nuptial bed, with a queen at his side."

"Dream on, sister. Father will address the issue, of that, I'm sure. He directed us to the nobles of France and now we are both at court, here. He is wily and has plans for us…he guided me into the bed with Henry and the outcome has helped to further his influence in broader circles."

"Father, as you say, is wily…on that I agree. But if father had his way, he would see me straddled by Henry and his false promises if he felt that he could gain royal approval. Father's motivation is power and a concubine of the king would sway his influence enormously; see how he has benefitted from his time with you and Henry. A second daughter…he would be second to none after the king himself. No, I will not be Henry's concubine, even to the wrath of father."

"As you please, sister, but I see no future for you if you defy father and retain this fantasy of becoming queen."

"Perhaps, not so much a fantasy, as you say, Mary. Why at this very moment, the cardinal is in Rome."

"Why is Wolsey in Rome?"

"To discuss if Henry's marriage to Catherine is legal."

"Legal! Of course, it is legal. How else would you describe a monarch marrying his queen in full view of the populace, with vows made before God, as anything other than legal?"

"Wolsey thinks that Henry should not have married Arthur's widow."

"Whyever not? Many a young widow stays married into a family one way or another. I believe that you are holding out too much hope on some pretext from Wolsey."

"No, it's not Wolsey, it is Henry."

"Well, Henry, then. Anne, don't be blinded by the truth."

"What truth?"

"The truth that Henry very much remains married to the Spaniard and conjectures by Henry, or Wolsey to the effect that the marriage is illegal, are not worth a jot. What is Wolsey going to say in Rome, huh? 'Excuse me Your Holiness, Henry would like you to annul his marriage to Catherine so that he can bed Anne Boleyn?' I think not, Anne…and you should come to your senses, for goodness' sake."

"I am not sure of the reason that Wolsey will give to the Pope, but he would not have made the trip, if he didn't have some just cause?"

"Anne, Wolsey goes to Rome for many an ecclesiastical purpose; annulling the marriage, even if it is mentioned, will only be part of the reasons why a cardinal visits His Holiness; besides, I do not trust the man."

"Unfortunately, neither do I…but he is all that I have to secure my rightful place beside Henry. Actually, I loathe the man, he is ambitious, deceitful, cunning…and of low-birth; a butcher's boy!"

"Yes, I agree that his low-birth does give one cause for concern being so close to the king…I wonder why Henry chose him and not one of the nobles to guide his hand?"

"It was his father that selected Wolsey, but don't think that the king can be so easily fooled. A low birth is of no threat to Henry. One of the noble families close to Henry, could begin to manipulate the king's hand to his own advantage and leave the king reliant on, and perhaps even indebted to, that family. A rebellion would not be out of the question and, with enough power, a new family line could rule this land."

"My word, Anne, you are close to Henry! Has he confided this to you…these are not your thoughts, that I know?"

"Henry is not just a man for sport and play, Mary. Perhaps, when you knew him in his younger years, he may have seemed somewhat naïve, but he has learned a lot since then, and as much as I despise the man, Wolsey has helped manipulate Henry's notions of who to trust and how to make decisions to his advantage. There is, and has been, many a plot to undermine the king's wishes for whatever political, or personal reasons, but Wolsey is astute and hears all the murmurings within the corridors of power."

"Perhaps, Wolsey manipulates the king's wishes to further his own gain and influence over Henry."

"Without doubt, but his influence and low birth do not threaten Henry, such as the likes of Charles Brandon, the Duke of Suffolk…and even our uncle, Thomas Howard, Duke of Norfolk. This isn't as far-fetched as you may think; don't forget Buckingham either, his threat was very real in Henry's eyes."

"But family ties…surely, father would speak against Howard, if that be the case…there are rules, Anne."

"In the world of power and ambition…there are no rules."

"Sister, sister…you really have grown-up! But aren't you as equally as conniving as those you've mentioned, if it is your intention to usurp Catherine?"

"I see it as pleasing the king and the king's wishes…"

"Which are to bed Anne Boleyn…"

"Which are to have a male heir! I shall become queen and give him a dozen sons, so that he can pick and choose his favourite. The union between Henry VIII and Anne Boleyn will produce the greatest Tudor monarch this country has ever seen."

"Well, I hope for your sake, Anne, that Wolsey finds the means to persuade His Holiness, otherwise you may become blinded by hate for that which you yearn and cannot have. What if the Spanish woman gives him a son...what then?"

"That is already too late...Henry has told me that their bedded days are at an end..."

"So, he seeks other outlets for his gratification...Anne, he wants a mistress, that is all!"

"...And an heir, Mary...and an heir."

"...Yes, and an heir. He thinks more for an heir than his escort. His queen is betrothed to him for that reason alone...and of course, for political gain. If, by any misguided chance, you succeed with your realms of fantasy, Anne, never show signs of fulfilment as his bed mate; he will see you as nothing more than a common whore. I made that mistake at our first union...I had been made to believe that was intensely satisfying to any man during his lovemaking, but the look of disgust on Henry's face showed me that I had been badly informed."

"But he bedded you again, did he not?"

"Yes, I quickly realised that this was not to his liking and so I pretended that the moans of delight were those of pain."

"Henry believed you, then?"

"After he had finished, yes."

"There is one major problem, though. As much as I wish to see Henry happy and with heir...I do not find his physical appearance, how does one say..."

"Appealing...?"

"Yes, appealing. I could lay with him, but I find that I need more...and Henry doesn't satisfy those needs."

"Anne, understand this, women at court...whether nobles or even queens, are for two purposes: to procreate and for the pleasure of men. Women were not designed since the time of Eve, for anything else, and men regard us as such. It is even written that God created a wife for Adam...she was for his needs, not him for hers. Man sees the '*Fanny*' as created by God for the use of man only...but there they are sorely misconceived; it was made for women too..."

"You mean..."

"Anne, don't be so naïve; your feelings of lust are as normal as a man's. That doesn't make you any less a woman, or even a person. We women also need an outlet for our desires and as long as men continue with this misconception, then we will need to fulfil these as best we can. Satisfy the king, but search for relief from other sources. There is many a young stud at court only too eager to oblige his mistress's needs."

"Mary!"

"Anne, do not be alarmed…but be discrete…and if no stud be found, the female hand is most pleasant."

Chapter 11

Thomas Wolsey settled down into the bath prepared for him after his tortuous journey to the Vatican. He had prepared himself mentally for his audience with Pope Clement, but his body needed the sustenance of the warmth of the *Tiber*. Easing himself into the bath, he let his mind relax as his body absorbed the soothing waters.

Norfolk, Suffolk, and had he survived the executioner's block, Buckingham; all would strike him in a moment should he be unsuccessful with his mission. Those ambitious, aristocratic hypocrites would disown him the moment that he failed, or shower him with adulation should he succeed. Yet, what a dilemma! Charles is Holy Roman Emperor and his aunt is the very person sitting on the throne of England. Henry, had already warred with France, and though at peace, the hostilities of less than a decade ago, would still be very much fresh in the minds of those involved and the old wounds could easily be reopened. Yet, Charles wanted control of France. Should he antagonise Charles, Spain, England's ally, and with a Spanish queen on the throne, could join forces with the French and bring England to her knees. It was not a situation that he liked, at all. What diplomacy could settle a dilemma such as this…and all because one man had decided that his loin was above all other considerations, irrespective of their outcome. The warm Tiber water ran down Wolsey's back, as the servant allocated for his comfort, emptied another jug into the tub. This wasn't a diplomatic mission, Wolsey thought, this was suicide.

"Your Holiness…"

"Thomas! a pleasure…Dominus vobiscum. In pace et amore Iesu Christi…"

"Amen."

"Come, take bread with me…and a little help from the fruit of the vine, perhaps? The granary is full and the fruit harvest abundant."

"Thank you, Holy Father."

The two ecclesiastical men of God settled down to an opulent feast, as the minions of the Vatican served them.

"You are here to enquire about my health, no doubt?"

"Ha, ha…Unfortunately, no…"

"Henry?"

"Yes, Your Holiness…Henry."

"Then it is he, who is concerned for my health….?"

"If only it were that simple. Holy Father…Henry wishes…no, Henry insists that he…that I, seek an annulment for his union with Catherine."

"A divorce, you mean?"

"Yes, a divorce."

"On what grounds, may I ask?"

"He believes that his marriage to Catharine is, and always was, illegal."

"Not so! His Holy Father, Leo granted them a Papal Bull, with his blessings."

"At the time, this was believed to be correct; that he could marry Arthur's widow. Indeed, it was welcomed with enthusiasm both from Spain and the English nobles."

"So, why the change of heart?"

"Henry remains without issue and believes that God has damned this union as sinful."

"From whence does he get this ridiculous notion?"

"Leviticus, chapter20, verse 16 quotes: *If a man shall take his brother's wife, it is an impurity; he hath uncovered his brother's nakedness; they shall be childless.*"

"Hm, a powerful quote, indeed. But his Holiness, Leo, must have acted with God's understanding and knowledge; and the blessing of this union must surely be with the Almighty's blessing, too."

"It may have been, perhaps, a poor receptive time between God and the Holy Father…an oversight?"

"…What is your take on this, Thomas?"

"I believe in the sanctity and purity of marriage; it is for eternity."

"So, you are not in favour, then, but seek to pursue Henry's will at the expense of your own beliefs?"

"I think that Henry may also be more interested in his relations with the Boleyn's, as well as his view that his marriage is not legal and that he lives his life as an adulterer."

"I have been privy to the affairs of the Boleyn's-an ambitious and ruthless dynasty, I believe."

"Ambitious indeed, Holy Father, and the girl, Anne, just a young trollop, exploited for the vanity and gain of the family."

"Hm, so more than just the wrath of God involved, then, and an alternative reason to hasten the annulment! Why not just take the girl as his mistress?"

"Oh, the cunning of the Boleyn's is without precedent. No bed without marriage, as the Earl of Wiltshire has hinted. After using Mary, his other daughter for the king's licentious means, Sir Thomas is too eager on expanding his influence throughout the kingdom. I believe that the man would sacrifice his own daughter if it suited him."

"So, an annulment would mean that Anne would become queen of England...am I not right?"

"Oh certainly! I think that I would rather see myself in hell, than see that hussy on the throne of England; though perhaps, *Purgatory* would suit better as a word."

"Yes, Thomas, be careful; the Lord hears every comment and every thought even before it has been spoken. Perhaps, it would be better to consult with Him? … It appears that you are not altogether at ease with your attachment to Henry?"

"He is my employer...and my king; anointed by God through his lineage. My points of view are inconsequential; his and God's are the orders to which I pledge my allegiance."

"Hm… but at this point in time, their paths may diverge… So, whose path will you follow… Henry's, or the Lord's?"

"Here, I need your help and guidance. You see, if I refuse to help Henry, then my demise is guaranteed. However, if I refuse to obey my conscience, and this is, I believe, the influence of my Creator, then my time in Purgatory will be very long, indeed.

"So, damned if you do and damned if you don't, then?"

"Precisely."

"It is the coin of Caesar again…"

"Render unto Caesar that which is Caesar's, and unto the Lord that which is the Lord's...except the head that is on the coin this time is Henry's."

"…And the head that may be on the block…?"

"…Is mine…"

"This does present a much more precarious scenario than mere ethical concern. Charles is now Holy Roman Emperor and is Catherine's nephew. The outcome of an annulment, could well create turmoil within the battlefields of Europe, irrespective of what God thinks. I cannot see that Charles would welcome this news with open arms; and, with Lutheranism rearing a very ugly head, mayhem within the Catholic nations would further advantage the cause of this plague."

"Henry is a loyal follower of the Faith. He has spoken strongly against Lutheranism. But he needs the support and agreement of the Holy Church."

"Have you any idea how Catherine feels about this; have you discussed this with her?"

"Unfortunately, this is the fly in the ointment; Catherine is adamant that her marriage to Arthur was never consummated; that Arthur was incapable, or merely not interested."

"So, a virgin until the marriage with Henry. As a virgin, Henry has no case whatsoever; but if the marriage was complete, then…"

"Leviticus, chapter20, verse 16."

"…Yes, Leviticus, chapter20, verse 16."

Chapter 12

"Your Majesty…Lady Anne Boleyn."

"Lady Anne, what an enchantment."

"Your Highness…"

"To what do I owe the pleasure…on such a fine day?"

"If it inconveniences not His Majesty, an audience is all I seek."

"Gentlemen, how do I possibly deny this fairest of all the blossoms in the land, an audience with her king?"

"Your Highness…My Lady."

"Gentlemen…Uncle."

The advisors, clerks and noticeably, the Duke of Norfolk, with courteous bows bade their leave of the court. Henry looked on as the group disappeared from the room. His eyes turned towards the woman before him, elegantly dressed in the finest of gowns of turquoise, with a lace scarf of white around her slender and young neck.

"My Lady…a walk in the gardens perhaps?"

"His Highness is too kind…that would be a delight."

The day was as bright as any had seen since the high winds and rains had brought chaos into the gardens of England. With protection from the high walls, the palace gardens had been spared the destruction of the surrounding countryside. Dismissing the gardeners from their duties, Henry strolled slowly with Anne beside him.

"Anne what news?"

"That is the same question I was here to ask you, Henry?"

"Sadly, Wolsey appears to have been unsuccessful in persuading Pope Clement to agree to this divorce…at this moment in time."

"Henry! Do you not control the man? Does he not owe you the loyalty of his office? How can this not be?"

"Anne, believe me, I am doing everything in my power to secure an annulment to Catherine, but the wheels of politics need to be trodden carefully…as do the wheels of the church."

"I am not convinced that the cardinal's wheels are turning at all! It has been three years now and what…nothing! Nothing but false promises and hopes of what might be if this…or might be if that. Henry, he is holding back."

"Wolsey is my staunch friend and Lord Chancellor and I believe that he is endeavouring to do his utmost to complete the task that I set him…what makes you doubt his good intentions?"

"I think, Henry, that he is against this divorce. I think that he is dallying and delaying, for whatever reasons…perhaps, he thinks that you will tire of me and that would make *his* life so much easier."

"Wolsey informs me that His Holiness says that he will consider the matter in due course; that there is much to ponder in light of the papal bull of his predecessor, Pope Leo."

"How do you know that it is the pope and not Wolsey speaking?"

"Wolsey is impartial…"

"Wolsey is not impartial, damn it! He is as partial as you can get. The man is as devious as he is fat. If it doesn't suit the man, then he will not pursue it. Henry, he has had your ear for nigh on twenty years and perhaps you are blinded to his true nature and motivations."

"My Lady, this is no way to speak to your king!"

"I am not speaking to my king…I am speaking to the man before me…the man that I love and long to be with; the man that I wish to lay with and succumb to his tender embraces; the man who will father my sons…and daughters, if that be God's will. This is the man to whom I am speaking."

"Then bed with me, Anne, let these dreams become a reality…let us create these sons that I so yearn for."

"Do you not already have a son, Henry…Henry Fitzroy?"

"Yes…"

"Born out of wedlock, as would be mine… Whatever happened to Elizabeth Blount, Henry?"

"Elizabeth and I became somewhat distant…"

"Yes, because my sister, Mary, came to court, I believe…"

"But she is well-cared for; married now to Gilbert Tailboys."

"But without influence, without recognition; without any of her affiliations with the King of England, save that of a son, whom you acknowledge…that is all that she has to show for her years with you…then along came my sister…then what, Henry…me, then who will follow? This is not how it will be…I will not be another one of your courtesans!"

"Anne, Anne, this is not how I feel for you. Unlike Catherine, the union into which I was coerced, with you it is love…true, deep, sincere and passionate. So, tell me what I must do to get you to believe me?"

"Get rid of Wolsey!"

"But Wolsey…"

"Is stopping the King of England producing an heir, a son, who may follow in the footsteps of his father and lead this country into further realms of greatness."

"Wolsey is…"

"Poisoning the mind of the man before me with his ambitions and motivations for what he feels is right for himself. He has been with you too long…he has blinded *you* to what you want, Henry, what you really want."

Henry pondered after Anne had left. Wolsey had been his resolute friend and advisor. No axes to grind, surely? Hadn't he strived always to put the king and country above his own personal and political desires? However, it had seeded doubt into the mind of the king. Henry gazed through the glass, slightly reflecting his own ghostly image as the clouds covered the sun transitorily. With King Francis now held captive by the Holy Roman Emperor Charles V, surely this was a sign from God himself to strike again at the French. With their king now a prisoner under Charles, it would only be a short war to claim the kingdom of France and unite England and her auld ally under the same banner. He needed funding to support his insatiable lust for power and dominance and his Lord Chancellor would see that the royal coffers had adequate means to support the conflict. After all, the previous skirmishes had always seen the French running; the navy; the army…the French had neither the skill, weaponry, organisation nor the belly for another battle.

The Dukes of Norfolk and Suffolk walked in.

"My Dukes! What news; how goes the rebellion?"

"Under control, Your Majesty. We have apprehended the main antagonists and they await their fate in fleet prison."

"Splendid…"

"But, Your Highness, far be it for me to support their cause…but, there is a strong distaste for this tax levy. The populace does not see it as justification to support another foreign conflict over which England does not need to become embroiled. If we were under threat…then yes, funding could be justified, but to search for a war…well, that does not bode well with the common man."

"Hm…Wolsey seemed confident that this funding would be most agreeable to the common man."

"Perhaps, His Eminence was unduly overconfident, Your Highness. Did he feel that he could just impose further fiscal burdens on the commoners of England, with impunity? If you pardon my boldness, this is not the first time that he has errored in the duties of his office."

"Name another, then?"

"The Eltham Ordinance…but, perhaps, the charges and trial of Buckingham were the most disgraceful activities carried out by Cardinal Wolsey, Sire. The charges were fabricated and those testifying against the duke had been paid handsomely for their testaments. Your decision to execute was based on these falsehoods…"

First, Anne, and now the Dukes of Norfolk and Suffolk; but these weren't the only nobles of the land that had spoken out against the king's chancellor. Henry mused for a few moments. Had he been wrong all along about the cardinal? Had he really been fooled into thinking that his Lord Chancellor was a devout servant of king and country?

"…I had been loath to mention it, Your Majesty, but, in confidence, Sir Henry Boleyn discovered, as Your Majesty's comptroller, anomalies in the funds deemed for the Exchequer."

"Anomalies…in what way?"

"As you are aware, Cardinal Wolsey has been heavily involved in the closure of those Religious Orders deemed corrupt and removing their wealth and assets."

"…And?"

"It would appear that their funds did not make it into the coffers of the Exchequer…they were directed elsewhere…"

"Elsewhere…?"

"…The assets were directed into Cardinal Wolsey's own foundations…into his great college at Oxford."

"Why was I not informed of this?"

"…So as not to denigrate his good name, Your Majesty…"

"But there was also his failure to secure the amnesty between the Boleyn's and the Butler's over the issue with the Earldom of Ormond and the arranged marriage between Lady Anne Boleyn and James Butler, if I remember it rightly…"

"Ah, yes, I had forgotten…"

"The what? He was involved with the marriage of Lady Anne to James Butler…?"

"Most instrumental, Sire."

Henry's mien changed visibly as he tried to supress his wrath.

"Thank you, gentlemen, you have given me much for reflection."

The two men bowed low before their king, turned and made exit from the room.

"You omitted to inform the king that the proposed marriage was ten years ago, I noticed!"

Chapter 13

It had been nearly three years since Wolsey's unsuccessful attempt at annulling the marriage between Catherine of Aragon and Henry. He was in disgrace and despatched to York to continue his duties as Archbishop of the diocese of York.

"Your Eminence."

"Yes, George?"

"Sir Henry Percy, 6th Earl of Northumberland, Your Eminence."

A group of men walked into the archbishop's office, fully armed. Moving before his men the Earl of Northumberland stood in front of the obese archbishop.

"Come to gloat, no doubt, Sir Henry?"

"Oh, more than that, Your Lordship; much more."

"Why the entourage, need a bodyguard against an old, defenceless man?"

"Let's just call it 'insurance,' shall we…hm? I have here a warrant for the arrest of a Thomas Wolsey, to be tried for treason."

"What? Treason?"

"Yes, you common, fat upstart. I said I'd get your head…and here it is-a warrant for treason."

"But treason against whom?"

"Mrs Briggs of Yarmouth."

"Briggs of Yarmouth!"

"The king, you fool. Who else can you commit treason against?"

"But…but, surely, Henry cannot consider me a traitor? I have served him faithfully for nye on twenty-years…and his father before him."

"Every rat must come to the surface sooner or later; even twenty-years later."

"But what grounds does he have for treason?"

"That will be put before you at the trial in London."

"Surely, I have a right to know of what I am accused? Show me the warrant."

"That I will not do…it contains articles of which you may not be permitted to see."

"Then I refuse to go…with you, or your henchmen; or anyone else that turns up unannounced, with seditious accusations…and without any just cause. Why, you may merely have a scroll that contains nothing but arse wiping's…See yourself out!"

"…Praemunire."

"Praemunire! What authority, other than the king's, have I ever obeyed?"

"Rome, perhaps…Your Lordship!"

"Rome? … This is Boleyn's doing!"

"Your undoing, more like…Your Lordship! Perhaps you hadn't considered the Norfolk's or the Suffolk's; after all, you don't have too many allies within the nobility."

In a state of shock, Wolsey, shook violently underneath his enormous array of clothing and robes.

"You chastised and humiliated me in your household when I was just doing my duty as your aide and advisor. All I asked for was the hand in marriage of the woman that I loved, and still love…and she loved me. Was there such a reason to chastise me so?"

"Perhaps, it was in the king's interest in that union that I became embroiled."

"An easy reply; blame the king!"

"However, I regret the voluminous manner of my berating. That was not justified. Besides, you are married now, Mary Talbot, isn't it?"

"How dare you! An arranged marriage, just to keep me from Anne, my real love."

"Mistress Boleyn, I believe, is now committed elsewhere."

"Yes, because of you; just as it suited you to cast away your own mistress, Joan Larke, when it suited you!"

"Joan was…was…"

"An embarrassment! Yes, with your high and mighty affiliations and ambitions, this woman was merely cast aside when it suited. She even bore you children. Do you see them, or know of their fates?"

"As with the king, it was better…"

"Oh, the king at fault again, is it! No wonder you have been charged with treason, you haven't the king at heart, only Thomas Wolsey! Get your house in order, pack…you have two days."

The moroseness of Wolsey was felt throughout Cawood Palace. An archbishop to be tried for treason! His close friends and confidants, Edmund Bonner and George Cavendish, felt the same distress as their master. The main difference being that the other two were unlikely to lose their heads, as Wolsey almost certainly would. Treason charges, despite the Magna Carter, were a tyrant's excuse for disposing of his enemies, legally. No arguments were possible against such accusations; after all, any such jury would have been selected by the very tyrant calling for justice. And Wolsey knew this. Having strived for the king and country, as well as for himself, Wolsey, in his mid-fifties was a spent man, in ailing health and prone to the pains of pending old age.

With increasing difficulty, his house as much in order as the two days had permitted, he climbed upon the animal to take him towards his doom. Accompanied by his friend, George Cavendish and chaplain, Edmund Bonner, the party moved slowly through York and towards London. Wolsey let his mind drift through the life that he had known since his youth. His father, a common butcher, had been so proud when he obtained his early degree at Magdalen College in Oxford, after completing his studies in Ipswich.

"A degree in Theology, father!"

"Thomas, your mother and I are so proud. Your path in life has been assured by God's good grace."

"And it is in His grace I shall follow, father. I have been offered the post of Bursar at Magdalen, but this is only the steppingstone; I shall seek Ordination and serve God and the people of this land."

Despite the solemnity, Thomas found himself smiling at his youthful memories, but then the reality of his immediate fate started him weeping. Oh, the innocence of youth, when the world centres on you and life is there for the taking. When dreams, aspirations and the excitement of hope, make each day seem like the world is made for you; the dawns that take on new beauties and the sunsets, new splendours. But, alas, time is not kind to age, as it wrinkles up your mortal frame and brings weakness to your senses and ambitions; those delirious fantasies of the young, that delude even the nobility of the land as time silently, but remorselessly, holds you in its final dance. The silence was broken as his chaplain spoke.

"How did you come to serve the late king, Your Eminence?"

Thomas's mind had drifted too far with the rocking of the saddle, as they ambled on through the wooded land. Nature's beauty beside him, which he had ignored and left unnoticed in his mercenary and relentless rise to power, now took on a new meaning, such as it had when a youth. Here was God's touch; here was God's gift to mankind-the trees in their swaying colours; the darting rabbit; the racing deer; the soft rain on the face; the elusive rainbow and the rolling sea.

"Your Eminence …?"

"Yes, Edmund?"

"You must have been far away?"

"Oh…did you speak?"

"Yes, I merely asked, how did you come to serve the late king, Your Eminence?"

"Oh, I was offered the position of chaplain to Henry Deane, former Archbishop of Canterbury, but he died after a year. Sir Richard Nanfan succeeded him and introduced me to his majesty. When Sir Richard died, Henry, that is Henry VII, asked me to join his service, first as secretary to Richard Foxe, then as advisor to the king, himself."

"An honour, indeed."

"Yes, I have been very fortunate. Just there in the right place, at the right time…perhaps not now, though…. Did you know that I have a place in Cheshunt?"

"Isn't that Hertfordshire, Your Eminence?"

"Yes, a pleasant country retreat. I visited there a few times and would like to return."

"Perhaps, after your stay in London has been concluded, Your Eminence?"

"…Perhaps, yes, perhaps."

The cortege stopped, as a light rain drifted in the air. One of the soldiers came to Wolsey.

"We are stopping here for the night, Your Lordship. You may take a stroll, but keep within eyesight, there are creatures here, both animal and human, that it would be better not to meet."

Strolling, with difficulty, the rain felt refreshing, but the squelching mud made walking difficult as the cardinal and his chaplain slid on the mossy ground.

"Perhaps, Edmund, we had better be returned to the others. The ground is somewhat challenging, especially for one used to the marble and stone floors of palaces and cathedrals."

The two men returned, and just as they entered the inn, Sir Henry Percy approached.

"A word, Your Lordship?"

"Come, Edmund, Sir Henry wishes to amuse us in chatter."

"No, Your Lordship …I think this conversation be better twixt just the two of us."

"Very well."

The two men took shelter in the welcoming warmth of the inn. Dismissing his men so that just the two of them were alone, he helped the man he loathed into a solid oak chair.

"I was, and still am, incensed with your despicable behaviour when in your service. But more than that, it was your refusal to permit my betrothal to my love."

"Your father was not in favour either, not just the king."

"The king! What do you mean, the king?"

Sir Henry withdrew his sword and placed it at Wolsey's heart.

"What do you mean, *the king*?"

"You can push that blade as hard as you wish, Sir Henry, my days are numbered, whether at the sword, or the executioner's axe, it makes no difference, my time in this world is closing."

"Then as your time is now limited, best tell me why and clear your conscience before God."

"Perhaps the time has come for my retribution. I have accepted the confessions of many; should it be now that I bare myself and my sins before a soldier?"

"The king?"

"Though I did not know it at the time, his majesty advised me to dissuade the union of you two, feeling that marriage would not be conducive to her presence at court with the queen. I did not realise then, but only later, that the king had his eye on mistress Boleyn, himself—*easy on the eye*, as he put it. Not wishing it to be made known of his ulterior motives, it was left to me to complete his licentious mission."

The sword pushed deeper into the cardinal's chest.

"You have now betrayed the king with your confession."

"I have only ever served him, even against my own morals and judgement, I have performed my duties as demanded of me. I am no traitor, my confession was not a betrayal; you asked for the truth, and as unpleasant as it may taste, you have it, spittle and all."

Sir Henry relaxed the sword and replaced it in its scabbard.

"My only apology is how I berated you—I make no apology for following orders."

"Then, perhaps, there is an outcome to this that will avoid any publicity, humiliation, or defamation to either the king, or yourself?"

"And how is that, may I ask? The trial will be a farce, and I may be too enraged not to bring the king to account for his actions."

"…That you do not make trial."

"…Not make trial, how is that possible? … Oh, no; life is given and taken by the Almighty. No other hand can be involved. As a soldier, your life in the Great Beyond may not be as assured as mine. No, I will not take my own life; I will face my Maker in the great hereafter in the knowledge that my life, though perhaps not as pious as it should have been, has been led in the belief and love of my Saviour."

"As a soldier, we too are faced with the imminence of death, but accept that fate without fear. You too, are a soldier, perhaps not as I, but you show no fear."

"No fear of the outcome; just perhaps a little apprehensive of the cold axe."

"I put it to you then, do you believe that if you had two choices, for example, take the road to the right and you will fall off the cliff, or take the road to the left and come safely home. Do you think that that choice is left to chance, or that God directs which way you will go?"

"I believe that the Almighty will always guide us onto the path of righteousness, whatever His motive, if the cliff path be what He wants, then the cliff path it be."

Sir Henry left the room and came back with two glasses of wine. He placed them down on the table before Wolsey.

"In front of you, Your Lordship, are two goblets. One contains a mixture of laudanum and Belladonna in the wine, the other, just wine. Which one will you choose?"

"Why the one without the laudanum and Belladonna."

"If you *had* to choose, as though your life depended on it, and you did not know which goblet had the poison, which would you choose-the one on the left, or the one on the right."

"I would pray to my Lord for guidance and let Him choose."

"Then, Your Lordship, perhaps you would consider that, perhaps, at the eventide supper, I shall have placed before you two glasses of wine. You may drink from the one on the left, or the one on the right, but one will lead to an early demise and avoidance of the cold axe, and the other to the joys of the fruit of the vine. It will be God's guidance which one you choose."

"An interesting proposition, Sir Henry, and one on which I will ponder. I believe that there is many a mystery at the hand of God and that He will direct me on the correct path; His will be obeyed."

"Tomorrow, you will arrive at Sheffield Manor and I shall return to Cawood. As a man of noble birth, I despise you, but as a soldier, I admire you. I admire the resolute character of a man who believes and follows those beliefs, even to the cliff path. We may not meet again but may the hand of God guide you."

With that, Sir Henry Percy, 6th Earl of Northumberland, arose, and giving a courteous bow, left the room. Wolsey became much disturbed with the discourse that had just taken place and retired to his room. He feared the executioner's axe, but suicide was not, and never would be, an option. He knew the outcome; this was a long, one-way trip to face Henry's 'justice.' Though he hadn't raised the issue with Sir Henry, he felt that the Boleyn's, especially that ambitious young hussy, Anne, had poisoned the king's mind against him. Despite all his achievements and success, it was this one failure that had brought his defamation. Henry's cock had steered his reasoning…as it always had done. The way to a man's heart, thought Wolsey, is not necessarily through the stomach, more likely through the fly.

With a roaring fire to keep out the November chill, Wolsey held the goblet of wine before him. He stared at the liquid inside. Yes, indeed he had a choice; he had always had a choice. Perhaps, his ambitions had blinded him to the real will of God. But then, he had served a king who had been appointed by God, hadn't he? He had always followed orders to the best of his abilities. Surely, it was God, who had guided him with every decision? But would God now steer him to his doom? Not my will, but THY will be done, he thought, again. Would he be testing God if he took up the challenge laid down by Sir Henry? On the other hand, *if* God had felt that this challenge was how He would see the depth of faith of his servant, then the gauntlet, should it be taken up? His chaplain walked in.

"Your Eminence."

"Ah, Edmund; a moment of your time, if you please."

Edmund Bonner walked across the room and sat down alongside Wolsey, facing the roaring fire.

"Edmund, are you a true believer in the Almighty?"

"Your Eminence, why such an outlandish question. I am a man of God, like yourself. My faith in our Creator knows no bounds."

"Then, Edmund, I repeat my question, are you a true believer in the Almighty?"

"Without question, Your Eminence."

"Then I wish to put to you a hypothetical theological question. If you were presented with two options to a dilemma, yet could by-pass totally that dilemma, or face the challenge set before you, do you feel that by facing that challenge, you are testing God?"

"Surely, that would depend upon the dilemma itself."

"If that dilemma were, for example, a man's life."

"I am not sure that I fully understand what you are asking of me?"

"Think of Abraham and Issac. God told him that in order to test his faith, that he had to take his only son and sacrifice him. Abraham could have ignored the demand, believing that it was the Devil talking to him. On the other hand, he could, as he did, accept that this was God's challenge to him, to test his faith."

"Genesis 22:1-18."

"Yes, Genesis 22:1-18. But suppose that isn't the way it was. We have been led to believe that God was testing Abraham. Could it have been that it was Abraham testing God?"

"Testing God...How?"

"By taking his son as a sacrifice to God; prepared, if necessary, to sacrifice Issac, not as a proof of his undying faith and loyalty, but to see if his lord and master would prevent such a senseless sacrifice. In other words, to stop Abraham murdering his only son?"

"We believe that wasn't the case, but as we do not know of the mind of Abraham at that time, your hypothetical scenario could be correct. But you cannot test God!"

"The Lord, our Saviour, was tested during His fasting in the desert."

"Yes, but that was by Lucifer, himself."

"But Lucifer is the tester against God, every time. It is not man, who is responsible for his own sin, it is the king of the Underworld, who infiltrates into the doubts and questions of a man's faith. Man is merely the tool of the Devil's own desires. The strong man; the believer, can cast aside those whisperings into the mind. The Devil seeks those who are weak."

"Are you suggesting that you are weak, then Your Eminence?"

"I trust not. But the Devil is whispering to me right now; he wants me to test God."

"Then you must ignore him-even at the sacrifice of a man's life, we do not test God."

"Consider this, Edmund, you approach a locked door that leads to paradise. The key to paradise is in one of two jars before you; in one there is the key, in the other a serpent. You know not which contains the serpent, but to get into paradise, you must choose one of the two jars. What do you do?"

"If this was the only way to get into paradise, I would pray with all my heart to my Lord and let Him guide me; for if I should select the jar with the serpent, it would have been because God had wanted me to; it would have been His test for me of my faith and His will that I chose the thorn of venom. My place in paradise would be assured because I put my trust in God."

"Hm…wise deliberation, Edmund…thank you. I believe that you have spoken God's own words to me, yet I could not hear them."

"Your Eminence, far be it from me to speak God's words to you. I am but His humble servant; it would be to you that He speaks."

"He has guided your mind and that what ye spake to me, were the words from God Himself. I cannot always hear Him, oft times he uses others to do His works."

With the doubts of the night now vanquished, Thomas Wolsey, Edmund Bonner and George Cavendish, began their journey to Sheffield Manor.

"The morning seems to have awakened your disposition, Your Eminence!"

"Indeed, George; I feel like a man released from his burden of responsibility."

"Good news, indeed, Your Eminence."

Edmund Bonner looked on, as the two men in front of him engaged in animated conversation. Last night, Wolsey had seemed morose, but today, there was a new-found vigour in his temperament. Today, he rode with strength, as of one riding to battle. What had he told him last night; that he *spake the words of God*? A strange conversation and outcome for a man riding to his doom.

Shortly before nightfall, Sheffield Manor came into sight. A glimpse in the fading November light, showed the welcoming torches lighting up the manor. The party proceeded towards the octagonal turrets and through the Norman arch, alighting at the entrance to the manor. With his household in attendance, George

Talbot, 4th Earl of Shrewsbury and his wife Elizabeth, greeted Thomas Wolsey, Cardinal and Archbishop of York.

"Your Lordship."

"My Lord."

"My wife, Elizabeth."

"Countess."

"The journey, no doubt, has been torturous?"

"The latter part, only. The day has been fine, as befits that painted by that Master Architect. Even now, the horizon displays His magnificence in an array of colours. But the chill, heralds the onset of a less amiable clime."

"Then, come join us in the welcome glow of the evening fire."

With arms linked, the 4th Earl and Cardinal, walked into the splendid surroundings of one of the several manor houses owned by this peer of the realm.

"I understand that you are on your way to London?"

"Indeed, but I must reiterate that my demeanour towards my sovereign remains, as it has always been, unimpeachable."

"This is, doubtless, as Henry feels. He has been coerced into this deplorable situation, by other less scrupulous voices. Here, I have his own correspondence, stamped with his seal."

Handing over the royal letters, Wolsey read, with some degree of incredulity, that the king wished him every comfort and that he was '...*to be treated, not as a prisoner, but as my good lord and true and faithful subject...*' Wolsey returned the letters to the earl and after warming before the blazing fire, bade his leave of his host, saying that he would take his evening repast in his own chambers, as the day's journey had started to bare down upon him. With a courteous bow, the archbishop, with his entourage, made his way to the area of the manor that had been bequeathed to him during his stay.

As he sat down to feast, one of the servants approached him and proffered him with two bottles of wine. Showing the archbishop both labels, he asked him which he would like served. Wolsey hesitated and asked him to leave both bottles and that he would decide later, during the course of the feast. Making his excuse to the others at the table, Wolsey went into his bedchamber and prayed.

"Is this my test, or Your test, oh Lord? Do not tempt me, I pray, as Thou didst with Abraham."

Then Wolsey remembered those letters … from the king himself, suggesting exoneration?

"Is it You who is trying my mettle, that I should choose eternal life, or eternal damnation? Guide me to Thy choice, oh Lord; let that choice not be mine, but Thine. I am weak, I am with sin and I beg that You look with favour upon Your faithful and obedient servant, who has suffered the pangs of injustice and condemnation in so doing Your work. It has always been Your will that I have strived to do and the trepidation of what lies before me, fills me with dread. I wish to do Your will, I want to do Your will, but I need Your hand to guide me. Whether it be the path to the cliff, or the path to salvation, please give me a sign, my Lord and Saviour."

Wolsey returned to the table. The fear which he had just experienced suddenly vanished as he handed both bottles to Edmund Bonner.

"Edmund, I believe that you are a man who has tasted the fruits of the vine and know the exceptional distinctiveness of the finest harvest?"

"Your Eminence, I must confess to having a little preference of some wines over others, that is true."

"Then, Edmund, which do you believe would suit the meal before us the best?"

Edmund Bonner examined both bottles and asked that the cork be removed from both.

"I will not partake of the fruit of the vine this eventide, Your Eminence. The day's travel has left little appetite. However, with the venison, I would recommend this vintage here."

He placed the bottle on the table and Wolsey indicated to the servant to pour the wine into his goblet.

"George?"

"Likewise, Your Lordship, the day has, alas, taken its toll on me also. I understand that the water from the earl's well has been blessed with therapeutic properties; perhaps I will partake of this."

With some degree of cordiality, the group feasted well. Despite the solemnity of the pending journey ahead, the discourse was vibrant, with lively banter. Bonner signalled to the servant to bring another bottle of the same vintage when he saw Wolsey's goblet empty and the bottle spent. There was even gaiety in the proceedings as the evening wore on. With the evening's course at an end, the party retired to their respective bedchambers and all succumbed to a good night's rest.

Spending much time in prayer during their stay, Wolsey declined to accompany the others in their pursuits of 'earthly pleasures,' such as hunting. He confined himself, almost to the point of becoming hermit-like, to his calling as God's representative to the people. Knowing that his time at Sheffield Manor was temporary, he started to prepare himself, psychologically, for his departure to face the 'justness' of his king and the wrath of the 'trollop.' Whether it was the tortuous emotional burden, the years of living from the fat of the land, or some other unknown reason, Wolsey took ill. It was at the table. Wolsey's demeanour suddenly changed and he expressed the others to continue, saying he would return shortly. His usher accompanied him.

"Your Eminence, what ails thee?"

"George, I am with some discomfort. I have been taken about the stomach with a thing that lieth across my breast as cold as a whetstone."

With his agony increasing, Cavendish left the cardinal and made his way to the earl's section of the manor and requested that Wolsey receive medication from the apothecary to relieve his aching. The formula worked, temporarily, and Wolsey made for the chapel to pray. During his prayers, Wolsey was hit yet again with increasing abdominal pain and the resulting black diarrhoea suggested to Cavendish, that this was more than a routine, digestive disorder. With empty bowels, the archbishop continued, but much weakened, with his daily routine.

The Earl of Shrewsbury called George Cavendish and informed him of the arrival of the guard to take Wolsey on to London. The cardinal's usher deftly approached the ailing archbishop.

"Your Eminence, Sir William Kingston and his guard have arrived to escort you onward. Your stay here has, I am afraid, come to an end."

"Sir William, huh; Constable of the Tower, I believe?"

"The very same; a regrettable escort for your travels, perhaps. But fear not the worst, our minds see only the darkest scenario; Henry will see that justice be done."

"Oh, of that, I have no doubt!"

With that, and with much difficulty, Cardinal Wolsey and his entourage, escorted by the Constable of the Tower and his 24 guards, began the slow move out from Sheffield Manor and George Talbot's care. Wolsey, clung on as best as he could, but both George Cavendish and Edmund Bonner could tell that the journey may have more serious implications than merely wearing him out. By the time they arrived at Leicester Abbey, Thomas Wolsey had become a dying man. On his deathbed, he whispered to his Chaplain.

"Edmund…there is not much time left in this domain for me. I have trusted my Lord and He, for whatever reason, has led me to the cliff path."

"Your Eminence, it is not for us to know the will of the Almighty, but whether the cliff path be it, fear thee not, for the love and care of our Saviour will guide thee and strengthen thee, in this thy darkest hour."

"Perhaps, then, this IS the will of God. For if the trial had borne fruit, then surely, despite my faithful service to my sovereign, my head would have rested on the block and my neck felt the touch of that cold axe. Perhaps, then this is not the cliff path after all; my Lord has led me to my salvation."

Sir William Kingston approached the cardinal, realising that with unfinished business at hand, he needed information that only Wolsey could give him. With dismissive mumblings, and with weakening voice, Wolsey continued:

"…Sir William, I have served the king faithfully, even in the weighty matter yet pending, but be well advised and assured that whatever matter ye put in his head, be prudent, for ye shall never pull it out again…George…"

"Your Eminence …?"

"I now see the matter against me and how it is framed; but if I had served God as diligently as I have done the king, He would not have given me over in my grey hairs. What hour is it of the clock?"

George Cavendish arose to ascertain the time, returning to the cardinal, he whispered:

"It is eight-of-the-clock, Your Eminence…"

But Thomas Wolsey was already dead.

Henry's Legacy

Chapter 14

The house was quiet and sullen as the group made their way to the small shrine; the *chapel room*, as those dedicated and frightened faithful, called it. The dark, mahogany table served as the altar, with two candles burning at each end. With heads lowered in veneration to the man of God before them, they settled quietly. The priest, speaking the Latin of the Eucharist, set the cross of the Lord in the middle of the table. Kneeling in homage and kissing the feet of the effigy in front of him, he lit the incense as he circled the table.

"Pax vobiscum."

"Et apud vos."

The Eucharist was nearly completed, when the first loud thumping at the heavy oak door was heard, reverberating through the house.

"Open, in the name of the king!"

Using hand-held battering rams, a second pounding followed, as the panic-stricken congregation collected their small items and sped through the corridors of the house. Being prepared for such an event occurring, the servants ushered those devout few into the upper parts of the house and into their own quarters. Before the third banging could be released, the butler opened the door and, with a courteous bow, ushered in the small garrison before him.

"Where are they?"

"To whom are you referring, captain?"

"Don't be innocent and smart with me, butler; those degenerate, devil-worshipers who denigrate the name of the king with their acts of filth and obscenity."

"To what acts of filth and obscenity are you referring? There are none here, but the servants and house staff."

The captain, with his men, forced his way through the open door, firmly squeezing the butler between his armour and the solid door. He turned back and pushing his face into that of the frightened, but composed man before him, shouted:

"Bring them all to me…now!"

As though rehearsed many times before, but with an outward calm, the shaking and nervous man slowly made his way through the house to the stairs.

"Private!"

"Sir."

"Take the first three men with you and follow that butler."

With their pikes, the four soldiers chased after the butler as he ascended the stairs. Using the stave-end part of the pike, one soldier forced him aside as they raced up the stairwell. At the first floor, two soldiers began to rummage through the rooms, whilst the remaining two chased up to the next level. On his own, as he ascended the third level, the final soldier, without due courtesy forced each door open.

"Who are you?"

The two women trembled as they hugged each other. Both bowing before the common soldier before them.

"Chambermaid, sir."

"And you?"

"Chambermaid, also, sir."

"How many chambermaids are there, here, then?"

"Five, sir."

Satisfied, the soldier left and forced his way into the next room.

"What's your position here, then?"

"Usher, sir?"

"Why aren't you downstairs then, ushering?"

"We heard you arrive and the master…I mean the butler bade us up here for safety, sir."

"Butler? Master? Well, which is it?"

"But…butler, sir."

"You don't seem too sure, eh? Come with me."

The soldier forced the frightened man out of the room, to the top of the stairs. Leaning over the balustrade, he shouted to his colleague below.

"Adelard, take this man to the captain and get that 'butler' too. Methinks they've got some answering to do."

Using the pike, he forced the, now petrified, man down the steps to his equally offensive comrade. Moving further along the corridor, he rammed open the last of the bedroom doors. There before him stood two women, and though one visibly shook, the other maintained a haughty air of arrogance and contempt.

"What is the meaning of this?"

Slapping her across the face and spitting into her eye, he yelled back.

"I will ask the questions, wench! Who are you?"

"Housekeeper of this house."

"And where is this 'mistress of the house,' may I ask?"

"Away in York, with Lord Shaw."

"How very convenient...And you?"

"Laundress, sir."

"Where's the cook, then? This place too small to have a cook?"

"She's in the floor below, sir."

Having rustled the two men before the captain, and accepting the explanations of the house staff upstairs, the four soldiers stood with their arms at the ready in the main hall. The servants, having been instructed to get on with their respective duties, moved cautiously through the house, as they continued with their relevant tasks. The usher descended the stairs to the cellar, as he searched amongst the dusty wine bottles for the quality Saint-Émilion, that had been demanded by the captain.

"So, 'butler,' or is it, Lord Shaw?"

"John Hoskins, butler, to His Lordship."

"Have you proof that you're this man?"

"Resident butler for four years, prior to that under-butler to the king at Hampton Court."

"So, the king can vouch for you, then?"

"It is highly unlikely, that he ever saw me, but his butler and Groom of the Stool, Sir Thomas Heneage, can vouch for me."

The answer, with respective contact names, seemed to satisfy the captain that the man being questioned before him was nothing other than whom he had said.

"I have very strong reason to believe that the *old religion* is being practiced in this very house that, I understand, was the former house of Thomas Wolsey, was it not-a strong catholic, himself?"

"I never had the privilege to meet with the His Grace. So, I am unable to answer this question."

99

"The question is that the *old religion* is being practiced in this house!"

"This is a law-abiding house, loyal to the king and whether or not any religion is being practiced, *old* or new, of this I am unaware."

"Perhaps, you would swear to this on the Holy Book, then."

"There is no practice of any religion here, old or new, so I am unable to offer you the Holy Book, captain."

With a degree of menace, the captain strode over with his face almost touching that of the butler, who smelled the foul breath of a man unused to the social graces of the aristocracy.

"In that case, then, perhaps we need to stroll over to the church of St Mary?"

"As you wish, captain, but it will make no difference to my reply."

With a feeling that torture would be unwarranted, as he felt that either through ignorance, or loyalty, the butler had nothing of use to offer in this discourse, he continued.

"So, where is the owner, then?"

"Lord Shaw is with Lady Shaw, visiting Richard, Duke of York. They have been gone two weeks now and are expected back next week."

"Richard, Duke of York? Wasn't his father, Richard of Conisburgh, executed for treason against the king…Henry V?"

"Yes, but you cannot hold the son responsible for the sins of the father."

"Perhaps not, but that does make me somewhat nervous regarding historical transgressions against the crown."

"Politics, affiliations, ambitions, treachery; these are not issues that concern a servant, captain."

"No, I guess they're not. Ok, John Hoskins, you may go about your business."

The butler arose and strode, with elegance, across the Great Hall. As he did so, the captain called out.

"I despatched the usher for some wine for me and my men, where is he? Taking longer than he should, I think!"

"I'll go to the cellar and fetch him, captain."

"No don't bother-I smell a rat! PRIVATE!"

"Sir?"

"Get to the cellar this instant and check out the usher. I think there may be more to this man than meets the eye!"

The soldier, leaving his pike, but drawing his sword, marched rapidly across the Great Hall and taking the butler with him for directions descended the stairs to the cellar.

In the cellar, the usher searched quietly amongst the dusty bottles, blowing the cobwebs away to see the labels. A noise startled him and, knowing that he was not alone, crouched and slowly made his way to the end of the row. With a gasp, he saw the eyes of a man peering through the racked bottles on the other side.

"Father! Quickly, follow me!"

Taking him to the end of the cellar and pulling at the ring in the floor, he opened the trap door that led down a flight of steps. Immediately above him, he heard the sound of heavy thuds as the feet of the soldier and butler descended the stairs.

"Father, take the steps. Follow to the tunnel's end; there is a stream-follow it to the hunting lodge and in the floor, there is a stairwell under a trapdoor such as this. It leads to St Mary's."

"God bless you my…"

"Go, father, now!"

Quickly and silently closing the trapdoor, the usher made his way back to the wine racks and picked out the nearest two wines.

"What you up to, eh? Why have you taken so long just to fetch the captain and us thirsty soldiers some wine?"

"It is not my area; it is the area of John Hoskins, the butler, and I wasn't sure which wine to bring. Here, I have a Saint-Émilion… fifteen thirty-six."

"I don't care if it's a Saint-Bernard fifteen thirty-turd, we just want something to drink-a reward for all the grief you lot have put us through."

Snatching the bottle from the usher, the soldier told the butler to bring enough for each of the men-a bottle each. With the two leading the way upstairs, the soldier followed them back into the Great Hall. Insisting that the cook prepare a small feast, the captain and his small garrison filled their bellies and drank the wine, until in a state of drunken stupor, they fell asleep on whatever items of furniture were available.

The priest, meanwhile, came to the stream at the end of the tunnel and, following the direction of the water's flow, edged his way as quietly as he could amongst the branches and brambles overhanging his water's refuge. He tried to stay at the water's edge but slid in the mudbank, soaking his shoes, socks and feet. Uncomfortable with the squelching water, he turned his head back and saw through the undergrowth a soldier guarding the outside of the heavy oak door of the manor. He removed his liturgical garments, folding them as best he could and with them tucked under his arm, crouched as low as possible and continued to push his way in the stream. His jacket started to get torn by the brambles and then, to his horror, found his path totally blocked by hawthorn branches draped in the water. The water continued gurgling on, but there was no way that he, or any man could pursue this route unassisted. Without means to cut the branches before him and afraid of being seen, he knew that he had no choice but to lever himself up onto the riverbank if he was going to continue with his escape. He turned his eyes towards the guard, now in the distance and felt mildly confident that from here he would unlikely be spotted. Slithering, like a serpent, he crawled for about twenty yards until he found the relative safety of the stream again, this time accessible. Sliding down the bank, he was just going to continue, when he heard the unmistakeable sound of the rhythmic marching of men. Pushing towards some undergrowth, he raised his head above the bank and saw eight of the king's soldiers pushing on towards the manor.

On the other side of the bank lay the remnants of, what appeared to be, a former manor, surrounded by an inaccessible, stagnant moat. Lowering his head again, he continued to make his way through the stream, made more difficult with the protruding rocks. Slipping several times, he saw, at least he thought he saw, the hunting lodge through the overhanging branches. With safety in sight, he was unaware of the path that he had created as he had slid through the grass earlier; but the men of the king hadn't.

"Take three men, corporal and follow that trail."

"Sir!"

Not needing to be camouflaged and hide amongst the undergrowth overhanging the stream, the soldiers made their way quite quickly along the bank of the brook.

"Corporal!"

"Soldier?"

"What do you make of this?"

He handed to his superior officer a piece of white cloth that had been hanging from a branch in the stream.

Hm…looks liturgical to me, eh?"

"Corporal!"

"Soldier!"

"I can see movement ahead in the brook."

"Chase!"

All four men withdrew their pikes from their shoulders and sped on towards their prey. Turning his head at the sound of the voices from behind, the priest saw the four military men in pursuit, as he drew alongside the hunting lodge. Scrambling up the bank, as though his life depended upon it, he grabbed the door of the hunting lodge and dashed inside. The floor was dusty and the trapdoor the usher had told him about was not obvious. He kicked at the flooring to shake the dust, but no trapdoor ring appeared. He looked down and saw all the evidence of his arrival, with wet shoes, mud footprints and stirred up dust. Outside, he could hear the soldiers collecting together.

"Where is he then?"

"Lost him, here, corporal. Methinks, he went inside the lodge?"

"Ok! You two, guard the door. You, come with me and search inside."

The priest, using the now, grey, liturgical gown of the priesthood, continued to dust all evidence of his presence. He cowered as he made his way into the room behind him, brushing his path as he went. Again nothing! The front door opened as the two king's men walked in.

"What do you make of that, corporal?"

"Hm, not sure. There're no obvious signs of any entry, though the floor does seem a bit damp underfoot. Continue the search, soldier."

The private walked stealthily from the entrance into the room beyond that contained some pots and pans, an open fire, with grate and firewood stacked in a pile. The corporal stayed near the door but cast his gaze around the dusty room. On his return, the two men walked towards the room that the priest had just vacated. Working his way quietly, but almost manically backwards, the priest's foot hit something hard. He turned. There, by his foot, was an iron ring. He pushed his middle finger into the ring and pulled upwards. With the creaking of wood, the trapdoor opened upwards, revealing a path of stone steps leading down into the pitch blackness.

"What's that?"

"Came from the next room, corporal. Sounded like a door closing."

The two soldiers dashed in, just as the priest closed the door and descended slowly and quietly down the steps. The air was dank and cold; he shivered. He could hear the two men running on the floor above him as they raced through the room into an end room, with a bed and wash basin. Two rats leaped up at the sound of the men and rushed through into the room they had just left.

"Ah! Rats! I hate rats. It was these rats!"

"Hm, possibly soldier, but you said that you saw the man coming into this lodge?"

"It was only a suspicion, corporal. He'd disappeared, so I couldn't think of anywhere else."

"What about the lake outside?"

"Possible, corporal, but it's not very deep."

"No, but perhaps deep enough to conceal a fugitive? Let's look outside."

As the soldiers strode back across the room, the corporal tripped on the trapdoor ring.

"What the…? It's a trapdoor!"

Pulling the door up, he saw the flight of stone steps leading down.

"Soldier, leave your pike and investigate."

Climbing down, the soldier slipped on the damp steps and landed with a thud next to the terrified priest. Backing away as quietly and as fast as he could, the priest could feel that the room was larger than he thought. The soldier stood up, painfully.

"Corporal, it's too dark down here; can't see my hand in front of my face. We need a light."

Limping, as best he could, the soldier reached the top of the steps and hobbled to his superior officer. His dagger blade had broken with his fall.

"You ain't going nowhere, like that, private."

"What about the search, corporal?"

"Here, help me drag that bed from next door. If there is anyone down there, then down there they will stay. The tomb of the unknown fugitive."

The two soldiers left, with the priest entombed below.

How long he had remained silent where he was, he wasn't sure, but the priest resisted the natural urge to escape from his interment. Eventually, hearing no noise above him, the man of God felt confident enough that the soldiers had vacated the house. Try as hard as he could, he was unable to raise the door above him, and he knew that he was trapped. As his eyes had now accustomed to the dark, with the small rays of light penetrating through the floorboards above, the priest realised that at the far end of what he thought was a room, was, in fact, not a room, but a tunnel. The tunnel that he had been told about as he made his escape from the manor? He had backed away from the soldier into a tunnel! No wonder the man couldn't see him! *The tunnel*…this tunnel? Did it lead to St Mary's as the man had said? The conversation had been rapid and brief, perhaps he had misheard, or misunderstood. Knowing that he had no choice, treading slowly and surreptitiously, with hands outstretched before him, the priest began to make his terrifying journey towards the unknown. In total black, he faced not only the fear of what lay ahead…the fear of those demons of torment, but the fear of his very survival. Reciting the Lord's prayer, he moved further into the abyss. As he continued with his recital, he found new strength and courage as he arrived at *lead us not into temptation but deliver us from evil*. Suddenly, his hands found the soft strands of a multitude of cobwebs that then brushed his face. He leapt back from this foulness and his fear rekindled. He urinated in his trousers and became ashamed of what he had done. He was weak…weak, and as a servant of the Almighty God, he should be strong. Here he was, just as a mortal man, suffering the same weaknesses as men; but he had to be strong. He was the shepherd of the people and the voice of God spoke through him, he could not be weak…not in their eyes and certainly not in his.

"Give me strength, Lord, please give me the strength to carry on. I am Your servant, weak and sinful and I need You to guide me through my fear and doubts. Please do not betray me…I need Your strength now more than ever. Lord, please hear my prayer."

He knew that this was not how it should be. He knew that this was the plea of a frightened man, asking for help in his time of need. He felt vitiated. Then, remembering the suffering as told of the Lord in the Gospels, he ended:

"Not my will, oh Lord, but let it be *Thy* will be done."

The sound of his own voice comforted him somewhat, and together with his final defiant prayer at his own weakness, he found the words of the *Kyrie* come into his head. He started to chant. Pushing the colourless garments before him as a large fist, he continued. As if his act of rebelliousness against his doubts had been the avowal that God had sought, his courage returned. His prayer had been answered by his selfless request. He even marched, rather than shuffled onward.

Unsure of the time, had he been walking minutes…hours…days…his outstretched hand hit a wall; had he reached the end? Feeling all around, his hand rested on a protrusion…a slab? Was this really the end? Was this the way to his survival? His heart started to race. Had his God heard his prayer? Had he been through the mountains of temptation just as his Saviour had been…and survived?

Not wanting to test his faith again, he had to climb the ladder of Jacob to reach his paradise. But first he had to find it. Had that protrusion been the first rung of that ladder? His trembling fingers searched around the cold stone that he had discovered and, with bated breath, came across a second, higher, cold stone. With a rising excitement, he placed his foot on the lower slab. The stone was solid and supported his weight. Edging his other foot forward and upward, the next slab was as solid as the first as he took his second step upwards. He stretched out his left hand, but there was nothing but air. Stretching out his right hand, he felt the safety of a wall and knew that he had to keep by the wall if he was to remain in this dimension of life. Now, resting his hand against the wall, he used his foot to seek out the next step. It was there! Barely, daring to breathe and with heart racing as though it would burst, he climbed higher. How many steps had he climbed? He was uncertain…but at least seven. In his mind, he could picture the drop from the height of seven steps. Though perhaps not fatal, it certainly would cause considerable pain and perhaps permanent disability! As he pushed on the tenth step, he felt a slight breeze on his face and thought that he could just make out a ray of light. At the next step, his head hit something hard and he realised that he was at the top. He pushed at the ceiling above, but nothing moved.

Meanwhile, back at the manor, the new soldiers arrived after an unsuccessful attempt at finding their fugitive.

"You're later than expected sergeant."

"Sorry, captain. We got delayed just away from here, looking for a suspicious character."

"Suspicious? In what way?"

"It appeared as if he was trying to avoid us, hiding down by the stream."

"Uncanny coincidence. I have been despatched here on orders that that pagan old religion is being practiced here and you espy a runaway? Hm…BUTLER!"

The entire household was brought into the Great Hall before the captain. With two sentries posted outside the main door and two guarding the entrance to the main room, the remaining soldiers stood around the room facing towards the group before them. The mood in the room was obviously one of fear, as the captain interrogated each one.

"I have more than enough suspicion that you have been practicing the old religion here, in this house. Is that not so?"

Two of the chambermaids wept openly, trembling at the possible outcome of such a discovery becoming proved.

"I will tell you, that the practice of Catholicism is death. It is also a treasonable act to harbour, or assist in the concealment of, any person practicing this despicable religion. The penalty for treason is death. However, as a reasonable man, I am prepared to overlook anyone here who wishes to come forward and give me information as to the whereabouts of any person they consider acting against the law of this land; they will be pardoned."

The two chambermaids continued weeping; others just looked on nervously. The butler, usher and housekeeper, remained defiant, almost aloof, that these men before them should be dictating to them how they should live their lives; how they wanted those in this house to betray their own kindred for the sake of a selfish, misguided, sinful, tyrant called Henry Tudor. They knew the truth and would remain loyal, but couldn't be sure about the others, especially the more menial staff. Selecting one of the weeping chambermaids, the captain began his interrogation.

"What's your name, then?"

"A…Anne, sir."

"Ok, Anne. Do you understand why I am here?"

"Y…Yes, sir."

"How long have you been in the employ of Lord Shaw."

"Two years, sir."

"Local?"

"Yes, sir…a Cestrian, sir."

"You realise the seriousness of practicing the old religion and keeping quiet about those that you know do, then? The result is death, probably at the block with the axe, though hanging is possible…I am a lenient man."

With uncontrollable emotions, the chambermaid wailed into her apron, shaking with fear at the prospect of such an end to her young life.

"I know…know nothing, sir. We just do our job as told…as told…"

With that, she howled hysterically and the captain knew that this was a pointless exercise. The other lower-ranking staff were equally unhelpful, more from fear than loyalty to their peers and the captain felt that they knew very little that would be of help in catching those foul practitioners of Catholicism. However, if anyone was to be able to betray those guilty of such crimes, he was convinced it would be either the butler, or housekeeper; the usher, he considered, as a too weak and insipid little man.

"Are you a believer in the Almighty, John Hoskins?"

"Without any reservations, captain."

"And a regular church-goer?"

"I practice the religion of this land every Sunday, captain."

"Good, then you, the housekeeper and me…"

"It is '*I*,' captain, not '*me*'."

"Listen, you arrogant little nonentity. The three of us; you the housekeeper and ME, we are all going to take a little stroll to yonder church of St Mary's, where the minister will give you the Holy Book onto which you can pledge your soul should you utter any falseness…understood!"

Accompanied with two armed soldiers, the five marched briskly towards the church, some ten minutes' walk away.

Pushing with all his might, the trapdoor would not budge. With the briefest of light penetrating the top of the stairwell, the priest had to use his fingers to ascertain if there were hinges attached. Running his hands around the top, he thought that he could feel the iron bars protruding below the stone door above. If this was so, then he had been pushing against the hinges! He tried again at the other end…nothing.

"Give thy servant the strength, oh Lord. Give him the strength to move from his entombment and live to serve you."

Using, again, all his might, there was a creaking as small rays of light penetrated the stairwell. Losing his strength, the door slammed over him and the blackness returned. With a deep breath, he pushed again and as the light re-entered, he pushed the liturgical garment into the narrow crack that had appeared above him. The rays of light shone down the steps that he had climbed and he saw that he was about twelve feet above the floor below. With another deep breath, again he pushed and forced the garments further into the gap and could feel the freshness of the air above. He dared not call for help, as help would only bring him back to those predators, who wanted to conceal the true religion being told to the people.

"Lord, push with me, my strength is not enough."

With a fervent believer in an Omnipotent Being controlling man's destiny, he pushed again, as the garments, now firmly wedging the door ajar, gave him the faith and belief that his freedom was but just another breath away. His hands now could penetrate above the gap in the door and pressing his crouched back against the stone, like Samson with the Philistines, he found the strength needed to open the door, as the sound of crashing reverberated above him. With the door now fully open, he saw the statue of St John, the Baptist broken on the ground. Shaking from exhaustion, he lay on the cold, damp ground by the empty tomb, weeping silently, and praying profusely his thanks to his Creator.

Picking himself up, he made his way into the main part of the church. As he arrived at the altar, the door at the far end opened with a loud grating noise, as five people entered. He dashed, unseen into the vestry and using water from the font to wash away the filth of the tunnel, donned on the garments of the protestant faith. There was a loud knocking at the door.

"Yes?"

"Rector, I have here two people who wish to pledge their souls before the Almighty, that they will tell the truth, the whole truth and nothing but the truth."

"Well, why bring them here?"

"We need the Holy Book, parson."

"Oh, I see. Yes, let's go out to the Nave. I have what we need there."

The man of God and the captain walked into the main church as the 'rector' searched amongst the shelves and came back with what he needed.

"John!"

"You know this man, rector?"

"Why, yes. A truly devout man. He attends here every Sunday. You question his sincerity?"

"I question his knowledge, rector, that is all. If, as you say, he is a truly devout man, then this shouldn't take long."

"Ask your questions, captain."

"Place your hand on the Holy Book. You realise that your very soul depends upon your reply…"

The butler looked at the book placed before him, then looking at the captain squarely in the eyes, hesitatingly, placed his hand on the book as instructed.

"Do you know of any person in the manor from which we have just come, who practices the old religion?"

"I do not."

"Do you know of any person in the manor who knows of any person who practices the old religion?"

"I do not."

"Do you practice the old religion?"

"I do not."

The captain brought the housekeeper before him.

"Do you know this woman rector?"

"Why it is Mary, housekeeper at the manor. Another pious person, captain."

Asking the same questions and receiving the same replies, begrudgingly, the captain left with the four others. As the door to the church closed, the priest smiled as he replaced the hymn book back on the shelf.

However, the captain decided that he needed an example…a display of strength and determination, to extract that information of betrayal. He had the groom brought before all of them in the Great Hall, as he did with the lady-in-waiting. Before the gathered throng, the kneeling groom trembled as the captain walked slowly in front of him; the woman seemed more resigned to her fate.

"So, tell me master groom, how long have you been practicing the old religion…that mire of popery?"

The sobbing groom mumbled an incoherent reply, as the captain nodded to one of the guards in the room. Drawing his sword, the soldier strode over to the pathetic man before him and held it at the man's neck.

"I repeat, master groom, either your next breath be your last, or it tells me of the filth that this house hides; how long have you been practicing the old religion?"

The stench of incontinence portrayed the act of a man beyond all normal self-control; a man in absolute fear for his own existence.

"Soldier…!"

"Master, tell them…I know nothing, nothing!"

"Master? Master? Why who here is the Master?"

The lady-in-waiting arose, as the usher came forward.

"I believe that you may be looking for me…"

"Why, Lord Shaw…and Lady Shaw; a delight!"

The sound of flesh succumbing to the metal blade, made the younger chambermaid vomit, as the captain drew his sword away from the falling corpse. Drawing the bloodied sword from the body, the captain likewise slew the arrogant woman standing before them.

"Despatch them in the vaults, Sergeant…and you…what's your name…?"

"A…A…Anne, sir."

"You, Anne, clean up this floor, this blood will stain our reputation as peaceful soldiers acting in the name of the king."

Richard Cromwell

Chapter 15

The constitution of the British Republic was on shaky ground since the despatch of the sovereign, Charles I. An arrogant, conceited and self-centred monarch, who deserved no less than the removal of his head from his shoulders for the way he treated his subjects, like a footstool. However, for all his flamboyance, it had left a void in the British edifice, notwithstanding that the king was not above the law of the land. His son could have, perhaps, simply taken the reigns after the decapitation of his father, but too many felt that after the bloodbath of the previous five years, this would only have continued the brutality, never mind about recriminations and revenge. With the commonwealth on a knife edge, it had taken a courageous and brilliant tactician and leader to take control of the country he loved, preventing complete anarchy. However, his time was waning and he needed to ensure that this green and fair land would continue in the beliefs and values of the Magna Carta.

"Richard?"

"Father?"

"You realise that with the death of Oliver, you now become my heir?"

"Father, it has been a source of concern for me for some time now. I understand that I have been somewhat a disappointment to you, but with two older brothers, I did not see my destiny extend beyond the field of sport, music and in the pursuit of game."

"Of those pursuits, I have it on good authority, you quite excel."

"I believe, father, that those interests in which one is passionate, these are usually well attended by the enthusiast."

"Indeed, indeed."

The conversation was interrupted as Henry Ireton walked across the room.

"Oliver?"

"Henry?"

"The Irish campaign-there appears to be some degree of unrest amongst the populace and your involvement is needed."

"Is that vital at this moment?"

"As Lord Protector, I believe that this requires your early intervention, sir."

"Richard, our conversation must continue in due course, but at the moment, I need to turn my attention to matters with Henry Ireton."

With that the Lord Protector and his son-in-law left the room. Richard pondered over the conversation, and the probable outcome, should his father be called to the Great Beyond before he and indeed, the country, were stable and established enough to prevent further disquiet and even, rebellion? After all, he wasn't his father and the characteristics that he had inherited from his mother didn't really suit him to the role that he was likely to have to play, in the event of any early tragedy.

That was eleven years ago. His father had deserted him, well if you can call death desertion? He hadn't been ready; he wasn't ready; and he was never likely to be ready; and now he was under house arrest in Whitehall Palace.

"Lieutenant-General Fleetwood and Major-General Disbrowe, sir."

"Gentlemen?"

"Sir, the country is now approaching anarchy with the current situation. There are many dissatisfied Royalists who wish to disrupt the commonwealth and reinstate the monarchy. Parliament refuses to fund the army; the army has excluded MPs from parliament and consequently have not been paid. Those guaranteed pensions by your father, have had their pensions revoked and, forgive me for saying, but unless you are prepared to take drastic action, for which there will be much accountability and, bear in mind, there is little trust in the outcome of another bloody mutiny, then perhaps, you should consider your position in the strongest possible terms."

"Gentlemen, I have thought of little else. Unlike my father, it was never my destiny to attain such a prestigious position as ruler of this country. It is not, and never was, my wish to have such a high office, with all the turmoil, tact and diplomacy, together with sleepless nights and fear of the next confrontation, that this has demanded. I shall, therefore, with immediate effect, resign as Lord Protector of Britannia and her commonwealth."

"A very wise decision, sir; and one for which the country, though not realising it at this moment in time, will be indebted. But perhaps before you commit to that final act, you must, first, dissolve the parliament and entrust yourself to the care and protection of the army."

"You will ensure my safe return to Hampshire, of course?"

With the third Protectorate Parliament now dissolved and the Council of Officers in control of the government, Richard Cromwell slipped into obscurity, or at least, from immediate scrutiny. Returning to his wife and family, at Hursley in Hampshire, he lived a quieter life, albeit one which had him constantly looking over his shoulder.

"Dorothy?"

"You're up early, Richard…working already?"

"Yes, I must finish these letters to Major-General Disbrowe and George Monck."

"There are moves to reinstate the Protectorate, then?"

"I think not…and even so, those reins of power and problems can be someone else's; life is too short and precious to forgo all other commitments, such as family and friends."

"Yes, the past ten months have been a blessing."

"Yes, such peace as I have not known since my brother Oliver died. God rest his soul."

"You will go riding tomorrow?"

"I am not sure; Fleetwood is due tomorrow and I do not wish to miss his arrival."

"Good news, I hope?"

"Good news is what I pray; bad news, however, is the more likely, otherwise why would such an important officer be attending me in Hursley?"

By noon the next day, Lieutenant-General Fleetwood arrived, with an escort of two soldiers. Though greeting Cromwell and Dorothy in an amiable and pleasant manner, both could tell that the officer had not come with information that would fall in a pleasing manner on the ears.

"…You are well aware, of course, that Monck has reversed Pride's Purge?"

"I had no idea; but the outcome does not surprise me."

"This will mean…"

"The readmission of those excluded MPs."

"Quite…so…"

"…The Long Parliament will be restored and demand for new elections to take place."

"Yes, with no doubt, many pro-Royalist MPs securing their place in the House."

"You don't consider, for one moment that they would reinstate the king?"

"I don't consider, for one moment, that they won't!"

"You, my father, my brothers and the common man, fought and shed blood for the divine right of our democracy; to uphold the writings in, and beliefs of, the Magna Carta. Has this all been for nothing? Are we to restore tyranny again?"

"I believe, Richard, that the common man will welcome back the monarchy. There is a new generation of young men who have not seen battle but may bear the brunt of a lost father. The uncertainty of times ahead may push for a change in the status quo. The nobility, who, don't forget, rule the land…the nobility would welcome with open arms the return of the king and his family."

"And what of you…?"

"I will be fine. I'll still have my commission, albeit with a lot of demand for some kind of retribution, but more, like, what of you?"

"It was not my decision to decapitate the king…I wasn't even on the commission that decided his fate."

"No, but your father was."

"Will they hold the son responsible for the actions of the father. They executed the man, not the family and certainly not the son."

"Be that as it may, you are dealing with an autocratic dynasty, who will see the entire campaign being responsible. Whether you dropped the blade, or not, will be of little consequence to your fate, Richard."

"That is not how democracy works!"

"Democracy be damned! This is the reality…and it will not surprise me if they see the whole bloody war as treason and those responsible, treasonable. And you know what they do with traitors, don't you?"

"My father is within his tomb…he cannot be held to account."

"Don't put it past the populace and the gentry to trial him in his absence. If he is seen as a traitor, then none of his family are safe."

"But yourself?"

"Just following orders; as I said, there will be some retribution, but I think my neck will be safe."

"Then I must…"

"Disappear, yes. As long as you are on this island, with a restored monarchy you will never be safe; not until they separate your head from your body. Be prudent, Richard, again these are dangerous times, but this time, you may well be on the losing side. I must return to London; I fear we may not meet again, and if we do, I hope it will not be alongside the scaffold. May providence guide and keep you safe."

"And you too, Lieutenant-General Fleetwood."

Richard Cromwell watched as the detachment rode into the distance. He was, by all accounts, now well and truly on his own. As long as he was alive, neither he nor, possibly, his family were safe. However, before they could settle on his family, they had to catch and trial him first.

"The discourse with Lieutenant-General Fleetwood, it went well, Richard?"

"It could have been better received, my love."

"So, not good news, then? Perhaps riding tomorrow will help address the disturbances in your mind?"

"Yes, I think that will assist in the clearance of all these demons-I may be gone awhile, but do not fret, I will be back before the setting of the sun."

Riding through his father-in-law's estate gave Richard Cromwell the solitude that he needed in this another dark hour of his time. He knew that Fleetwood was correct and appreciated the time that he had given him to plan for his immediate future. He had contacts throughout the land, but this land wasn't the one he needed. He had also connections within the continent, and the continent may well be where he would be headed, should Fleetwood's predictions come true. However, though France was the nearest and most likely sanctuary, Cromwell knew that Charles had also been given refuge on the continent, France being one of the European countries who had befriended him; so, tread with caution he must.

With the pro-Royalist Parliament duly restored, it was only a matter of weeks before the monarchy would be reinstated and landing at Dover on 25 May 1660, the king-designate stepped foot once again on England's shores and on 29 May 1660, his 30th birthday, he was proclaimed sovereign of England and all her dominions.

"Dorothy, it is time."

"Richard, no, no!"

"He is too involved with his own vanity and establishing his advisors and council. My attention, will be someway off, so I must make haste before this becomes one of his priorities."

"It is as we discussed, then? But how will I contact you; to what address and when?"

"Should…when the king's men arrive, they will entice, cajole, even threaten for information of my whereabouts. They will endeavour every way possible to bring me to account for my father's deeds, even though I believe that he, above all the English nobles and gentry, was the most patriotic…and loved this land the most. With my anonymity, you will not be able to divulge any information, even under duress. I will contact you, perhaps under a pseudonym; but this I promise you…I will return; my tomb and my heart remain in this fair land."

"Will you say farewell to the children before you go?"

"The night before, I shall tell them that I must go away on business and may be gone for some time. As with you, they will have no secrets to keep from those in high office."

"Richard…I love you. I love your beliefs and your gentle, wise and forgiving nature. This, you don't deserve, as nor do I. But fate is the grasp that holds us close and who are we to untangle from that grip? May your courage and good fortune rest with you, until God deems that we should be together again as one."

July 1660, Richard Cromwell left on the tide for France. His ability to speak several European languages gave him an edge and with his link waiting at Calais, he stepped under the summer sun onto the soil of France.

"Bonjour, Alain."

"Monsieur, Richard, enchanté."

"We are going to Paris?"

"Non, tonight we will stay in Calais, I have reserved accommodation and tomorrow, we will start our journey to Alsace; Paris is too dangerous-many are loyal to your king Charles and your father and his family were not seen in a good light."

Richard had been used to both the splendour of palaces, as well as the less salubrious places found on the battlefields. The hotel in Calais was neither, but it did afford him the comfort of feeling free. Though a protestant, he held no strong views upon religion and the fact that he was in a strong catholic country did not affect his opinion regarding the hereafter. As far as he was concerned, there was only one God and the path to paradise, though often stony, could be trodden by any number of tracks and they all ended in the same place. After travelling to Alsace, he meandered slowly south until he arrived in the Languedoc area of France. As a visiting Englishman, *John Clarke*, younger brother of Sir Richard Clarke, he found himself of much interest to the nobility in France, and though trying to keep a low profile, was often invited to banquets as 'John Clarke of Huntingdon.'

"Mesdames et Messieurs, Armand de Bourbon, Prince of Conti."

And with that, the gaiety of the evening continued in the normal deceitful and snobbish fashion of the French aristocracy.

"Ah, our English noble."

"Your Royal Highness, Prince of Conti, a pleasure to make your acquaintance. But I am not of the nobility; just a simple Englishman, journeying through your beautiful land."

"Come, come, no modesty, please. This is the court of the Bourbon family and all are welcome…"

Then whispering into his ear continued:

"…though may I say, most here have ulterior motives, n'est-ce pas!"

And with that let out a loud, aristocratic, false laugh. Richard smiled and knew what he meant. Most people in the room did have ulterior motives; a contact here; some gossip there; but all with one motive, to rub shoulders with, and hope to gain in some way from, the French aristocracy. He did notice some glancing eyes in his direction from, though not necessarily restricted exclusively to, the fan-waving ladies of the court. It wasn't what he had wanted, but in order to maintain his incognito, he had to accept that by word of mouth, his journey through this land would be made known to the hierarchy of France. Clapping his hands, The Prince called out to the throng:

"Let's eat!"

Leading the way, Armand de Bourbon, Prince of Conti entered the lavish dining room, accompanied by the entire group of, Richard estimated, forty people. Dismissing an ambitious socialite beside him to the far end of the table said, "Non, non, I wish the Englishman to provide me with news from abroad, I have heard you all now, and I seek fresh gossip! Please, sit here, John Clarke of Huntingdon."

Though somewhat taken aback, the embarrassed courtier bowed and made his way to the end of the table as Richard set himself down, next to Armand de Bourbon, Prince of Conti. Turning his head towards the prince, he felt a hand rub his thigh and turning immediately to his left noticed it was not one of the fan-waving ladies. Pushing the hand abruptly and forcibly away, gazed at the wigged head of one of the assemblages, who continued in a pretend conversation with his partner.

"Ha, ha, ha…John Clarke of Huntingdon, this is the French court, you have to, how do you say in English…laisser-faire. Ha, ha, ha."

"I am sorry, Armand de Bourbon, Prince of Conti, it is not what we are used to; I was shocked somewhat."

"You are married then, John Clarke of Huntingdon?"

"No…" Richard lied. Better, he thought, to keep his past well and truly concealed, otherwise, probing questions may lead to his identification.

"Well then, perhaps you prefer one of the ladies to sit beside you? Marcel, exchange seats with Angèlique."

This time, the hand resting on his thigh *was* one of the fan-waving ladies. Richard neither encouraged, nor discouraged the contact, but knew that with time and no conversation taking place, the hand would ultimately lose interest, which eventually, it did.

"So, tell me, John Clarke of Huntingdon, what news from this island of yours? I have heard much turmoil is taking place?"

"Well, Prince of Conti, we have a new sovereign, Charles II."

"Ah, yes, Charles. I had the pleasure to meet with this exceptionally fine fellow and his family when he was exiled here in France. Such a tragedy that you English have to decapitate your king, only to replace your 'republican' ideals with his son!"

"A tragedy, indeed; it left a bitter feud within the commonwealth, after replacing the monarchy with republican ideals. But, as a nation, perhaps we were not ready for such dramatic changes."

"Well, that Oliver…though he was a traitor and a villain, was a brave man…had great parts, great courage and was worthy to command; but that Richard, that jester's hat, was surely the basest fellow alive; what has become of that fool?"

"I believe that he was betrayed by those he most trusted and who had been most obliged by his father."

"Ah, the intrigue of the English. I have heard it said in many circles, that within your monarchy, no one is safe; even your cardinal…Wolsey? Yes, Wolsey, Thomas Wolsey; he was murdered, n'est-ce pas?"

"That is not as I have been informed, Prince of Conti. The loyal servant of Henry was accused of having been traitorous, and the accusations were weak at best, but he did not make it to trial, so no account can be given one way or another."

Aggrieved, without displaying his true emotions to the Prince of Conti, Richard left the next morning and continued his journey further south, before heading into Italy.

Five years after receiving the overwhelming news of his wife's death, and twenty years after his rapid departure into unknown territory, Richard Cromwell, still under the pseudonym of John Clarke, returned to his beloved homeland. Europe, like England, had been plagued with the devastating 'Black-death,' and London severely destroyed by the ensuing 'Great Fire.' Times were very different from those that he had left behind. In fact, the London that he knew was no longer the London that he saw before him now.

With age very much on his side for maintaining his anonymity, he still retained his alias as he meandered through the streets of London. A new cathedral was being built to replace the old gothic building destroyed in the fire atop of Ludgate Hill, by a well-known architect and its circular nature was most intriguing and quite different from the conventional cathedrals scattered throughout the land. With masons and carpenters very much in attendance, he edged his way around the circular frame. Already its size was enormous and shadowed every other building around.

"Sir?"

The master mason approached Richard as though he were an intruder, but with Cromwell's attire as obviously being a man of some significant means, he broached him cautiously.

"Magnificent!"

"Indeed, it is, sir. A masterpiece if you don't mind me saying so."

"How long has this construction been underway?"

"Why close on six years now, sir."

"…And its completion…?"

"Hopefully, during my lifetime…perhaps, another ten years."

"Trying to reach the heavens, then? Who is the architect?"

"You've not heard, then…why, Sir Christopher Wren! You must have been absent sometime then, sir?"

"Yes, I have been on the continent-missed all the excitement with Pudding Lane and the devastation that caused."

"Would you care to see the plans, then sir? You seem to have an eye for taste? And, if you don't mind me saying so, seem to be a bit above the ordinary gentleman, sir."

"That I would like very much, if you have the time to spare."

Taking Richard to a shack at the back of the construction, Richard gazed in awe at the splendour and scale of the plans laid before him.

"I am absolutely speechless. This…this building is absolutely bravura; it is a true masterpiece."

"Now, perhaps this has been planned, or a perhaps, it is just a coincidence, but the height of this cathedral is 24 rods and 16 inches."

"What is so special about that, then?"

"Well, in the unit of feet, that is exactly 365 feet!"

"So…one day of the year for every foot!"

"Exactly, sir! Planned, or a coincidence?"

"Well, your guess is as good as mine, but there may be more hidden secrets within this construction than we may ever know! Well, I must away; 'tis far to Charing Cross?"

"From here, sir, perhaps an hour on foot."

With that, Cromwell made his way slowly towards *The Golden Cross* and his rendezvous with Thomas Pengelly. The two had hit it off immediately, when a chance encounter had brought them together in Italy and they arranged to meet at the coaching inn next time Richard returned to London. Richard knew that his friend may be several days away, as the unreliability of the tides and weather made it almost impossible for an exact schedule to be met. Two days later, arriving at Greenwich, Thomas Pengelly made his way to the coaching inn and his engagement with his new friend.

"Thomas!"

"John, my friend! How goes the day?"

"Fine, fine. A jug of ale?"

"Make that two; I'm as parched as a dried thorn on a rose!"

Settling down to a renewed friendship, the two men engaged together in the merits of travel, politics, religion and, within the hour, the splendours of English ale.

"John, you are staying where?"

"Well, I have an estate in Hampshire-Hursley to be exact and thought that I may return there."

"Is there anything that presses your return in attendance?"

"No, not really. My wife died five years ago, my family are dispersed to heavens knows where, and only a solitary return awaits me."

"Then lodge with me, my friend."

"Lodge with you, Thomas?"

"Yes, yes, yes. I have modest accommodation in the country-Cheshunt and would be overjoyed to share this with a friend. However, first, we can travel to Finchley where I have my London abode, as I still have unfinished business, both in the city and abroad."

"You have a wife, I believe, though?"

"Yes, and a son; Thomas also. Rachel, my wife, she is the daughter of Lieutenant-Colonel Jeremy Baines. She would be delighted to have the company as I am often away with my work."

"Lieutenant-Colonel Jeremy Baines? Wasn't he an officer in the'42-'49 Civil War?"

"I believe that he is the very same, though we have never talked about that conflict. After all, I was barely off the breast at that time!"

The two men laughed, but Richard felt slightly uneasy at the prospect of one of his father's officers being able to recognise him-albeit 30 years later.

"You see your father-in-law often, then?"

"Not too often nowadays, he succumbed to the 'Death' in'65!"

Perhaps, it was the gratifying effect of the ale, but despite it being such a remorseful subject, both men roared with laughter, until tears were streaming down their cheeks.

"Thomas…I must apologise. I…I did not mean to laugh at the demise of your father-in-law. Please forgive me."

"Nothing to forgive, John. A harmless mistake, and one, which knowing Rachel's father, he would likewise have found in need of mirth. Apology not accepted-it was not needed, my friend. Now, what say you to Finchley…hm?"

The next day saw both men in a more subdued frame of mind as the effects of English ale still lingered, together with a disturbed night's sleep.

"John, will you join me for breakfast?"

"I fear, Rachel, that the events of yestertide, have had a deleterious effect on my appetite. But thank you, all the same."

"Ha, ha…will you men never learn the problematics of inns and ale houses?"

"For one not too accustomed to the ambiance of the English tavern, I must confess to being a little naïve."

"Thomas was the same, but he should be more adapt than you with his constant socialising and business."

"The same? Thomas is up?"

"Up and away! Yes, he had affairs to attend this day and may not be back before the clock strikes eight, this eventide."

"Oh, I had no idea. In fact, when he invited me, I must confess to total ignorance of the future-immediate and near."

"What will you do today, then?"

"Well, once this pounding in my cranium disperses, I may consider my options. But pray, tell me, what does one do in Finchley?"

"Finchley is a hive of toing and froing. Sellars Hall has been rebuilt and there is much activity with society moving away from the heart of the capital to these quieter quarters. Even Finchley is not as I remember it but five years ago. We have been invited to attend Richard Utber's opening of the Hall and, hopefully, Thomas will have returned by then, but whether or not, please come."

"Would that be agreeable to Richard Utber; after all, I have not had an invitation?"

"Oh, without question. Richard is a close friend and he did mention that should Thomas not be available; he would guarantee me good company!"

The next few weeks passed quickly and very affably. Rachel and Richard became close, particularly with the consistent absence of Thomas, and were often seen out together. Rachel was glad to have the regular company of a man and despite suspicions, gossipmongers held their distance and refrained from any innuendoes. Richard, likewise, found the company very much to his liking, having suffered twenty years of near isolation. Finally, Thomas's business reached a level where he was not required for several weeks and he returned for a prolonged stay in Finchley.

"John, as much as I love being in Finchley, I am not needed again for several weeks and would propose that we journey to the country. As mentioned, I have a modest accommodation in Cheshunt. The air is clear and the noise less prolific than here-and there is more chance of game and sport, near Wolsey's old house. What say you?"

And with that, Thomas, Rachel, their son and Richard began the day journey to Cheshunt. Some of the domestic servants went ahead of the group to prepare the house for the master and his family. The *Parsonage* was less grand than the house in Finchley, but it contained all the essentials and some degree of luxury. Richard stepped from the carriage and sniffed the air. Yes, this was definitely more acquiescent. As an active man keen on sport, he was eager to investigate further.

"Well, John?"

"Charming, absolutely charming."

"Good, good. Today we shall gather our bearings and tomorrow, perhaps a little investigation? I have two fine mares, both dapple-grey, and both in need of the exercise that we shall give them."

"Rachel, she doesn't like to ride then, Thomas?"

"The daughter of a lieutenant-colonel, not liking to ride! When I first met Rachel, it was on a hunt and I must say, it was me trying to keep up with her, not the other way round! Nowadays, though, she prefers the carriage, but I wouldn't put it past her to take a jaunt on one of these beauties."

We walked towards the meadow and there, in the distance were two of the finest dapple-grey mares that I had seen. Just beyond the enclosure at the end, I thought that I could make out a small stream. With night beginning to make its way into the sky, the two men turned to go inside, passing the stables on the right. The smell of fresh straw and the lingering odour of horses was appealing to both of them.

Entering through the small arched doorway, the freshness of the twilight was replaced by the welcoming warmth of the large fire facing at the far end of the room. Unlike at Finchley, the ceilings were low, almost to the point of being reached by standing on a chair. The dark-oaked beams and panelling, gave an Elizabethan feel to the house, as did the leaded casement windows and vertical and diagonal timbers. The candles had been lit and the dancing flames created an eerie spectacle as a multitude of shadows wavered on the walls.

With the delights of roasted venison and red wine now completed, Rachel busied herself with her son and the domestics, whilst Thomas and Richard settled down with a decanter of port before the blazing logs. There were certain similarities between the two men, both being born and raised from more humble stock. Perhaps, Richard having the edge, with a father who had already made his way into the world of men and power. Nevertheless, the determination of both to attain better status, whilst maintaining an empathy for the common man, was probably the most likely bond that linked the two and made their friendship more genuine. Neither had a strong affinity for religion, but with due protocol, kept a regular attendance for service every Sunday.

The next day saw both men mount their steeds and trot amongst the woods surrounding the area. Returning to the track leading on to the London Road, they picked up the pace and with a steady gallop found themselves in the region of Theobalds Park. Dismounting and leading their horses, they strolled for a while taking in the smell of the woodland, with the white of the silver birch, the strength of the beech and the majesty of the oak. Though Richard enjoyed both the company and the sport of riding, he felt slightly uneasy with the surrounding area.

"Theobalds Palace stood there, John."

"…And those three buildings…?"

"Palace House, Grove House and the Cedars. The original palace was demolished…it demonstrated too much the opulence of the monarchy at the cost to the common man. King James and even Queen Elizabeth resided there, but after the war, it was taken down. Did you know that Charles I drew up his plans for the war here, and then rode to Nottingham to raise his standard for the beginnings of the hostilities?"

"Those feelings of hate, I sense that here…in the land. I feel the wrath of those determined to keep, at all costs, their lavish lifestyles, to the suffering of the common folk. I sense the anguish of the brutality of those times…come let us move on…"

Slightly taken aback at his friend's reply, Thomas let his mind drift as the two horses penetrated deeper into the woodland.

"Well, will you return to Hampshire, or do you think that you have found a new home, John?"

"My estate is but a memory to me now. This feels more like home…and as I said, I really have no pressing need to return to Hursley."

"You know, I have had many a contact over my years, but none that I can say meet within an inch of our friendship. I feel as though we were childhood friends, such is our comradeship."

"Indeed, Thomas…'tis how I sense as well. My trips on the continent have made me realise just how English I am and how I have missed my home. My wife, without question, was truly my best friend and even now I miss her, as though her passing was yesterday; and yet *our* comradeship has renewed my strength in, and my commitment to the hope of a fresh beginning and a new life ahead."

"Well spake, John. You have not considered seeking a seat in the Commons, then? An original thinker and good orator; your presence would be of much benefit to our fellow man."

"'Tis not the avenue that I seek, Thomas. My experiences of past do not tempt me onto the paths of justice for the populace. My oratory rests with the likes of you and Rachel. In the public eye, I am of poor rhetoric. I can serve the citizens better by not being beholden to dogma and creeds laid down by the ambitious and heinous cretins that currently rule our land."

"You have strong views, my friend-as mine, no less!"

"I feel, Thomas, that the injustice of the decades has been due to men's wishes to gain for themselves at the expense of all others; for their own glory, gratification and vanity. No less do I think of the people of this land, but mine is but one small voice amongst the shouts of the ruling class. I would never be heard."

"But one small voice, together with a thousand small voices, makes one very big sound, does it not?"

"Yes, 'tis true if you can trust those thousand voices to all sing together. Not all, but a few, will stand and not falter, but most…well, my experiences of past, as I said, have seen the frailty, as well as the apathy of the human spirit."

"You must relate to me, sometime, those experiences that have made you so saddened towards your fellow man. However, soon I must away, though I have a few weeks here in Hertfordshire before business beckons me again, but will you leave after my departure, John?"

"How would you wish me to answer…with honesty and as a friend, Thomas?"

"I would wish you to answer, as you said, with honesty…and as a friend."

"Then, with honesty, I would wish to reside here, with you, Rachel and little Thomas. This feels to me like the family that I once had…and lost. I do, with honesty, feel that this place, I could call home."

"Then reside! Rachel, I know, for she has spake her mind to me, has said how comforting to have the companionship of a fellow intellect, with whom she can speak to without ridicule, or fear of rebuff, if her conversance is not totally correct. She is a highly intelligent woman and needs the stimulus of lively debate;

and you with your experience and interests have awakened her soul to the thirst for knowledge. Reside, John…reside."

"Your grandiloquence is too persuasive, Thomas…reside I shall!"

"Splendid, splendid! Tomorrow is the Sabbath, and we shall give thanks to the Almighty Himself for the bringing together of our acquaintance."

"There is a cathedral nearby, then Thomas?"

"Nay, cathedral, nay; but across the path from my modest abode, there is the church of Saint Mary, the Virgin. It will be there that we shall hither and celebrate."

The few weeks that Thomas allowed himself the freedom from his work were the happiest in many a year that Richard could remember. Here, truly was a friend and family in whom he felt, at last, able to fully relax and be himself…with the exception of his true identity. Even that, he thought, he could divulge, and as candidly as he loved Thomas, felt obliged to conceal the truth of his family. Yet, Thomas was sincere, was he not? Twenty years a fugitive; twenty years of concealment; twenty years on the run; even his name was a lie. What if the man that he had befriended had one moment of weakness, despite their bond…and it was a bond-a real bond, but what, if despite all their camaraderie, it was one area of politic that was divisive? This he could not and would not risk.

"John, come walk with me, I have something of interest."

The two men, as Rachel looked on, walked together as two brothers. She had seen the wonderful change in the husband before her in those few weeks together. Albeit that absence from his work may have aided the situation, but this was more than that. She loved the man that had brought the family together even closer than before and, notwithstanding the absence of a blood-bond, felt that the man accompanying her husband had been the true contributor to this new-found happiness.

"John, I must away the morrow."

"Away! No, say that this is not so?"

"Yes, I am afraid, even now, that I have been absent for too long. I shall return to Finchley soon after the sun has lightened the sky and hope that you will not be too long behind."

"I shall escort your family as soon as Rachel and Thomas feel that they can suffer the journey home."

"Home! This is home! Since you have been here, this has been a true home! I see Finchley now as a place of interest and work; but THIS is home!"

The two men crossed the track leading to the gothic church of St Mary's and traversed through the cemetery until alongside this former catholic church of St John, the Baptist.

"What is it of interest, then, Thomas?"

"We are a little way off yet, but we shall pass the gate onto the track opposite and through the woods."

Alongside the track, Richard noticed a swampy area to his left with the higher wooded ground to his right. The track finished after about 300 yards as they approached a broader road, much wider than the path from the church of St Mary, the Virgin. Though woods still covered the landscape, a gap opened before them.

"Look to the left, John."

Turning his head and looking through the gap in the trees, Richard could make out a magnificent building of red brick about 200 yards distant.

"Rather splendid, Thomas; who lives there?"

"Well, it was the Shaws residence until recently; but now remains unoccupied."

"Oh, you didn't fancy this yourself as your country retreat?"

"Not likely! It has history, you know; and I am not too sure that I would like to be involved."

"History?"

"There are reports back from the local servants that the place is haunted."

"Haunted! Who would wish to haunt such a magnificent building?"

"It was Wolsey's residence, you know?"

"Wolsey…the cardinal?"

"The very same."

"I had absolutely no idea; what history indeed! Come, let's look closer!"

The grounds were open and with no bordering gate, entrance into the gardens was easy. Without ownership, or residency, the once resplendent gardens were now overgrown and in need of attention. The house, though from the distance breath-taking, close up had a feeling of menace. The two friends turned their backs on the house and surveyed the landscape before them. Fifty yards, hence, the land fell away into the swampy ground that they had walked alongside. To the left was a stream, gurgling its passage through the woods. In the distance, they could make out a moat and a small manor house on raised ground.

"Well, this is history. Such history! Wolsey, Lord Chancellor to that ruthless monarch…here!"

"How much he lived here is uncertain, but yes, this was his own property."

"And yonder manor house?"

"Unknown also. There is an air of mystery about this place, make no mistake. Perhaps, if I spent more time here, then I would have unravelled some of its secrets; but it certainly is a place of shadowy associations."

"'Tis a shame that you must away the morrow; I would so dearly have liked to have stayed and seen more."

"Then you shall. I am away on the tide from Portsmouth after my return to Finchley. There can be no reason for you to return until you are ready. You could even stay here longer if you wish. My voyage will be unpredictable, but I hope to be back before spring has embraced the daffodils."

Thomas had been absent for well into the second week and, surprisingly, Rachel took to the saddle of one of the dapple-greys. Richard was more than happy to accompany her, as her curiosity and own experiences made her an entertaining and invaluable consort. Dialogue was constant and losing all track of time, Richard suddenly found them to be back at Theobalds Park. Though there was no foundation to his feelings, he again sensed an air of apprehension as they dismounted and led their horses onwards.

"Rachel, if it is all the same to you, perhaps we should return to the Parsonage?"

"If you so wish. It will take well into the hour if we allow our steeds to stroll with us. Is that the reason that you wish to return?"

"Partly, but I feel also less than tranquil here."

"Why is that…has Thomas been talking to you about the hauntings?"

And with that, Rachel let out a small chuckle, perhaps enough to make Richard feel somewhat self-conscious at his own inward weakness.

"Why, yes, he has had occasion to mention the hauntings at the manor, but not here. No, I merely have this feeling of hostility; a disquiet within these woods."

"But we have been riding in the woods for well into day, why now and why here?"

"Think of me as disconsolate, perhaps, but there is something to which I feel a foreboding. There is a menace in the breeze on the leaves."

"I will chasten you no more then, let us return."

And again, Rachel let out a broad grin that made Richard feel a little humbled at his own weakness. However, Richard did not feel at ease, even with the knowledge of their slow return. Though it was only a twig that snapped underfoot, Richard was attune to a whispering, almost husky, breath nearby and the cracking wood made him even more sensitive to his surroundings. Their two dapple-greys nodding their heads in unison as they ambled on, blew vapour from their nostrils as their warm breath met the cool autumn air. Feeling the warmth from the animal beside him, gave Richard a little more courage, but he could not shake off this feeling of ominous presences within the undergrowth and high in the branches. The lane, at times, was almost covered with searching tendrils, seeking to establish new foundations within this most unwelcoming place. Richard had with him a small dagger and, at times, needed to cut through those penetrating vines to clear a way home. If it hadn't been for the obvious presence of a mud track, Richard would have considered himself well and truly lost and would have turned back the way that they had come, even though it meant returning to the place that bore menace. With a final rasping, as though gulping for air, the whispering sounds faded into the thicket and the sun shone through the leaves above.

"Shall we remount, Rachel; the track is clear and the horses rested?"

"The walk is good, John, but with the afternoon sun fading, perhaps it is for the best."

Dropping the reins of his dapple-grey, Richard offered his hand to steady Rachel as she started to mount her steed. Their faces drew close as she readied herself for the vim to push herself from the ground. Suddenly, she voiced a niggling that had been inside her since first they had met.

"John…excuse my boldness, but your face…it has a familiarity about it."

"Really? Oh, surely that cannot be…we have met only since Thomas brought me home all those months ago."

"No, it is not that. When we first met, I thought that I had seen you in the distant past; not to talk to, no, not an introduction, but somehow it was as though I had known of you?"

"Well, keep pondering, Rachel; I would be interested to know from whence that idea came and to what association I had to give you so vivid a recollection of my past."

Richard helped Rachel onto her horse, but the content of what he had said was anything but the truth. He was slightly unsettled that perhaps she had seen him in her youth, as a man of extreme importance; a man whose father's body had been exhumed, decapitated and whose head was still spiked at Westminster

Hall, as a traitor to this land. Though they had left the dark fear of the woodland and the overhanging branches, Richard was again at unease with this latest possible revelation of his past. They let their dapple-greys meander at their own pace and spoke not a word; Richard's mind being occupied with thoughts of him being discovered and Rachel wondering where and why she felt that she had seen her companion and friend. As the horses led on, she recalled how very little they knew of John Clarke; did he really have a sinister and dark past; were there things best left unknown; who really was this man her husband had brought to their home? A small copse lay ahead and passing by, the track joined a more significant lane.

"There, John…that is what Thomas inspired into your mind; such feelings of devils and goblins!"

Rachel pointed to the right and, following her direction, Richard saw again the magnificent manor that, once owned by Cardinal Wolsey, Thomas had shown him but a short while before. Richard raised himself slightly from his saddle and turning around, took in the scene before them.

"Ah, yes! We, Thomas and I, came from a different direction…the manor was on our left."

"That was the track that leads to St Mary's, that he brought you on. We will pass by and then this lane will take us back to the Parsonage."

They turned to the right and at a slow trot passed by the great house on their left. As they did so, Richard felt a slight apprehension, as he had when Thomas had brought him here. A second larger track at the end of the lane brought them back into the land that Richard now recognised. Though not as grand as the house they had passed, it had a welcoming feeling and Richard was glad to dismount and enter into the warmth of a comfortable house…a home; almost, he felt…his home.

Chapter 16

With the welcoming return of Thomas Pengelly, the two friends took every opportunity to enjoy one another's company and would often spend days out together, either in riding, or some other activity involving sportsmanship or mild competition, such as playing croquet and bowls.

"See this courtyard, John? On my travels, I came across a game called '*Tennis.*' Fantastic fun. Apparently, played by the French monastics back in the 1200's. Henry…the Tudor, that is, loved the game. Mind you, that was probably before he felt that there was more exercise to be had in bed."

"Why the aspect of the courtyard, Thomas? Is this relevant to the Tudor king?"

"Heavens above, no! I was merely adding some history to the game. I take it that you have never heard of the game before?"

"Heard, yes; but not participated."

"Well, the courtyard would make an excellent place in which to play the game."

"How does this work, then?"

"We will use some curtains, suspend on twine and drape these across the courtyard."

"…And then…?"

"We use a ball that I have had made with sheep's wool and tied in leather."

"So, what happens…?"

"I stand on one side of the net and you on the other, then with these paddles, we hit it across the net and whoever misses the ball and cannot hit it back over the net loses."

"Ok…sounds interesting; let's give it a try."

After nearly 40 minutes, two tired, but contented men walked wearily back into the Parsonage, sat on the wooden bench in the kitchen and, without pausing for breath, downed a full flagon of cider.

"This…this *tennis*…I think I am too old for this, Thomas! Ha, ha, ha."

"Nonsense! We played as though our lives depended upon it…and saw it through! Ha, ha, ha."

"Perhaps, again tomorrow, then after a good night's rest?"

"Absolutely…perchance a little wager, then…just to add some spice to the challenge? What say you?"

"My very own thoughts, indeed!"

"John…I am overwhelmingly indebted to you for staying here as a companion to Rachel, whilst I have been away. I have seen a transformation in her countenance and her wit is sharp. This is in by no small means thanks to you, dear friend."

"Thomas, it has been no hardship on my behalf, I can assure you. As you correctly say, Rachel has a wit akin to…Baron George Jeffreys."

"Ah, the *Hanging Judge*!"

"Hanging Judge?"

"Where have you been, John? Notorious for keeping to the letter of the law with no compassion, whatever. Another flagon?"

"Is this in advance of tomorrow's game, then?"

With that, the two men finished a second bowl of cider amid a roar of laughter.

"Thomas! Are you leading our dear guest astray?"

"Ah, Rachel, my dear…heaven forbid, it is our dear guest who has been leading your husband astray!"

"Rachel, I must confess to being part of this conspiracy; the onus is not entirely your husband's."

"A small bowl, my dear?"

"Perhaps, best left to the men, methinks. No, I shall partake of the juice of the apple."

"But *this* is the juice of the apple!"

"Without the need of the ferment, I mean!"

The conviviality continued, with Rachel succumbing to a Médoc during the course of lunch. Post lunch celebrations became more subdued as the effects of two flagons of cider and the lunch wine took their toll. Rachel left to attend to the house staff, leaving the two men engrossed in more thought-provoking dialogue.

"What know ye of Theobalds Park and the woods, Thomas?"

"Some, as I mentioned to you recently. Residential home to Queen Elizabeth…and the Scottish king, James, but otherwise not a tremendous amount as that area is rather away from here. Why ask?"

"Rachel and I had been riding a few hours and found ourselves at this point. As before, those feelings of hate that I sensed before, returned. I did not like it at all and became, somewhat, unsettled."

"Frightened, you mean?"

"No…well, yes; though I did not want to alarm Rachel, I felt an unease there and suggested that we return here."

"Did she rebuke you?"

"Most robustly!"

"Yes, she is not one to hold the unknown and unseen close to her heart. Very much down-to-earth…and a God-fearing woman."

"That is the problem, Thomas…I don't think that God was present there…or if he was, so were others not beholden to Him."

"You are not the first to mention that place, John. I have heard it from other sources…reliable and sensible men too. The air has a sense of melancholy and mishaps have been told to take place there with greater frequency than is the norm. I have had it told to me that the hunt will not venture there as the hounds refuse to go beyond the hamlet of the Bury…and the Dark Lane perhaps has its name labelled for more than just the overhanging copse."

"If the truth be told, Thomas, there were whisperings and noises that I did not feel were of this world."

"'Tis at the end of the manor, someway off, as is the Dark Lane. Maybe the influence of the house extends there?"

"Whether, or no, Thomas, 'tis not a place I would wish to visit too frequently."

"There is many a sailor's tale, that speaks of serpents and other monsters of the deep, that are also reportedly not of this world. Perhaps, the forests and oceans share a common mysticism of which the Holy Book has forewarned us- not to tempt, dabble with, or communicate. Perhaps, your encounter was a warning, John?"

"A harmless ride; taking in of the good Lord's air; I think that there was no attempt to tinker with, dabble, or participate in anything other than His magnificence and the splendour of His bounteous gifts before us. I fail to see what warning was warranted."

137

"Not a warning against His benevolence…no, a warning from sources that recognise not the guidance of His word."

"Maybe, Thomas…maybe."

"Come! Enough talk of Dark worlds-I have another venture for you!"

"As well as the tennis?"

"Oh, yes; tennis is a *must*; and the wager on! No, there is an interesting place not far, as the foot falls, to which we will away and visit the morrow."

With the day's activities and the considerable consumption of alcohol taking their tolls, the two men retired to their chambers and arose late the next day. The weather had turned from the crispness of the winter's day of yesterday, to the damp and cold of the English season. The wager, not being possible, and the pending return to Finchley of Thomas, gave a morose feeling. Thomas busied himself in his study with the planning of his return to Finchley and then his journey to Southampton. Rachel found Richard, reading in the library and sat herself down on the chair facing the fire.

"John, we must not, I insist, detain you here. You have a home and family in Hampshire, I believe? Surely, you must want to sojourn back to your home and kindred? From a selfish point of view, I would be distraught should you wish leave; the difference that you have made to our lives; Thomas…I have not seen Thomas as vibrant and of such amiable disposition as he is now; and this I am of no doubt, is due to your company within our family."

"Rachel…your words are so kind. Yes, you are correct, I do have kindred in Hampshire. However, after my wife died, I felt no desire to return-the place had too many memories and the bitter thoughts of returning there left me in no doubt that I wished to start a new life without the associations with my past. The pain would have been too great."

"Then, John, you shall remain as long as you wish, dear friend."

And with that, Rachel placed her soft hand on the back of Richard's and stroked it soothingly. Richard felt an anguish inside of him. He so dearly wanted to see his children, albeit now adults, but the fear of returning and being recognised overruled his desire to return to his estate at Hursley. The anguish, though, was a two-edged sword; he also felt another desire at the touch of Rachel's hand and politely, with a gentle patting of her hand, withdrew his and arose.

"I shall seek my friend; he said that we had another venture to face; though heaven knows what he has in store?"

As he passed by the small leaded-window, Richard saw the rain pelting down. The drops fell onto the top pane and rapidly ran to the base before dropping onto the ground. Some drops remained where they fell, being blown into place as though they had been held by some unseen force. As much as he loved being here in the Parsonage with his two dear companions, gazing at the outside weather caused his mind to wander. How had it come to this? If his brother, Oliver, hadn't died, his life would have been so different. He would have had a wife and family with whom he could indulge and enjoy. And Dorothy…oh, Dorothy, so cruelly taken, as with his own life; at least the life that he might have had. The love for his children, as with Dorothy, was unsurpassed, but he had to forgo all of life's accepted pleasures to hide like a thief in the night. Though he had used several pseudonyms, he nearly let slip on one occasion by introducing himself as '*Richard*,' but had recovered quickly enough to continue with 'Clarke'; Richard Clarke. He had now become accustomed to replying to the name John Clarke. It was unfair; it was unjust. The fortunes of the State were what dictated men's lives and he had been dealt a prejudicial hand of cards.

"Ah, John!"

"Thomas! I was on my way to find you."

Thomas looked out of the window.

"Alas, my friend, I feel the God of the weather is against us today; and the morrow, I must away."

"No venture, then?"

"…Nor tennis, either, damn it! However, whence the weather returns to the crispness of the winter's day again, perhaps you would consider the little investigation yourself?"

"Interesting; what is this investigation?"

"Just after the church of St Mary's, lies a token track; as we passed the wicket at the end of the churchyard on our way to see the Great House of Wolsey."

"On the left…?"

"That's it; on the left. Follow this track to the marsh…about 30 yards and then turn left again along a wooded lane; barely recognisable as a path. At the end of this path, about 100 yards, you will find an old, deserted abode."

"What is so fascinating about this old abode…is this the venture that you mentioned but yesterday?"

"It is. This old building is believed to have been the lodge to Wolsey's Manor House, but now remains deserted."

"Well, who owns the house; they must surely know?"

"Unknown, I'm afraid; that's what makes it so intriguing; possibly owned by the Crown. There are rumours…as there always are, that the house has bad vibrations…and there exists somewhere in its cellars, a tunnel. People will not venture near it, especially at night. Animals, too, avoid its proximity. I viewed it once and felt somewhat uncomfortable."

"Akin, perhaps to the Great Manor…?"

"…yes, somewhat; there appear to be certain similarities twixt the two buildings. As it is now, one cannot see the connection, but in Wolsey's day, perhaps…?"

"Enthralling; I shall venture there on the first available day."

With that, both men together with Rachel, settled down and accepted the accustomed English weather with due grace. With the onset of a miserable English winter, mostly dank and uninviting, the first available day was well beyond the boundaries of February. Thomas had been absent for most of the time since he had mentioned the *Lodge* and the tantalising prospect of the discovery of this mysterious place teased Richard's imagination. There was, though, a degree of hesitancy since that feeling of menace that he had sensed a few months back when at Theobalds Park. If there was any relationship between these two locations, then he wasn't sure whether he wanted to find the *Lodge*. He was no coward, but the unknown world of the macabre was not one for which he held an affection and felt that it was best left alone.

"John, what a beautiful spring day! I must away to the Abbey at Waltham for the diurnal, why don't you advantage yourself of this glorious moment and take in the fresh air?"

"Rachel, this was the very thought that I had been considering, since I observed this captivating morning. I shall in due course enjoy the splendour of the day."

"Will you take the dapple-grey?"

"No…I think that I will enjoy the moment without steed…as nature intended; just the senses to take in the bounteous display of blossoms and the advent of new life."

The insect world was awakening from its winter dormancy and the air was alive with youth and fresh hope. The smell in the air was vibrant as was the sound of the pulsating arthropods. After the prolonged cold, dank and dark season, this, indeed, was a beautiful day; a day just to feel alive! Though still weak, the sun shone through a cloudless sky, as the early morning dew twinkled on the grass. The skeletal branches of those young saplings awaiting their moment to display their splendour, stretched out, reaching for the touch of nature to bring them from their unanimated slumber.

With Rachel away in the carriage to Waltham, Richard began his stroll along the lane leading from the Parsonage. In the soft earth, the fresh marks of hooves and carriage wheels. Looking behind, Richard saw another set of tracks…his own as he walked on. Arriving at the road leading to Enfield, Waltham and London, Richard crossed over to the other side and into the grounds of St Mary's Church. Several of the gravestones were weathered and sloped away from their original placement, forced over by centuries of winds and rain. Richard ran his hand on the moss-covered stone marking the resting place of Mary Jaco…? Wife and mother of ….? Born 1415, died 1478. The elements, as they had already done, would eventually erase all evidence that *Mary Jaco…* had ever existed. As he moved on, Richard noticed the remains of a fallen and broken stone statue bearing the markings of '*St Joh…*' but as with the grave-stone to *Mary Jaco…*, the winds and rains had worn away the evidence to whom the statue had been dedicated. In its place, a tree branch had fallen, laden with moss and ivy, leaving the tomb beneath almost invisible.

Richard arrived at the wicket gate and turned to his left after leaving the cemetery. If Thomas hadn't mentioned it, he would not even have known that this was a path. With his small dagger, he cut away the penetrating branches crossing this track, and, as his friend had said, a wider path stood before him. He turned again to his left and, though the path was more established and wider than the track that he had left, emaciated brushwood still restricted his move forward. The sun shone through the overhanging twigs, casting a mystique of shadows and light causing Richard to squint with the contrasting glare. A branch smacked him across the face, causing him to stop momentarily to recover from the shock and pain. He turned around and though the leaves were yet to make their appearance, he could scarcely make out the path that he had trodden. In a few weeks' time, he thought, he would have been totally lost and this place inaccessible. He struggled on and, without warning, through the frames of the woodland, he saw a derelict building of wood and stone.

The *Lodge*, he surmised, and made his way to the frontage. To his left appeared to be a shallow lake, but with foliage growing through the water, it made it feel more like a swamp. Richard then noticed something that he had overlooked as he had arrived here…there were no trees around the house. Moss and wild grasses grew nearby…but no trees. He sensed no malice and circumnavigated the house. Facing the lake stood a door, with wooden steps leading up. Walking along the decking, he arrived at the gable-end of the house, with wooden steps leading down to a brook. The fast-flowing water twisted and turned as it splashed over stones and bracken that had been washed down from further upstream. Leaping onto the muddy bank, he completed the tour of the house as he made his way back to where he had started. The only entrance, he inferred, had to be the door facing the lake.

He made his way back and pulled at the handle, but the door remained fast. Twisting the handle and trying to push on the door, yielded no success, either. Richard next twisted the handle and with his shoulder gave a sharp and forceful jostle. With a large crack, Richard's right leg fell through the hole, as one of the planks gave way and splintered into several fragments. Cautiously, he pulled his leg up, as he rested on the floor. The protruding splinters may perhaps easily have torn through his skin and gashed his leg and, though bruised and painful, he found that he could, with caution, still walk, albeit with a slight limp. He noticed that the door now stood ajar. Pushing it fully open, he stepped into a room with barely discernible features, as everywhere was covered in a grey dust from years of neglect. On some grey shelving, he could make out the shape of some pots and pans; perhaps this was the kitchen, he thought. With a loud creak, he pushed open the door leading into the adjacent room. It, too, was devoid of any resemblance of what it may have been in its former youth. He returned to the 'kitchen' and noticed a wooden stairway leading to the upper part of the house, but decided that, with what he had just experienced outside, he would leave until another time to investigate. Turning to his left, he entered another room, not particularly grand, but somewhat larger than the room he had just left.

Beyond, Richard could see a doorway with an open door and vigilantly moved forward. Though covered in all forms of dust and decay, as he peered in, he saw the unmistakeable form of a bed in the middle of the room! What? Was this a bedroom? Surely, bedrooms were usually on a higher level away from the activities of daily chores? An infirm person, perhaps, who couldn't make the difficult ascent for the tranquillity of the storey above? But what would an infirm person be doing in a hunting lodge, if this was a lodge, that is? And why the bed in the middle of the floor? Despite the bright morning outside, there was little light penetrating through the almost opaque windows and Richard decided that he would return to the Parsonage and come back with more adequate means to investigate further. Thomas had been right; this was a venture!

"Ah, Rachel, how has been the day?"

"Grand, John, thank you. The Abbey at Waltham is most splendid…and enlightening. And what of you?"

"Interesting, indeed, Rachel! Thomas, a while back, mentioned to me of a hunting lodge near to the church of St Mary. With some difficulty, I came across it using his guidance and found it to be quite captivating. To be sure, I intend to return at a convenient time."

"Thomas has mentioned this place before, but I have never trekked there; the appeal is left wanting."

"That I can understand. The place is without interest, with the exception of the discovery of something new. There is an allurement within the place which draws me back, but I will need some items to assist in my search. Perhaps, I may take the ash butler and lantern?"

"Take the steed, the lane leading up to the house can be easier reached from the bottom, than through the track by the church; and yes, take what you need for your adventure!"

Though the next few days were uninviting, the sun eventually shone through and Richard, with an excitement building up inside him, made his way to the 'Lodge,' three hundred yards from the *Lordship*. The dapple-grey turned right at the corner of the bend before the hill and after thirty or so yards, turned right again up the track leading towards the *Lordship*. Though wooded, Richard was convinced that he could hear the sound of running water to his left…the brook that he saw when he came before? Perhaps, this is why the land is so boggy, he thought? As the tree-line stopped, so did the steed. Richard could see the house to his left, but the horse refused to move onward. Directly in front was the track that Richard had taken a few days earlier, but with the oncoming spring, the shoots on the branches now made his previous path almost impossible to view, and impassable to follow. Tying the horse to the nearest accessible tree branch, Richard took those items that he needed from the saddle-bag and made his way to the house. The front door remained open, as he had left it, and avoiding the gaping hole that he had made in the flooring, he stepped inside.

Using the horse-hair brush, he began sweeping away some of the dust, to gain a better observation of the rooms and the items laying around. The saucepan shape, after cleaning was indeed a saucepan, perhaps of pewter, though there was a hint of copper on the base. He pushed on a latch and the door opened onto a rather basic wooden stairway, somewhat wider than he had expected. Holding onto the banister, he tiptoed up and arrived at a large landing with a small, rusty candelabra suspended from the ceiling, though there were no candles in the holders. Everywhere was black, with timbers protruding through charred flooring. There had obviously been a fire here at some stage. Three rooms were attached to this main landing to his right and in front, but to his left, there was an extensive corridor that led onto further rooms. Richard started to make his way to this corridor but stopped suddenly in his tracks. With his foot on the edge, he looked down into a large gaping hole in the flooring, preventing any access with what tools he had brought from the Parsonage. Though bright outside, Richard decided that he needed the help of the lantern that he had carried with him; this near disaster, had brought home to him the need for increased vigilance, and so he lit the lamp. Though the shadows cast ghostly images beyond, Richard was convinced that he could see that the length of the flooring was riddled with gaping holes. But then his eyes caught sight of a horrendous image. There, by one of the holes in the corridor lay the unmistakeable form of a skeleton. This truly was a macabre scene and though not a believer in the occult, felt that he wished for the safety of the floor below.

Making his way back downstairs, he went into the room with the bed in the middle of the floor. He placed the lantern beside the window and, brushing away the dust, cleared enough to ascertain that this was a grey sheet on top of a feather mattress. Looking down at the flooring to ensure that there were no other jeopardies, Richard noticed a ring protruding from the floor under the front leg of the bed and using his horse-hair brush, swept away the dust from around the area. Bringing the lantern over, he saw the unmistakeable signs of a narrow gulley all around the leg of the bed, forming an almost perfect square. A trapdoor!

It was wide and long enough to permit a body to enter through it. His heartbeat quickened its pace at the thrill of what he had just uncovered. The bed was heavy, though, and Richard, as fit as he was, had difficulty moving the frame away from its resting place. With brute force, the bed finally scrapped along the floor and freed the trapdoor from its concealment. With a heartbeat that sounded like a military drum going into battle, he hooked his finger under the ring and gave a gentle tug. A small, but definable gap appeared within the gulley by the ring and with a second, much stronger tug, he pulled the trapdoor open. Bringing his lantern over to the open cavity, Richard gazed down at the stone steps leading to an earth floor below. With a heart beating so fast that he felt that his sternum would collapse, he sat down on the bed to recover his wits. Standing up, his legs shook, as did his whole body and again he had to sit down, shaking visibly on the mattress. Of all the quests that he had experienced in his life, this was undoubtedly the most thrilling. Even the ride into battle did not compare to what he felt right now. Was he entering into the world of the unknown? Did others know of this secret passage? What was it that Thomas had said…believed to have been the hunting lodge for Wolsey's Great Manor House? Was the world of Wolsey at his feet right now? Did the famous cardinal know of this passage; or even, had he arranged for its construction? To what purpose had he built such a secret room…or was it that – just a room? Perhaps, his imagination had got the better of him, after Thomas's briefing about the rumours suggesting the manor being haunted. Perhaps, this was just a storeroom; a convenience for keeping food and supplies fresh and out of harm's way? But then he recalled how but just a few months ago, he had felt frightened on his journey to Theobalds Park. Was there malice within the region, not just at the manor?

Placing the lantern on the floor, Richard faced the opaque window and stealthily placed his foot on the first stone. Stooping and holding onto the rim of the opening, he placed his second foot on the lower step; he was now completely on the stones. The third step was as solid as the other two and Richard grew in confidence that his footing was hard and would not give way as the wooden flooring had done. By the sixth step, he was now at head height to the floor above and his next step down would take him into this cavernous, dark and forbidding abode. Reaching for the lantern, he twisted his body and held the light beneath him. He could not yet see the bottom, but the scattering light showed that the room was not of insignificant proportions. Holding onto the steps with one hand, whilst keeping the lantern held tightly with the other, Richard continued his descent.

Reaching the bottom, he looked up at the opening above him and estimated the height to be about twelve-feet. Swinging the lantern around, he noticed the room to be about the size of the smoking room at Finchley. The walls were damp and the atmosphere, dank. The smell of mould permeated the room. On the floor near the foot of the stairs, he saw what appeared to be the end of a rusty dagger blade. Pushing the lantern ahead of him, he tentatively brushed his hand against the damp walls, feeling his way as he moved around the room. Suddenly, his hand hit an open space; there was no wall! Bringing the lantern in front of him, he could see that he now faced a tunnel, just big enough for a man to walk through without stooping. Edging forward, he kept his eyes towards the ground. What was that? Something brushed his foot and with the scurrying of feet, he saw a large rat disappear into the shadows. Richard knew that he had made himself nervous by facing the unknown, but did not believe in the phantoms of the night; all inexplicable phenomena had a reason, and were not attributable to some unseen entity haunting the passageways in the dark. He could not, though, explain the feeling of dread that he had experienced at Theobalds Park. Despite reassuring himself that no spectre existed, he found that his heart was beating at an incredible pace and that the quivering shadows on the tunnel walls were due to his shaking hand; but this did lead rise to a vibrant imagination, and though he fervently dismissed all notions of unseen hands threatening him, he could not help but wish that he had not decided upon this venture. Moving even deeper into the void, the light started to dim as the candle wick lowered to just above the surface of the wax.

Richard noticed in the flickering faint light, another set of steps. As he reached for the third stone, damp like everything within this chasm, he noticed on the fourth step, cloth…like the fabric worn by the priests of the Old Faith. It seemed to have been ripped from the main garment and, with the passing of time, fragmented in his fingers at his touch. Mounting the steps, Richard reached up at the top and could see, as he moved the lantern in a circular motion, that above him was another trapdoor. Pushing with some force, the stone above would not move. He climbed down the steps, placing his lantern on the floor and ascended the stairway again. With his shoulder wedged against the door above, faint shadows danced on the roof as he pushed with all his might, but the stone would not budge. Placing his dagger in the gaps around the stone, he cut as best as he could. Pushing again with all of his strength, he was unable to move the stone and, frustratingly, in the end had to concede defeat. Despondently, he dismounted the steps, picked up the lantern and retraced his steps along the tunnel. The light from the lantern was barely discernible and with a final glimmer, terminated itself. With any assistance from the lantern now gone, Richard was in total blackness and had to feel his way along the passage; this really was now an abyss! His imagination now took hold of his logic, and his strength-of-mind was severely put to the test as he slowly moved on. He heard the same scurrying as he had previously and something tangible rested on his leather boot. He could feel a warmth where the entity rested and then a grinding as the gnawing rat tore away at the warm leather. Richard kicked his leg in the air, but the rat clung on. With a screech, the animal released its grip from his foot as Richard kicked his boot against the wall. Amidst the scurrying of feet, Richard ascertained that this rat was not alone, but a final squeal, as he inadvertently trod on the now dead rat and slipped over, sent his self-control into a frenzy. Hearing the shattering of glass, as the lantern smashed onto the floor, he picked himself up, rigid in fear. A pain in his hand told him that he had cut himself on the broken glass and the scurrying now grew louder as the rats smelled the fresh, warm, blood oozing from Richard's wound. Grabbing his dagger and swooshing it about as he edged forward, he stumbled onwards, not knowing if there were other tunnels that he had not noticed earlier, or whether this was the only one that would lead to his salvation!

He heard the multitude of rats now behind him fighting, as they feasted on the dead rat. Staggering, almost at running speed, Richard thought that he could glimpse a greyish light ahead and prayed that this would be the trapdoor and steps steering to the world of light and normality. At last, he entered the room at the end of the tunnel and there, in front, were the stone steps and open trapdoor guiding his path to freedom. Mounting the stones, his head finally surfaced above the floor and as he stepped onto the solid floor, vowed that he would leave the pursuit of the unknown to others in the future; this was not his calling. Closing the trapdoor and trembling, he made his way outside and stood on the wooden porch. Looking towards his steed, he swore that he saw the tree by his dapple-grey uproot itself and move slowly towards him. Wide-eyed, Richard slapped himself as the hallucination dissipated, leaving his horse still tethered where he had left it. Slowly, and very despondently, Richard made his way back to the Parsonage and the comfort of a home.

Though with a preference for Cheshunt and the Parsonage, Richard, Rachel, Thomas and young Thomas, flitted between Finchley and the Hertfordshire countryside. Though regarded as a friend, with the passing years, Richard was now accepted almost as one of the family; young Thomas calling him 'Uncle John'.

The dreaded day that no one wanted finally arrived. Richard, now being in the twilight of his years, sat at the bedside of his very dear friend, nearly twenty-years his junior.

"Open the drapes, John; I want to see the light."

Getting up slowly, Richard moved over to the sash window, as Rachel took her husband's hand and kissed the back as she rubbed it against her face.

"Father…I…"

"Hush…Thomas. Never, in a lifetime…could a father be so proud of his son. Use your inheritance wisely…and make good your life…but care first and foremost for this woman beside me."

The weak winter sun, low in the sky, shone with all its glory through the sash window, illuminating every item within the room with an intensity that made it seem as though they glowed themselves. Richard stood to one side while father, son and wife hugged and wept together.

"I would like a few moments with John, please."

Kissing the dying man before them, Rachel and Thomas arose and left the room, hugging Richard as they passed. Moving over and kneeling beside his bed, Richard placed his ear close to his friend.

"It has been a good life, John and…one for which I have…no regrets."

"Indeed, my friend, and also my good fortune on us meeting as we did. 'Tis cruel, though, that you should depart so young."

"Ours is not to reason with our Maker. Mine is…but a small chapter in the great book of life and that chapter…is coming to its end. The day is good…though; bright with the promise…of life to come…and go. Do you realise, today…is twelfth night?"

"The wise men find the Saviour…I hadn't thought of it, but yes, today is twelfth night."

"…John did you ever find the *Lodge*; I meant to ask…but overlooked it?"

"Yes, I did…just the once."

"…And venture inside…?"

"Yes…ventured inside?"

"…And…?"

"'Tis not a place I will venture again, my friend…there was a menace in the air, which I did not like."

"…Tunnel…?"

"Yes, I found the mythical tunnel, but not so mythical now; it exists. I walked some distance to its terminus, but the exit remained closed to me and I know not its location to the outside world. Did you venture there, then, Thomas?"

"…Soon after we moved to Cheshunt…but…I found no tunnel. The place did have a haunted feeling, I remember…but I left quickly and did not explore…John, I wish…to ask you one last favour…"

Richard, took Thomas's hand in his, and as Rachel had done, kissed the back.

"Ask, my friend and it will be done."

"You have been…a good friend…a loyal, faithful…and…good friend and what I ask is as a friend. Look after Thomas, he needs…guidance, but has…a good and willing heart. Please take care of Rachel…as a wife, if need be. She has adequate means, of that…I have ensured, but I am afraid that…as her age increases and her frame stoops…that she will need all the help you can give…and she needs companionship, John…and that I cannot…give her now."

"This, I promise to you, Thomas. As long as I live, I will look after your son and take care of Rachel. She will want for nothing…but we are friends, and as that it will continue. I have no need of a wife, Thomas, mine was taken too long ago, but Rachel is like a sister to me, and as a sister, she will remain."

Thomas weakly took Richard's hand and with great effort, drew it to his mouth and kissed it.

"…Thank you, my dear, dear friend…"

"God bless you and keep you, Thomas…I love you and will cherish your memory…always."

The time was almost upon them, and Richard stepped outside to the weeping pair. Beckoning them to the open door, he uttered one word:

"…Please…"

As they went in, Rachel turned to Richard.

"…Are you not coming inside, John?"

"I have said my goodbye, Rachel…It is for you now to rest with him in his passing."

Richard, quietly closed the door, but could hear the softly spoken pair say their farewells. There was a hush, perhaps ten seconds…twenty seconds, and then the wail told Richard that the end had come; his friend had gone.

Life was never the same again after Thomas's passing, but true to his word, Richard cared for Rachel and her son as a brother and uncle. Malicious rumours spread that there was more to the arrangement than depicted publicly, even to the point of suggestions that Richard was, perhaps, more than just a surrogate uncle. With his previous position before his rapid retreat to the safety of the continent, Richard had accrued much knowledge with contacts and the manipulation of the law, used both for profit and for the common good. Using all his previous experience, he guided young Thomas towards the *Bar*, after his admittance to the *Inner Temple*. His enthusiasm and commitment to his work resulted in Richard and Rachel being, for the large part of the year, left to their own devices, as he was obliged to spend most of his time in the city.

"Rachel, it pains me to say to you, but I have a commitment to which I must address without delay."

"Why would it pain you, John…?"

"Because I must away to Hampshire and may be gone for some time."

"Oh…but you will return…?"

"Return? Oh, yes, I will return at the earliest opportunity…how could I possibly not return. It troubles me such that I should leave you now, without company…of which I know you so much desire."

"John, I will survive…Thomas, though husband, was absent many a month, but I was left blessed with our son. Your residence here, though much desired, was not with us in our early years and yet I survived…as I will again. But, if it at all be possible, please return at your earliest convenience."

"I will, dear Rachel, this I promise. It warms my heart as I gaze upon you, to see such radiance. Why, it is like a bud that comes to blossom."

"It must be the spring air, John. After the loss of Thomas, and with the dark and cold of winter, it is now time for full vigour…perhaps, that is what you see before you…?"

"Indeed, it must. I shall take my leave before the rising of the sun the morrow"

"So soon! I thought that we may awhile the morrow with a jaunt on the dapple greys?"

"Alas, Rachel, that jaunt must await my return. Here, a toast to our next acquaintance…"

With that, Richard arose and pouring a small port from the decanter, handed one to Rachel.

"…And to a safe journey and an early return…"

It was well into the autumn before Richard returned to the Parsonage, with rapturous joy at being at *home* again. Rachel went to great him after being informed of his arrival.

"Rachel, I have missed you so…"

"…And I you, John."

"It is *so* good to be home…with friends and companions."

"You have been sorely missed, John…and missed a wonderous occasion!"

"To what wonderous occasion have I been absent from, then…?"

"Come, I'll show you…"

Walking through the house until they came into the small nursery, a small sound could be heard.

"Oh…now I understand! You have found solace in caring for a baby, Rachel?"

"More than caring, John…endearing and loving!"

"Endearing…? The baby…to whom does it belong…who is the mother?"

"I am, John…"

"You…you! Rachel, how is this possible?"

"Before he became unable, Thomas and I still had our intimacies…in fact, a blessing, a true blessing.

"Oh, what wonderous news indeed! He…she…has a name?"

"She is called Elizabeth. I named her after my grandmother."

"So sad that Thomas never knew of her…he would have been so proud…"

"Yes, he would, but that is not to be, but with Elizabeth, my daughter, I have found new happiness…almost as though he dwells here in her."

"…And if I may be permitted, Rachel, I shall care for her, like with Thomas, as if she were my own…I owe that to my dear, departed friend, no less…"

"John…I am overwhelmed…but part of me had hoped…and if I may be so bold…felt assured, that this would be your true response."

"May I…?"

Lifting the baby from the cot, Rachel kissed, caressed and handed to Richard her new-found love. Without removing his gaze from this tiny, warm and beautiful young girl, Rachel saw the countenance of a friend; a true and honourable friend; a friend that would move heaven and earth to love and protect all those that he cared for from harm.

Jaunts on the dapple-greys became replaced with promenades and carriage rides as young Elizabeth grew. Her presence always filled the rooms with joy, as her inquisitiveness nearly always led to amusing surprises and outcomes. Her character, was like that of any curious child, invariably seeing the humorous side to any scenario and despite her living a life of comfort, she was empathetic with those of inferior social breeding. She would often be seen in the company of Charles, the gardener's son; the pair, at times, almost as inseparable as brother

151

and sister. Her insatiable curiosity led Rachel to have some concerns that she was tending too much towards traits usually displayed by boys, that could have repercussions as she developed into a woman. Though not actively discouraging his company, Rachel did, whenever possible, find excuses that prevented her dallying with young Charles.

"...John, as much as I like young Charles, perhaps his familiarity with Elizabeth should be discouraged?"

"I see no cause for concern, Rachel. See how gleefully she plays. If we were to discourage such an association, what would she do...mope around the house? No...I think that the freshness of her youth would be placed in jeopardy, should we remove that joy that she has found. She causes no worries, or frets of any kind...and her vibrancy and happiness are a joy to behold. Indeed, it is her youthful contentment that is so infectious"

"Perhaps, I am being too cautious, John, as would any mother who cares for her child's future, but I am concerned that she will not be seen in the light of a desirable woman of means, should she not display the character of a lady, let alone a woman. Why, just the other day, I saw her hanging upside down, with her legs dangling over a branch of the beech tree"

"I guess Charles taught her how to do that?"

"No! She called to Charles and said to him, 'try this, Charlie, it's fun'."

"Perhaps, we could replace this joy with another joy, to which she would be equally compliant, then?"

"I am sorry, John...I follow not your suggestion?"

"I believe, Rachel, that you have family on the Borders?"

"Yes, I have a cousin who has some acreages of land in the foothills of the Wrekin."

"A gentleman farmer, no doubt?"

"Yes, the family moved to Shropshire when Dudley was but a boy. Why do you ask?"

"Perhaps, we could away to the Borders then for the summer? The change of scenery always does the spirit good and Elizabeth will have the rolling hills of Shropshire to explore. Her voracious appetite for discovery, will overcome her sadness for leaving here."

"John! What a splendid idea. I shall write to Dudley this instant."

Though initially remorseful at the thought of leaving her home and Charles, the thrill of the journey to pastures new saw Elizabeth excited with the pending arrival of the departure date and, unable to contain her elation, set a rift between the two children, as Charles felt forsaken at the prospect of losing his childhood companion.

"Be not sad, Charlie…I'll only be away until the harvests."

"But, Lizzie, I will have no one to play with. Father and mother are always too busy with other things. Life here will be so dull…"

"Then think of new games to play, for when I return. Perhaps, you could help your father…he is not so young and I see how he stoops as he stands. Perhaps, you could do his stooping work…?"

"Yes, but it's not the same as playing with you…"

"I am sorry, Charlie, truly sorry, but mama has made up her mind to go…and I have no choice; besides, it will be quite exciting to live on a farm, with all the animals…"

Charles did not appear on the day of departure to say 'goodbye' to his friend, though the face at the cottage window as the carriage pulled away and into the distance portrayed all the emotions of a child whose world had fallen apart.

Summer had started early and after a particularly severe winter, the warmth was a welcome blessing. Both the world of habitation and animals found new vigour and form in the embrace of the sun. Arriving in the foothills of the magnificent Wrekin, Rachel, Richard and Elizabeth were welcomed warmly by Dudley and his wife, Johanne. Their brood of five children gave the house a happy and lively atmosphere. With her cousins in playful and joyous mood, Elizabeth soon forgot about Charles and the six were often absent most days, before returning well into the early evenings, ravenous for supper.

"Mama, thank you so much for bringing me here…it surely is the best time of my life."

"Elizabeth, it is your uncle John that you should thank; it was his idea."

Embracing her 'uncle' as though he would break, she slid her arms around his neck and kissed him firmly on the cheek.

"Thank you, Uncle John…thank you."

The warmth of her young body and the innocent clasp around his neck brought a momentary tear to his eye as he recalled all that he had missed in his earlier years; but now, now he had once again been blessed with a new family. He looked and smiled at Rachel and then dropped his gaze down to the young form curled up before him, but her eyes were already closed; and with that, the day's toll took over and, still with her arms around his neck, she fell asleep. With a contentment that she had not felt in a while, Rachel placed her hand on John's and, like Elizabeth, kissed him on the other cheek.

"Yes…thank you, John…thank you."

Without rain, an early harvest was calling. Though not directly involved with the everyday running of the farm, Dudley still retained an eager eye on the labourers that Bennett, his farm manager, brought in to work the land. Overtly, a kindly man, though he was not one to be on the wrong side of when riled.

"That's a fine girl that you have there, Rachel."

"Yes, she is a true blessing, Dudley…but what about your brood?"

"Huh, huh…indeed; like yourself, a true blessing."

"Dudley…you have been more than generous permitting us to stay throughout the summer, but I feel that we have taken too much of your time. Perhaps, the morrow, we will make ready for our return to Cheshunt…?"

"The harvest starts tomorrow…at least wait until the grain is in; 'tis a time for great celebrations…and this year the good Lord has deemed it fit to have a harvest in abundance, methinks!"

The next day heralded another magnificent morning with the household up as the sun rose above the horizon.

"Elizbeth…we are going up Caer Gwrygon today…do you want to come?"

"What is kayer Gw…n, Robyn?"

"Caer Gwrygon, Elizabeth…ha, ha, ha…It is Welsh for this hill before us; we call it the 'Wrekin.'"

"It looks fun, yes, let us go!"

The initial enthusiasm eventually gave way to the realisation that for the spirit to reap in the glory, the body had to endure the pain.

"Can we rest, Robyn. How far does this hill go?"

"Elizabeth, we are nearly at the top…it is not far, but believe me, the reward will be worth it. Shall I tell you the story of Caer Gwrygon, perhaps it will help with the climb?"

"Please, Robyn…if only to take my mind from this pain in my side."

"Well, a Welsh giant called Gwendol Wrekin ap Shenkin ap Mynyddmawr, who hated the English, decided to kill all the people of Shrewsbury. He dug a shovelful of earth and set off towards the town, when on route he met a cobbler. The cobbler had a sack full of shoes for repair and the giant asked him the way to Shrewsbury. The cobbler asked the giant what he was doing with the earth that he was carrying and the giant said that he was going to dam the river Severn and flood the town. The cobbler told him that it was a very long way to Shrewsbury and showed him all the shoes that he had worn out since leaving the town. The giant decided that it was too far and dumped the earth here and went off in a huff."

"Ha, ha, ha…a good story, Robyn…"

"And see, Elizabeth…we have reached the top…did it help, then?"

"…Why, yes…the pain has gone. I must remember that story and tell it to Uncle John."

Robyn, his three siblings and Elizabeth arrived at the top of the Wrekin. Elizabeth gazed in awe at the view before them. Turning from south to west and to north, view upon view stretched before them; only the horizon stopped her seeing farther. The east was covered in the trees that they had just climbed through to get to this spot.

"Robyn! This is magnificent…truly magnificent! I have never seen such beauty before…why we must be at the top of the world!"

"Very nearly, Elizabeth…there, in front, you can just see the Welsh Hills on the horizon and if you look slightly to the right, in the valley, is the town of Shrewsbury; but come here…let's walk towards the north."

Following her cousin, Elizabeth trod carefully as they approached the edge of a steep slope leading towards the fields far, far below.

"See…there; just there…"

"What am I looking at, Robyn?"

"Can you see the workers in the field?"

"Why yes! I can see the people shifting the hay…and the horse and cart."

"That's the hay waggon; but can you see the boy at the front?"

"From here I wouldn't know, boy from girl, or man from woman…but, yes, I can just see a small person at the front…is he feeding the horses?"

"No…that is Tom. He is holding them Shires steady. They are tossing the corn into the cart and Tom will lead them Shires to the barn."

"Oh, so that is why Tom didn't come with us today?"

"Yes, father told him the farm is to be his, but he has to learn how to farm, first. Now look into that field nearby, Elizabeth…"

Turning her gaze to the adjoining field, Elizabeth could see the defining lines as the sheaves were scythed down.

"Why do the women work in the field, Robyn?"

"They take the cut corn and stack the sheaves, a bit like wigwams, to dry, then later, they'll thresh the corn and use the hay for bedding and food for the cattle in the Winter."

"Robyn…I absolutely love it here…I really, really love it…"

"…Mother said that you will be going home soon, though…"

"Yes, I know and it makes me so, so sad. Don't get me wrong, I love my home…but here, here it is so different. It seems so carefree and natural…being with the animals and birds and…and…"

Elizabeth found tears streaming down her face as she realised that within the next few days, they would leave this paradise, perhaps forever.

"Don't be sad, Elizabeth. I'm sure that you will come back again, now that father and Aunty Rachel have been united…"

"Yes, I am sure we will…"

"Shall we return and watch Tom and the others in the field, then?"

"In a moment, Robyn…let me look one last time before we go down…I want to keep this scene before me forever."

Descending through the trees, they eventually came into the open land where stubbles of once pristine corn had been blowing in the breeze. Crunching their way through into the next field, the hay waggon stood, with Tom at the front as the workers' tossed their pitch-fork loads into the waggon.

"…And you, young lady…"

And with that, Elizabeth squealed with delight as a strong arm lifted her and threw her onto the corn. With tossed hay mounting in the cart, Elizabeth tramped around, keeping her body above the rising sheaves. Robyn, Tom and the others laughed…they knew what it was like to be showered in hay.

"C'mon, miss Liz…let's get 'e down from that tha' wicket."

The same strong arm lifted her gently down and placed her onto the stubbled field. The sun had started to lower behind the Wrekin and the cart, horses and corn took on an orange hue as the heat of the day started to weaken.

"That'll do, Tom. Off t' store. Mind 'e don't get 'e larst…there be scrumpy and hog t' night, 'e know!"

"What's scrumpy, Robyn…?"

"Why missy, it be nutin' but pure apple juice. You awt t' try it…"

"Don't 'e be getting' that poor lass on t' 'em bad ways, Gerald! You ignore him, miss Liz, 'e awt t' know better; 'tis bad for 'e…take me word."

The laughter was contagious as everyone took on the good-natured banter.

"You'll be staying for harvest celebrations, Elizabeth…I hope. 'Tis probably the best time of the year. There'll be music and dancing and feasting…and scrumpy!"

"Oh, yes, yes, yes, Robyn…I will ask mother; I'm sure she will agree…though I am not so sure about the scrumpy…!"

Rachel had already been persuaded by both Dudley and Richard that harvest supper was not to be missed, and though teasing Elizabeth with her pretend indecisions, gave the answer that Elizabeth was sure that she would give.

The hay waggon arrived and the Shire horses were dressed in the finest garlands of wild flowers, freshly picked that same morning. As tradition dictated, Dudley, as 'Lord of the Manor' did not lead the procession, but the workers of the fields led the way with their foreman steering the waggon at the front. The hat on top of his head bore a corn dolly, as two of the workers walked in front to the sound of their fiddles. The gaiety of the occasion was unprecedented within the world that Elizabeth, and indeed, even Rachel and Richard had known. Dudley, had set a grand table made from the bales of hay and Johanne had kept her servants busy preparing the feast…a thanksgiving to the good Lord for the abundance and completion of this year's harvest.

With due reverence, the corn dolly was removed from the hat and laid at the end of the bailed-hay table. With the kitchen in full vigour, an abundance of meats, vegetables and puddings were set on the table, as both food and ale were consumed in significant quantities. Dudley, did not exert his position as Lord of the Manor, but let the workers enjoy the rewards of their hard labours in the free ways that they knew. Suddenly, above the noise of the merry making, a drone could be heard. The laughter and banter abated immediately, as Elizabeth and all at the table turned their heads towards the sound. There, at the end of the courtyard sat a lone musician, and immediately he was accompanied by the two fiddlers that had led the hay waggon earlier. The chorus of approval was made by everyone as the three musicians set the tone for the remainder of the evening. Thudding of tankards and stamping of the feet, followed the rhythm of the music, as the raucous joviality continued. Elizabeth, could not but help herself as she, too, clapped along to the tunes. Some of the group stood, as best as they could, and leaped around as the musicians played.

"Dance, Elizabeth?"

"I…I don't know how to…I've never been taught, Robyn," though, secretly, she had hoped that it would have been Tom who would have asked her.

"Oh, there are some dances that have no rules…you just get up and move to the sound of the music…see, look how your feet tap to the sound!"

Elizabeth looked down and sure enough, her feet were tapping out to the rhythm of the fiddles.

"Well, I…?"

"Come; I'll show you the swing and we can swing to the music. Now, grip my hand…that's it and place the other one on top of our clenched fists with my other hand…good. Now swing around with me and tap your feet to the fiddles…"

Rachel placed her hand on top of Richard's, as they watched Elizabeth squeal with delight as she swung around the throng with Robyn. She gazed at Richard and kissed him on the cheek. She looked at the small gathering; each one without a care in the world.

"This is a different world entirely to what I have known all my life, John. See how freely and gaily they enjoy the occasion and each other's company."

"Rachel…I could not have imagined such a scene as I witness now. In all my travels, surely there was never such contentment as this. Formal dances…correct attire…polite conversation…protocol…the falseness of my attachments of the past. This before me…this is as pure and honest as any man, or woman can be. See how they care not who is Lord of the Manor…they just…they just…enjoy."

"Mama…will you not dance with Uncle John?"

"Your mother and I just like to watch you and the others enjoy the music…besides, we have never been taught the country dances."

"Mama…may I have some ale, please…I am so thirsty?"

"No, Elizabeth…you may not…"

"Please, mama…Uncle John, can you persuade her, please?"

"I agree with your mother, Elizabeth…but perhaps a small glass of cider would suffice…?"

Without pausing for breath, Elizabeth emptied the entire content of a glass of cider and, with a hiccup, followed this with a somewhat unladylike belch.

"Elizabeth!"

"Sorry, mama…"

And with that, the ecstatic Elizabeth Pengelly took Robyn for another round of swinging to the sound of the fiddles. A young girl, about the same age as Elizabeth, stood by the musicians and the music stopped. Again, with a drone starting the music, one of the fiddlers began playing a somewhat slow, but melodious tune as the girl danced with a clickety sound to the melody. Looking down, Elizabeth noticed that her shoes were made of wood and shaped in a form that she had never seen before.

"What is this?"

"The girl is Letecia and the man beside her, with the pipes, is her father. They came last year-they are from way up north. They travel down from their home every summer, harvesting on the way."

Elizabeth looked on entranced, as Letecia danced rhythmically to the melody of the fiddle and the steady beat of the drone of the pipes. The clogging sound as her wooden shoes tapped on the courtyard was the magic of the spectacle before them; but all too soon the dance stopped to rapturous applause from the small throng, with their ruddy faces and beaming smiles. Elizabeth ran over to her mother.

"Mama, I want to stay here forever..."

Rachel caressed her daughter, holding her head gently against her chest.

"Elizabeth...the evening has been enchanting and our stay with cousin Dudley has been truly wonderful. I have so loved being here, but we cannot abuse the hospitality and kindness of our cousin and so, I am afraid, the morrow we must away."

Elizabeth knew that their stay here amongst the rolling hills of Shropshire was temporary, but still did not want to hear the foreboding news of their departure. She clung on tightly to Rachel.

"...And besides, you can get back home to Charles..."

"I don't feel the same about Charlie, since I have been here, mama. At home, Charlie was the only friend that I knew, but here, with all my cousins, I have found new friends..."

Rachel raised her eyes to Richard and gave him a knowing and grateful smile.

Their return to the Parsonage was also accompanied with a change in the weather as the season started to mellow into the beauty of autumn. The green leaves of summer started to blend into the deeper reds and oranges associated with the onset of less joyful weather. Elizabeth was no longer the playful, mischievous, tomboy of the past; her childhood had started to leave her, as the change in her appearance and manners, slowly, but irrevocably, matured; it was as nature intended.

With the onset of adolescence, Elizabeth was sent to a boarding school for girls.

"...Elizabeth is a bright girl and she needs more than I can teach her."

"I agree completely, Rachel. She *is* bright, she is inquisitive-always seeking answers to her multitude of questions. Upon reflection, I see her in her childhood and, even without realising it, she was as curious then as she is now. I have seen many a fine lady in my sojourns and most of them were raised into the manner for which they were bred; polite conversation and raising a new breed of nobility. But, Elizabeth, is way above them; she has the mind as good as any man and should be encouraged to use her wisdom and intellect to the benefit of humankind…a bit like her mother, I believe."

"…John, you mock me!"

"Nay, Rachel…I am in earnest. Before my good friend, Thomas, left this dimension, he requested that I should challenge you in debate. He was very aware of your great understanding and wished that I should enhance this as best as I could."

"Indeed, you have John…you have been a true friend; a good and true friend…and to Elizabeth, why you have helped raise her as though she were your own…"

"I owe it no less to the memory of Thomas…and, of course, you."

With age now not being on Richard's side, previous leisure and pastimes requiring the enthusiasm and energy of youth, became merely fond memories, as both he and Rachel, preferred the comfort of the fireside sofa and, when the weather permitted, a slow amble around the nearby lanes. The spring of 1712 had been pleasant enough, but with the onset of summer, Richard's health deteriorated to the point of both knowing that he, too, was to submit to the Lord's calling; the only blessing being that he would again be with his dear friend taken so young and his long-passed wife, Dorothy.

"Rachel, I am afraid to say that the promise I gave to my dear friend, Thomas, I may soon have to break."

"To which promise, pray tell me, John was that?"

"…The promise to care for you…and young, well…not so young anymore, Thomas."

"Thomas has need of you only as a dear friend; he is secure, and the fine life he has moulded will see him comfortable. I, on the other hand, do need you…as I needed Thomas. 'Tis a cruel taskmaster that gives us a moment of joy, only to take from us that moment and replace it with the frailties of age."

"…And Elizabeth, I will no longer be able to serve and steer her along her chosen path…she has still much youth and I will not be here to guide and assist."

"John…Elizabeth is now old and mature enough to seek her own way. She has needed you so much in her younger years, but now…now she has to learn to fight her own battles…and you have given her that strength of character to ensure that she will. John, you have done more than guided her…you have been her fortitude and given her the wisdom of your years. She is the evidence of your legacy and will not be wanting."

Richard moved closer to Rachel and clasped his hand around hers. He could feel the warmth of her hand through his own trembling and cold fingers.

"John, you are so cold…come, let me get you a blanket?"

"Nay…I have no need of a blanket; no blanket can bring back the warmth to an old and weak body. What I need now is the warmth of our friendship…that will bring me more comfort than any blanket…"

"John, what ails you? I sense that you are troubled?

"Rachel…I have to…I have to confess my soul before you; before my Creator deems it time to call me home."

"Confess your soul before me…whatever is it that you have borne, that warrants such a confession?"

"…I have lived a lie; lived a lie with my two dearest friends…and it is a burden I must shed before my voice can speak no more…Rachel, I am not…and never have been John Clarke. It has been my pseudonym…my security…my safety, from those that would do me harm. My real name is…"

"…Richard Cromwell…yes, I know."

"You know?"

"Yes, I have known a long time."

"…But…but how?"

"The day I went to Waltham Abbey, they had just received some leaded stained-glass windows to replace those deemed not fit, or too old. Laying on the floor were several of the removed panes. I asked the abbot who the picture represented. For his discretion and complicity, he received a generous donation for the replacement glass."

Rachel got up and went into her cellar, before returning with the window.

"Do you recognise this…Richard?"

Richard gazed at the image of his father. Around the face was engraved 'Oliver Cromwell.'

"But…but that is my father, not me."

161

"The similarity between you two is irrefutable. With the sudden disappearance of Richard Cromwell from public view all those years ago, I realised why I thought that I recognised you when you helped me onto my steed. It did not take long to know that my suspicions were truly founded"

Richard gazed at the coloured glass depicting almost his own image in his prime.

"I…I had no idea, Rachel. My father must have arranged for the engraving, when he was Lord Protector. How it came to be at the Abbey, I have no idea."

"You have kept your secret far too long, Richard; it surely was a burden almost too heavy to bear!"

"I lived in fear and trepidation from the moment the king returned. The tide had turned against the commonwealth and the desire for the return of the monarchy, meant that those who had perpetrated the revolution, were now seen as nothing more than criminals and traitors. My father, devout in his faith and a true believer in the rights of the common man and the wrong of the sovereign in his treatment of his subjects, was treated with the contempt of the wicked. Had they sought and found me, would they have cut and disembowelled me and leave my head piked on *Traitor's Gate* for the world to see, as they did my father? But…but did Thomas know?"

"My father held both you and your father in the highest regard and felt that you had been unjustifiably and sorely treated. He served under your father and, like him, believed in the good of the common man. But Thomas, as much as I loved him, I did not know which way his allegiance lay. The incivility of civil war can bring out the extreme in any man, as you know, and I could not be certain of the depth of emotion that my husband had towards the monarchy and the commonwealth. You, Thomas and I…ours was a special friendship and I dared not risk putting that bond in jeopardy; so, he remained unaware of your true identity…even to his last breath. But, John…I mean, Richard, I have felt so honoured to have known you and been given the opportunity and time to care for you and keep you and your identity safe. How could I, or anyone, possibly know the hardships and burdens that you have had to bear; it would surely strip a man of his soul to the depths that you have been."

For the first time ever, Richard wept openly. The relief, the trust…even the love that he had been shown, broke him down. For the first time in nearly fifty years, he could finally live with a conscience, free from the guilt and burdens that he had known for most of his life; it was a chain cut free. Rachel moved close to Richard and gently caressed his head and laid it in her lap, as fifty years of anguish finally exuded from the man before her. Richard searched for her hand and gripping it firmly said two words:

"Thank you…"

Time stood still as Richard and Rachel let the moistness of their sorrows run their course. The caress of friendship was at last relinquished, as Richard raised his head from her lap and looked at her tender eyes, moist like his own.

"Rachel…dearest Rachel; this relief permits me now to ask one last favour…a favour that you may deem too macabre to grant…?"

"Speak, Richard; any '*macabre*' favour cannot be as horrific as the strain that you have borne."

"My estate…and the family that I have not been allowed to know, are at Hursley, in Hampshire; but my home is here…with you and my memories of my dear friend, Thomas. The home I once had has sufficed me in financial comfort, but the memories do not hold me dear as they do here. I wish, therefore, to be buried here at St Mary's…"

"But that is not a concern at all, Richard…why should this be so *macabre*, as you call it?"

"My resting place must remain unknown. If those who sought to persecute my father should find my last abode, they may well disentomb me and leave my soul in purgatory…and the Turnpike of Temple Bar awaits further traitor's heads for the populace to gaze upon."

"Dearest Richard. My loss will be your passing, as it was with Thomas, and your wish is but a small token of my love for you. But this is not *macabre*."

"It is if I lay in an unmarked tomb and not under a headstone in a false grave."

"…You mean…?"

"Yes, upon my death, lay me to rest in in the soil of St Mary's and send an empty coffin, save for earth of my weight, to my estate at Hursley. Should those that seek to violate my body be so determined to complete their gruesome task, it will be an empty coffin that they will find. The Angel of Death will know where I lay."

"And the pastor of St Mary's will want to know who is buried here…he will not accept an unmarked tomb."

"It will be the tomb of *John Clarke*. But delay the carving of my name; tell the rector that there was an error and it will be corrected; and in the meantime, leave the monument unmarked."

"As you wish, Richard, it will be done. But where do you wish your tomb to be?"

"Lay me on the south side towards the west, where I may be able to see the setting sun. There is a spot I had set my heart on, but not believing that this could ever be; not without you knowing my true identity."

With the onset of age weakening his body, Richard once again lay his head in the lap of Rachel. Here, before her, was the reality of the frailty and mortality of man. With only memories now to keep her depth of passion alive; a man who she would have gladly have claimed as husband, had Thomas not wooed and wedded her, lay in his fading repose. Using her sleeve to erase the evidence of her sorrow, she caressed Richard's head; a man of unappreciated and unrecognised strength, whose resolve and love of his fellow man had kept the country that he loved, safe; even at the risk of his own life. As she thought on, she realised just how indebted she, and indeed all the men, women and children of this land were, to this dying man before her. To hero-worship would be an understatement of what she felt right now. This humble, pure and tender man would pass into the unknown without the pomp and triumph that he so deserved; for, unlike his father, the role that he had taken on had been thrust upon him, and against his own wishes. Indeed, he was a true king in his own right.

With difficulty, and with a servant to support him, Richard and Rachel strolled slowly into the grounds of St Mary's. Passing the church on their right, Richard stopped at a spot in the late afternoon sun so that he could witness, perhaps for the last time, the sacred soil under which he will lay.

"See how the sun shines and warms the earth just here; and how the sun's colours intensify the green of the grass and the shadows of the branches from the sky above? It is here that I wish to be laid for eternity."

"I can visualise no better place, Richard; by the fallen statue of *St Joh*...I cannot make out the name. It is here that I shall have your tomb built."

The final days were difficult for both Richard and Rachel; Richard from the pain of his transition and Rachel from the pain of her loss. But finally, the everlasting peace descended upon this once great and mighty man, as the countenance changed from that of a living being, to that of an entity now eternally at rest. This time, it was Rachel who laid her head in the lap of Richard laid out in his sombre repose, but unlike Rachel a few weeks before, Richard could not caress in comfort the weeping woman before him. With her request granted by the rector of St Mary's, the gravediggers went about their grisly work.

As they completed the trench, unnoticed, a small clod of earth gave way; too small, though, to reveal a stone staircase descending into the abyss beside them.

With the illusory task completed by her servant, on a cloudy Tuesday, 17 July, 1712, the coffin of Richard Cromwell was placed in a hearse and slowly transported to his estate at Hursley, in Hampshire. On the top, imbedded in a brass templet was engraved:

Richard Cromwell Esquire
4 October 1626-12 July 1712

Within the hour, another hearse arrived at the Parsonage, as the body of Richard Cromwell was laid gently in his final abode and the lid nailed into place. His body, resting under a brass templet engraved with:

John Clarke
4 October 1626-12 July 1712

…was removed from the hearse, then carried by the pallbearers to the open trench and lowered into the tomb as the pastor read out the burial sermon. Throwing earth from the mound beside her onto the resting coffin, Rachel then pushed her fingers to her lips and with a kiss, the last that she would ever give him, gently lowered her hand towards the open space, turned and walked back home.

Chapter 17

It had been five years since the death of Richard Cromwell and Elizabeth was approaching her 21st birthday; a day from which she would no longer be subjected to the authority of her mother. In those five years, Rachel too, was slowly surrendering to the weakness of old age.

"Mama, I miss Uncle John...he was so good to me; and I know that you miss him too."

"Whatever has brought this on, Elizabeth? But yes, you are right...I do miss Uncle John."

"I was thinking about cousin Dudley...it was at this time of the year that we went to stay in Shropshire and I remember falling asleep on Uncle John's lap...I miss his embrace and kind and wise nature."

"Yes, he was an exceptional man...that is true."

"But I also miss not knowing my father...I wish, so wish, that I had met and known him."

"...But you did meet and know him..."

"Mama! Father died the year that I was born...how could I possibly have known him? Do you mean in my dreams...or as a ghost! Mama...are you, are you well...?"

"Elizabeth, you are to be twenty-one in a few days and you will have your independence. You will be an adult and responsible for the actions and consequences of an adult...as am I; I will no longer be your guardian...but I will always be your mother...."

"Mother! I could not wish for a better mother...why no one else in the world can have a better mother. Why is our conversation so sombre and mysterious? It should be joyful that I am to be of age!"

"Elizabeth...I have been terrified of the moment that I should have to face the truth with you, but decided that for your adulthood, there should be no more secrets between us."

"Secrets! Secrets! I have no secrets…and you have no secrets that I am aware of…until now."

With difficulty, Rachel arose from the armchair and walked across the room.

"Where are you going, Mama? Are you sure that you are well…?"

"Most well, thank you, Elizabeth. I shall return within a moment."

Elizabeth Pengelly was startled. She had never seen her mother in such a serious and mysterious mood. She got up and paced the room. In fact, Elizabeth Pengelly had started to perspire and saw that her hands were shaking. Indeed, her whole body had started to tremble as she awaited her mother's return. Opening the door, there was no sound and Elizabeth walked out into the corridor, but heard no noise. Walking out of the front door, she gazed across the field where years earlier, two dapple-greys had chomped on the tender grass. The late afternoon sun, with all the colours that reflected nature's glory, brought no relief to the anxiety that she felt right now. She, too was terrified…terrified of whatever 'truth' her mother had to tell to her. Hearing the door close from the room that she had left, with a tension building inside her to breaking point, she returned. There, again sat in her armchair, was her mother.

"Elizabeth…here is the picture of your grandfather…"

Elizabeth took the stained-glass window and gazed upon it.

"Why, it looks like Uncle John…Uncle John! Mama! Is…was Uncle John my father…my real father?"

"Yes, Elizabeth…he is."

"But…but why? How could you…how could he…?"

"It is a complicated story…"

"You…you…you had a lover…Uncle John, behind my real father's back! How could you?"

"I understand that you are upset…and shocked, but as I said, you are no longer a child and deserve to hear the truth…"

"The truth! The truth! You have lied to me all these years and tell me that I deserve to know the truth! How dare you?"

"Please, Elizabeth. Please, listen and try and be calm and form judgement when you have heard the truth."

"…And Uncle John! Kindly…wise…more like deceitful…and cunning…and malicious! I hate the man that you call my father!"

Rachel, for the first time that Elizabeth had ever seen, wept. Elizabeth's emotion of anger changed to one of disparagement. She arose, throwing the stained-glass window onto the chair and stormed out of the room. Her trembling had turned more violent and grabbing a nearby vase, threw it onto the floor as she ran out of the house and into the late afternoon air. With her head in a spin, she wandered away, not knowing whither she was going. Off through the lanes, through the churchyard of St Mary's and down a small track that led to who knew where? She didn't care; her world had been devastated! Those people that she had loved …and trusted had, in their own selfish and carnal ways destroyed all that she held most dear; her cherished memories of home, love, kindness and gentleness…all had been taken from her in that instant! Her mother…her uncle, deceiving her 'father,' the man that she had wanted to know. Her mind was in total turmoil as she approached a clearing in the woods; there before her was a small lake…a lake around which grew no trees. To her right was an old, deserted house. Her violent emotions abated somewhat with the curiosity before her. She turned to her right and strode up the steps to the front door, which was partly open, but stopped in her tracks when she saw the wooden flooring in front of the door splintered and broken.

Elizabeth stepped to the side of the gaping hole and found that she could just reach the open door. Sliding her body by the wall and keeping an eye on her feet, so as not to fall, she reached the handle and pulled herself in. Suddenly, a myriad of thoughts went through her mind as she gazed into the unkempt and filthy room. One thought, in particular needed an answer and she realised that she had to see her mother…immediately. Dashing back the way that she had come, she reached the front door as the evening candles were being lit. Rachel was in a distressed state and could not conceal her emotion as Elizabeth walked in.

"Mama…when was I born?"

Sobbing, Rachel took several moments before she was composed enough to reply.

"You know when…September, the sixth of September, sixteen ninety-six."

"When did my 'father' die?"

"To which father are you referring…your real father, or the man that you believed to be your father?"

"Your husband…Thomas Pengelly."

"January, January the sixth, sixteen ninety-six…"

"Then he was incapable of fathering me…he was too ill…"

"…Or already gone, Elizabeth…"

"Oh my God…he was dead before you and Uncle John became lovers?"

"Uncle John and I were never lovers…"

"Not lovers! And yet he fathered me? I don't understand!"

"Are you ready to listen, now…ready to calmly and sensibly listen…as a mature woman?"

"…Yes, Mama. I need answers…so, I will listen."

"Your father, Uncle John, met my husband, Thomas Pengelly, many years ago in Italy. They became the closest of friends…almost like blood-brothers, such was their bond. Your father had spent many years on the continent and during his time abroad, lost his wife…a death that he never overcame. Because of his business, my husband was away for many months at a time, but had arranged with your father to meet up when he next returned to these shores. Because of the death of his wife, your father, though having his home in Hampshire, was torn by the bitter memories of their lives together and was loath to return. Thomas encouraged and persuaded your father to remain as our guest for as long as he wished and many a happy day they shared. We were united together in a bond of love and friendship. Your father became my escort and companion during those long months when Thomas was absent, but at no time was there any impropriety…none at all! I loved my husband as deep as any woman can love a man and when he passed…when he passed, I was inconsolable. I needed comfort, real comfort, and your father provided me with that. He held me fast as I bewailed the loss of Thomas…and yet your father felt the loss of Thomas as much as I. It was…and had never been an affair…or an act of lust…we were never lovers, but your father had been without a woman for so many years, the proximity of our bodies together…that…that his natural instinct when in contact became as nature intended; but he felt so guilty afterwards, even though Thomas had asked him to take me as wife when he passed. Your father is as true a friend as there can ever be…and there has never been any union between us since that moment of despair…"

"But why did my father never acknowledge me as his own daughter, mama?"

"He never knew…I led him to believe that you were conceived between husband and wife…"

"…But he must have known with my birth date…?"

"He was absent during my term; he had to away to Hampshire, returning after your birth, and believed the baby to be Thomas's… He cared for you as his friend's child…and that is a true, true friend."

Elizabeth, like her mother, found the succulence of her sadness also displayed, and searched for her sleeve to remove the river of tears falling gently down her cheeks. With a mixture of relief and pathos, the two women embraced as mother and daughter. At last, she found not remorse, but comfort in the tale related to her; but it still did not make sense why her father never knew the truth.

"Mama…why did you not tell my father the truth…surely, it was his right?"

"Yes, it was his right…and it was my encumbrance that I kept the truth from him. Your father felt guilty for our union, but he was consoled with the fact that Thomas had wished for me to be comforted…it was that request from his friend that overcame his guilt; it was momentary. But, should the truth have been known, then he would have had a lifetime feeling culpable. He cared for you as his friend's daughter, but how would he have felt if he had known the truth! He would have seen his guilt every day."

"Mama…I am so sorry for how I treated you; I should have known that you were not as I had fleetingly thought…I should have listened to your explanations."

"Hush, Elizabeth…You had every reason to react as you did…believing, after what I had said, that I was capable of acts of indiscretion and deceit…But there is more that you have not yet heard."

"Mama! I am not sure that I can take any more surprises…Will what you tell me…also shock me? I am just coming to terms that my real father is Uncle John…"

"…Richard…his name is Richard…"

Elizabeth sat at her mother's knee dumbfounded. With her lips slightly apart, she gazed into an abyss…the abyss of her own life. A life so full of warm memories inexorably being torn apart.

"…Richard! Richard? Why did papa change his name to John?"

"What know yea of the Civil War?"

"We have been told at the seminaries that the king was unjustly and brutally murdered at the hand of Cromwell and all those traitors that followed him and his wicked ways."

"I was not even a child during those terrible times, but my father…your grandfather, fought alongside those people that you call traitors…"

"Mama…I had no idea…"

"So, do you think that your grandfather was possibly one of those treacherous bandits that have so maliciously been defamed?"

"I…I…"

"My father, Lieutenant-Colonel Jeremy Baines, fought side by side with Oliver Cromwell. The king, Charles I, was a tyrant and egoist, who used the people of this land as his footstool. To accommodate yet another venture, he raised the people's taxes, even though they were already overtaxed…they could take no more. Whilst he lived in comfort…lavish comfort, I may add, the common folk of this land starved. Yet the pompous and selfish monarch cared for none bar himself, his family and his friends. He was brought to account for his actions and given many an opportunity to recant before that final decision to end his reign and his life was taken. It was no butcher's slaughter…the king had created the chaos and savagery that the war…the people's war, had brought and those 'traitors' as you call them…those heroes of this land were prepared to give their lives for the sake of the land that they loved…truly and really loved. And now we have monarchists again, teaching those in their care the biased untruths that have been dictated to them."

"Mama! You talk almost as a traitor yourself!"

"I am no traitor, nor was your grandfather…nor Oliver Cromwell…nor Richard."

"Richard…my father!"

"Elizabeth, there is no Pengelly blood in your veins; it is Cromwell and Baines…Oliver is your grandfather and Richard is his son…"

If the news that Richard was her father had not been enough of a shock, the information that she was now processing sent Elizabeth Pengelly-Cromwell into a state of numbness. She couldn't speak…she couldn't even digest the enormity of what her mother had just told her! Rachel looked on at her daughter as she sat stupefied on the floor beside her. It took several minutes before Elizabeth found the will to speak.

"Did your husband, Thomas, know of my father's involvement in the war, mama?"

"No. He knew, obviously, that my father had fought for the Roundheads, but where his true allegiance lay, I was not sure…so I kept that information from him."

"But as Richard Cromwell…he must have known…surely?"

"No. Your father travelled under the guise of John Clarke…and that is how Thomas met and knew him. He remained ignorant of Richard's true identity."

"…But how did you find out?"

"Perchance during a visit to Waltham Abbey, I came across this stained-glass window of your grandfather...I worked out the rest; besides, Richard never, ever spoke about his past, or himself, except that he had an estate at Hursley in Hampshire and that his wife had died when he was on his travels."

"Did my father know that you knew his true identity, Mama?"

"Yes, shortly before he died, he confessed to me who he was, but I already knew. It was a burden that he had borne for fifty years and the relief as he told me brought out his emotional vulnerability; fifty years a secret; fifty years in hiding; fifty years a fugitive...now the truth was laid bare and he could for the first time in fifty years relax and live the truth...the chain of fear had been removed...and now he lays at peace in an unmarked tomb."

Elizabeth could control her emotions no more and wept as of one in bereavement. Rachel stroked her daughter's head as it rested in her lap and her sobbing continued.

"You see, Elizabeth...you did meet and know your father...and what a wonderful father he was too!"

"Mama...oh, mama...what a...what a..."

But the tears flooded out any coherence of what Elizabeth wanted to say. Rachel too, now wept...but it wasn't the tears of despair; it was the tears of relief and joy...the truth...the tears of truth.

The shadows of the day had long since gone and the shadows on the walls were those of the flickering candles. How long Elizabeth and Rachel had remained embraced was unknown, but the small flames still flickering, suggested that the night was well-established. With sleeves and skirts dampened from their tears, Elizabeth looked up at her mother, still stroking her hair and smiling.

"What was my father really like, Mama?"

"You knew him as he really was; kind, gentle and wise, very wise...but perhaps there were parts that you never knew...his courage and selflessness. At one time, he was the most powerful man in England...and probably could have remained so, but relinquished all that to avoid another bloody war. The carnage that his father endured, had torn England apart and he was selfless enough to forsake his position and keep the country and people that he loved and cared for at peace. Elizabeth...he should have been a king...his was a true passion and belief in his fellow man and was concerned deeply for all those under his care...as you know."

"...Then, beneath that tomb that has no name...there lies my father!?"

"Yes, Elizabeth, your father lies at rest beneath that tomb."

Taking to her bed, Elizabeth lay in the dark thinking of that wonderful man who was… no, who *is* her father. He may not be able to enfold her anymore, but he will never be seen in anything but the present; he *is*…and *will always* be her father. With memories now warmly embraced, she pictured all those times that she remembered being with him and her mother…perhaps the Shropshire memories being amongst her favourite; the view on top of the Wrekin; thrown onto the hay waggon; the harvest celebrations; drinking cider; dancing with Robyn…how she wished that she had danced with her father…. But she remembered seeing her mother take his hand and how she had looked at him on that most perfect of evenings. The shocks of the day and the contentment that she now felt, sent Elizabeth Cromwell into the land of dreams. The torment and then the calm raised voices in her head as of one reciting; almost as a chant:

I kissed the waves and watched them cry as the seagulls screeched a sad farewell;

The hillside top of green and white bade me to stay no more.
I followed in the furrow deep, as the grass bent before my fall
And lay there as the day turned night and hid me from myself.
Seek no more the wind then cried, as sadder will yea yet become,
The night turned day…the day turned night as truth and lies intertwined.
In the rain, in the shine, I walked on as one now found…
But lost was I and did not know and once more on that soil did fall.
The voice of truth was never heard as the lies unwound and spake the most…
The lies, the lies those dreadful lies that keep the truth from ears and minds.
'Neath the sod, that cold, cold clay, the corpse lies still as before…
But the heart beats on as once so young and from the grave will rise once more.

She awoke to the sound of the cockerel.

"Did you love my father, Mama?"

"Yes, I loved Richard…as a friend; as one who loves a brother."

"But I remembered how you took his hand and gazed at him when I was dancing…did you love, I mean really love my father, Mama?"

Rachel needed time to reflect. Her answer had to be honest; yet she needed her daughter to see the truth, the absolute truth, but the words needed to be exact.

"I loved Thomas, even until his passing, and yet, I loved Richard as a friend. When those times happed that he was absent, I was most disturbed…yet I knew

173

it was his companionship that I missed…his wit, his conversation, his company. Thomas, was the man who had stolen my heart and while he lived, it was he that I loved as a woman loves a man. After your birth, I began to see in a different light the man who committed to his care the daughter that I loved. He made no demands and was always there to care for us. When I saw you dancing, it was one of the happiest times that I can remember since Thomas's passing and, as I gazed at Richard, I knew that I had fallen in love again…he was no longer a friend… he was the man that I loved."

"Mama…oh, mama…"

"Now, Elizabeth, I have one more surprise for you…"

"Oh no, mama…I cannot take any more!"

"Hush, Elizabeth…this is a surprise that will not shock…but I hope that you will welcome with open arms…"

"Promise me that it will not be like yesterday…my heart could not take another day of revelations!"

Pushing a box towards her daughter, Rachel smiled.

"Open the box, Elizabeth…this is the surprise that I had planned to give you…"

Removing the ribbon and paper, Elizabeth tentatively opened the box. Inside was a key.

"Is this a key to Pandora's Box, Mama?"

"No, it is the key to your independence. You are to become a woman and will have your own life and your own independence…and your own home."

"A home…My home?"

"Yes, your own home."

"Where is my own home, Mama?"

"Well, that will be for you to decide."

"But why can't I stay here, with you?"

"When I am gone, this will be Thomas's home-father deemed it in his will; he knew not of you, otherwise provisions would have been made."

"But brother Thomas will ensure that I am cared for?"

"Of that, I am certain, but you will be dependent upon your brother. With this key, you will place no burden on anyone else and live your life as you wish."

"Oh, Mama…"

"…And I have ensured that you will have enough fiscal means to support yourself; you will need no man, save for the man that you love…"

Elizabeth took both of her mother's hands and stared into her mother's eyes. "Thank you, mama…thank you."

As she held her mother, a thought entered her mind.

"Mama, I think that I know the house that I want. When I stormed out yesterday, I came across an old deserted house near the church."

"Yes, I know of it; both your father and Thomas mentioned this…I believe it has some historical merit. Though Richard never spoke of it, I believe it had quite an effect upon him…and Thomas believed that there was some association with Cardinal Wolsey."

"It is deserted and needs complete repair, but it has a certain appeal…and I would be but ten minutes' walk from you, here…Mama, what do you say?"

"Well, certainly if you have set your heart upon it…but we would have to search for the owner and he may not be willing to sell…though, upon reflection, if what Thomas told me is true, then there may not be an owner, save that of the Crown…hence the neglect. If that is the case, then the Crown would be only too willing to sell and help boost the exchequer. I believe that your brother may have some influence in these quarters…I shall contact him forthwith."

"And this window…the portrait of my grandfather will be seen by everybody who comes to visit…it will be a shrine to his memory…"

With hope and joy in her heart, Elizabeth walked through the churchyard of St Mary's and approached an unmarked tomb. She lay the small bouquet of flowers that she had gathered and kneeling down, placed them on the headstone.

"…Uncle John, it is I, Elizabeth. I have news for you that, I believe, you are unaware…I am Elizabeth, your daughter. Mama told me yesterday and I now know what a wonderful person lies here, beneath this soil. Papa, papa…oh, how I love that sound! It makes me so proud to have known you and now I can see just how much you have sacrificed and suffered for this land…for England, the land that you loved.

Do you remember our time with cousin Dudley…? That surely was the happiest time in my life…and I remember how mama looked at you…. Do you know that she loved you…not as a sister, or a friend, but as a woman? Yes, she loved you as much as I love you now. Though you lie beneath this soil, I know that your heart grows young, and one day you will enfold me again in your young, strong arms. Until that time comes to pass, papa, your memory will never die…you will always live; you will live in my thoughts, my dreams, my awakening, my sleeping…and should it be deemed that I shall have children, then they too will know of the greatness of their grandfather. Be not sad… one day we shall be as one…one day when you are young again."

Goff's Lane

Chapter 18

On 15 February 1957, three years after the fire had devastated our house, we left Lordship Road and moved to a fairly new terraced house in Goff's Lane (No. 5). It was a Friday and the day was brisk. I was 8-years old and took the bus fare that my mum gave me. I found it a little worrying, as the bus fare to school was $1^{1/2}$d (old pence) and the fare to the new bus stop, which was two stops further on, was 2d. I was worried, as my mum had given me the exact fare and if she had got it wrong, I didn't know what I would do. I was excited to be living in a new home and so grateful to be leaving that fearful house in Lordship Road. Perhaps, not the most popular of pupils amongst the teaching staff, I was quite upset at the reply that my form teacher, Miss Rogers gave me:

"Miss, we are moving house today, Miss."

"Oh, that's good news, Ian. Will you be moving to a new school?"

"No, Miss."

"Oh…what a shame."

In those days, teachers were allowed to give minor corporal punishment, which the sadistic and narcissistic Miss Rogers seemed to relish in-especially with me, as I would regularly have a transparent, plastic ruler wacked over my knuckles. However, an equally, perhaps even more so, naughty boy, Brian Boys, would be sat upon her knee, whilst she tickled him. Brian had blue eyes (like me), blonde hair (unlike me) and an angelic face (unlike me), which allowed him to get away with the same misdemeanours that got me into trouble; especially as we were in the same gang…*his* gang.

Upon reflection, I am amazed that an 8-years-old boy was given bus fare and had to make his own way to and from school! But then again, mum couldn't drive and the only car that we had, my dad needed for his job. Even though people would be aghast at the concept of such a scenario today, it seemed quite normal to me at the time.

At that time, the distance between Lordship Road and Goff's Lane seemed to be vast; actually, it wasn't. I didn't know at the time that there were short cuts, but later realised that, as the crow flies, Lordship Road to our house in Goff's Lane was actually the same distance from Lordship Road to Cheshunt Great House. In fact, we now lived only about 400 yards from the manor, and I could just see the Great House from my bedroom window.

A new boy from Scotland joined our class, and though we weren't friends when I lived in Lordship Road, when we lived in Goff's Lane, I found out that our back garden gates almost touched one another. As a result, we became friends (and remain so to this day, even after 64-years) and it was his mum who walked her children to school, with me alongside, using the shortcut that made taking the bus unnecessary. This shortcut passed another junior school, Dewhurst St Mary's, but a short way behind Dewhurst St Mary's was a well-established house, *The Old Parsonage*. Though I had no concept at the time, I was living alongside some deep-rooted British history.

Living in our new home, I did not suffer the terrible and frightening dreams and experiences that I had in Lordship Road. Here, for the first time I could actually relax and live a life free from the influences of the unknown and unseen. Whether my former residence was the cause or not, I don't know, but I became fascinated by the things not of this world and took to reading books about the supernatural. Both my parents were staunch Methodists and Sundays were held in strict accordance with the teachings and beliefs within this religion. The Sabbath was treated with respect and no merrymaking was permitted on the *Lord's Day* – I wasn't even allowed out to play in the garden, and the only excuse that I could give for being outside, was to cut the lawn. Though Saturdays were fun, the onset of Saturday evening heralded twenty-four hours of shear boredom. I took to reading the bible, as well as the compulsory trip to church, and began to query the authenticity of the *Holy Book* before me. I started to question the inconsistencies and apparent contradictions in this revered book and slowly started to turn away from the beliefs and upbringing that my parents had fought to instil in me.

The thing is, I wanted to believe in Jesus; life would have been so much easier, as death would mean the chance of life; but to disbelieve, meant that life was finite, frail…and terminal. Theirs was unshakeable belief, mine was unshakeable doubt. The concept of Jesus, I still hold dear, but the divination of this man is the area from which I digress.

Though it began when still at junior school (Burleigh, in Blindman's Lane), because of school friendships, I started to venture towards Lordship Road and beyond into the Bury Green estate. Quite neatly laid out, most of the estate was made up of social housing. At the same time, Harry Webb (known globally as Cliff Richard) and a few of the Shadows, lived on the estate, but I was too young to appreciate his potential stardom status, albeit that we went to the same school (Cheshunt Secondary Modern). At the very top of the estate, the housing ended and the tarmacadamed road led into an unkempt, potted and unadopted mud lane. Overhanging trees grew on either side of the lane and with a few school friends, we made our way slowly down the lane into unknown territory. Though the conversation was jolly and lively, as you would expect from a group of 10-year-olds, I did not feel comfortable with the course that we had chosen; and if it hadn't been for their company, I would not have ventured beyond the end of the constructed road. However, we continued until there was a clearing and sunlight shone through the overhanging climbers and branches. To the right was a stagnant swamp and try as we may, we could not venture farther than about twenty yards, as our shoes became bogged-down in the squelching mud. Making our way back to the track, we turned to our right and continued on, but the joviality had stopped. It was as though all of us felt some kind of trepidation, but were not willing to share this sense of foreboding with the others.

Suddenly, we came across a monument in the depths of the woods. I did not know it then, but discovered soon after that it was *Temple Bar*. The building was heavily covered in overhanging branches, ivy and other undergrowth and climbers. It did not at all resemble the magnificent monument built by Wren and standing proud in the heart of London for 200 years. Heavy, solid, wooden doors barred the way into whatever secrets lay behind those great gates, but above the doors were spikes. We stood there fascinated. How was it possible? What sense was it to place an arched, stone monument in the middle of nowhere? We were at the right age for discovery, but the wrong age to appreciate and understand this magnificent piece of history before us. It was just weird. We went up to the gate and banged on the solid door, demanding to be let in. The monument was obviously old and so we mimicked mediaeval characters in our encounter with this gateway to who-knew-where? I didn't mention this to the others, but after my first knock on the wood, I only pretended to knock afterwards, as I did not like at all the sensation of the feel of the door. As entry through this arched gateway was impossible, we tried to clamber to the sides, but the thicket was just too dense; it was almost like *Sleeping Beauty*, where the prince tried to cut his way through the impenetrable undergrowth, only to find that as he moved on, the woods closed in behind him. With this thought in mind, I grew scared and moved away from the great door into the free, open space directly before the arch, but I wasn't the only one; the others moved back with me.

"No point going in there; no way we can get through."

"Yeah, rubbish door!"

We laughed, but I could feel an unease with the others too. No one wanted to be the first to admit that he was frightened and felt uneasy with the strange structure before him.

"Wonder what it is?"

"Yeah, makes no sense; why put a silly door here…in the middle of nowhere?"

"Spooky, though…"

"Yeah, spooky."

"I bet it goes into an enchanted forest and…"

"Come on, you've grown out of that namby-pamby stuff…all right for girls and babies, but not us."

"Well, explain it then?"

"It's just a gate going into someone's garden…innit."

"Garden? Here?"

"Look, I have no idea; it was just a suggestion…'is all."

"I like the idea of an enchanted forest behind…whatever, even if it be just for girls and babies."

"Yeah, well…"

And with that, relieved, we turned around and made our way back to Bury Green.

Sometime later, it was in June, a fair came to Cheshunt and made its base in the playing fields about 200 yards from our house, in Goff's Lane. This was the era of the *Teddy Boys*, and these thugs were the precursors to the future *Mods*, *Rockers* and *punks*, of which my generation should be ashamed. I walked in fear, as once espied, you couldn't be certain that you would get home without being ruffled and bruised, as this seemed to be the favourite pastime of these hooligans. The generation that had bred these contemptuous teenagers had served in, and returned from, the most catastrophic war the world had ever seen and the freedom that their offspring had was a surprise; one would have expected a cohort of polite and respectful adolescents after what their parents had had to face.

This was the late 50s and the music from the fair was exciting and enticing. Under the sound of '*that'll be the day*' and other rock and roll songs, I rode the dodgems paying with the mediocre pocket money that my mum and dad gave me each week. Though the riffle range and other side shows added to the *fun of the fair*, it was always the rides that thrilled me the most. I had just won a goldfish from a side-stall, and was ecstatic with my prize. Still with the pounding music in the air, taking my 'winnings,' I started to leave the fair, only to be confronted by a group, with their greased-back hair, drape jackets, drain-pipe trousers and winkle pickers…the uniforms worn by the mafia of our time.

"Where you goin', mate?"

"Home."

"Nah, you ain't goin' 'ome…you're staying with us."

"No, I'm going home."

All stood where they were, with cigarettes hanging from the corner of their mouths, like James Dean, as though they'd practiced this macho image many times before. With the flick of the back of his hand on my head, the red-draped jacket lout said, with a sardonic smile:

"Nah…perhaps you didn't hear us too well, runt; we said you are staying with us."

I was now surrounded by five thugs, who prevented me from making any kind of escape. A few other people looked on, but the human reaction of self-preservation took precedence and they moved away from the prey that these predators had secured. I looked up and there before me was Cheshunt Great House; ominous, secure, solid and safe; which I was not, right now. It somehow helped distract me from the precarious position that I was in. And here, within the once grand, hallowed and eloquent gardens and land of one of England's great historical figures, stood a brash and noisy fair with the bullies of this era. How 400 years had changed the ground that I now stood upon?

"What's this…been fishin'! Ha, ha, ha…"

And the other morons joined in the laughter that nobody even them found funny; it was their means of scaring and threatening people, like me; a pretend façade. With that, a violent hand pushed me on the shoulder, whilst another equally violent hand snatched my prize.

"Oi…leave 'im alone."

183

A solitary voice called to my defence above the rock and roll permeating all around.

"You want some of this, dad?"

My defender's voice spoke no more and disappeared into the throng.

"'Ere Matty, you want 'is fish?"

"Yeah, I fancy some fish an' chips an all…"

"Come on, share it around, Matty…"

And with that, they chucked the bag with the goldfish amongst themselves, but I knew well before it happened what the outcome would be. With a splodge, the bag was thrown onto the floor and the water burst out, leaving a small flapping fish to live its final moments amongst these hooligans of our society. Their raucous guffawing summarised the level of intellect that stood towering before me. These banes of our community would somehow be eventually humbled into the reality of life and the need to survive…or end up serving at Her Majesty's pleasure. I was frightened, but the emotion that ruled at that moment was something else. I was so upset that I couldn't take home my prize and show my mum and dad what I had won at the fair; it was the emotion of pride…being proud of what I had achieved. I saw a weakness in their attack as they pursued their superficial chortling; they had taken their eyes from me and, as though they were looking around for some kind of applause at their ultimate crime, I forced my way through the defenceless gap between two drape jackets and freedom…well, almost. Pushing my way through, ruffled the two teddy boys I had squeezed between and they turned and chased after me.

"You little sod!"

Being smokers and probably prone to very little exercise, I was, at first able to dash ahead, especially as I was quite a sprinter. I looked behind, and one of them had given up, bending and wheezing; the other however, was a fast sprinter and, throwing his cigarette down, burst after me. I was but seventy-yards from my house, but a thought occurred to me as I was running for my life, that if I made it home, the thug would know where I lived and perhaps bring his mates to break a few windows and cause disruption to our front garden. To my right, ten yards ahead, was the service road that led to the backs of all our houses. He was catching up with every step and I knew that the vandal behind would overtake me before I could reach safety. Just before I reached the service road, I slowed down to allow my pursuer to catch up with me and, as he was in arms reach, I stopped and bent down. Over he went, knocking me down, but his momentum sent him into a headlong spin and he came down on the pavement with a thud. I was sure that he was injured, but I wasn't taking any chances and sped along the service road, only to see him get up and continue the chase. However, he had been injured and started to hobble and I knew that I had beaten him! After thirty yards, the service road had a bend, that then led up to our back garden. At the bend, I could see the fair 70 yards away, but with a fence across the end of the service road, made access impassable without scaling the barrier. I stopped, pulled down my shorts and waved my bum at him.

"You little sod; I'm gonna get you!"

"Yeah, perhaps…but not today, teddy boy!"

Though I had lost my prize from the fair, I did feel quite euphoric having escaped and even beaten one of the ruffians. I walked into our back garden feeling quite content.

The next time that I ventured towards *Temple Bar*, a year or so later, I went with different friends; I had moved into senior school and was now with a group that had never experienced this neck of the estate by the woods. Perhaps, I was a bit more brazen, after all, not only had I made this journey before and knew how the land lay, I was also a bit older and my voice had started to break; I was getting to the stage of life, when being brash and not showing fear, were necessary requirements if one wished to secure and maintain street credibility. It was called youth; the era that most adults detest. The day was overcast, but pleasantly mild and I decided that I would pass my old house in Lordship Road. I had, with recent developments and the building of a school just outside St Mary's Church, found a route that avoided the main road towards Bury Green. I stopped outside 20A and the front gate was open, allowing me to see the stained-glass window of Oliver Cromwell that had fascinated me when I had lived here. Though this part of the house and grounds felt safe, I remembered the other side where I had felt unsafe and terrified. I recalled my feelings of dread at being alone in this house; of the times when I had been so scared of the unexplained happenings, phantoms and dreams. I recollected my first moment of being frightened…the jumping tree; a thought that I tried to dismiss as fantasy, but believed it to be so true. A myriad of thoughts flew through my brain in those few moments of reminiscing my previous life here and I was so glad, so relieved, that I didn't have to walk through that front door anymore.

"Ian James…Well, bugger me."

I turned around.

"Mickey…Mickey?"

Yeah, what you doin' here…thought you'd moved on. Missing the old times?"

It was Michael Soall…five years older than me. He was the street gang's leader. I always looked up to him, though I had been too young and insignificant to be part of his gang. Being so young at the time, he looked out for me and if anyone threatened me, Michael stood up to them.

"Just passin'. Goin' on to Bury Green…see some mates. What about you…what you doin'?"

Michael had left the Secondary Modern early and had taken up a job as an apprentice mechanic in a cycle repair shop. He was also wearing a yellow drape jacket, but was not one of the thugs that I had encountered at the fair the year before. With both the age difference and my absence from the street, there was little else to talk about, but just before parting he asked:

"You still at Burleigh?"

"Nah, at the Secondary Modern, now."

"Oh…watch out for Miller; he's a kiddie fiddler."

I did not understand what a *kiddie fiddler* was. However, I did eventually find out.

"Oh, ok; I'll be careful."

And with that we said our goodbyes. However, I was still impressed with Michael Soall; he epitomised the guy that a young male teenager would idolise.

I walked to the beginning of the Bury Green Estate and met up with the friends, as arranged. We slowly meandered through the estate and, unlike the year before, the conversation was mainly about girls, football and music; the trivialities of childhood, were now a thing of the past. At the far end of Bury Green, we began our stroll along the mud track, and though less intense than before, I still felt uneasy as we made our way through the overhanging trees. This time, there was no bright sunlight piercing through the leaves and branches to brighten the gloomy wood and track. As we descended a gentle slope in the lane, we saw ahead, a police car and a group of people scouring through the quagmire that I had been through the year previously. A feeling of dread immediately came over me and I started to tremble.

"What's that?"

"Police."

"Yeah, but what they doin'?"

186

"Looks like they're searchin'."

"What they searchin' for, though?"

"My dad said that a girl was missin' and had been murdered."

"Murdered…That's like when…you know…?"

"Yeah, killed."

"Oh, that's 'orrible."

"Yeah, I know…"

We continued onwards talking about the police searching the woods for a dead girl. Then, in front of us, almost completely hidden by climbers and tree branches, was the monument.

"What is that?"

"My dad says that's *Temple Bar*."

"*Temple Bar*…isn't that a place in London?"

"Yeah, me dad says that they brought it 'ere hundreds of years ago…you know, keep it hidden."

"Why keep it hidden?"

"Oh, 'e wasn't sure, but said it was used to keep traitors 'eads an all. See them spikes on top of the gates…well they cut off peoples 'eads and stuck 'em up on them spikes."

"Ooh…'ow horrible. Your dad sure knows a lot, then dun' 'e."

"Yeah, 'e's good with stuff like that…knows a lot, me dad."

I gazed up at this grisly piece of our history and began to understand why I had felt such a revulsion before. I must have sensed its past even though I had never heard of *Temple Bar*; but the fact that it had been used as a traitor's deterrent was in its own right, terrifying.

"Me dad says it was built by *Wren*."

"What, a bird?"

"Nah, 'e was some kind of builder, you know, durin' King 'Enry."

"What the 'ead chopper."

"Yeah, 'im."

"Oh…"

"Come on, me mum said that I 'ad to be 'ome by six for me tea."

"Yeah, mine too."

With that, we turned around and made our way back up the track towards Bury Green. We again passed the police car, but any evidence of a search was hidden from our view by the thick coppice. I couldn't help but wonder if they uncovered the dead girl…if there was a dead girl, that is.

Puberty had certainly taken hold of me in a big way. I had become captivated by the girls in my year; they had taken on a new awareness that seemed to be equally, if not superior, to my interest in football and the other boys that I hung around with. We had entered into the athletic and cricket season for the final term, before our summer break. The deputy headmaster, Mr Miller, who to me, resembled somewhat Stirling Moss, the racing driver with his small moustache, appeared to be an enthusiastic sport's teacher and often would take us boys for whatever sport was being practiced at the time. It hadn't occurred to me during the autumn term, when, on one Saturday after a practice rugby session, Mr Miller said that we could take our showers in the girls changing rooms, as these had the luxury of individual cubicles, rather than the long corridor that we had in the boys changing rooms. This was a thrill indeed and we relished in this new found freedom. Ultimately, there remained just the three of us and Mr Miller, who was showering in one of the cubicles. Whatever the reason, it ended up with him playacting and holding us against the shower as he threatened to turn on the cold tap. I thought no more about it until, in this final summer term, whilst in class waiting for Mr Salmon our maths teacher to arrive, Paul Boswell turned to me and Steve Letts and said:

"Miller's a homo."

"A *homo*! No, he isn't."

"He is…listen; when we finished cricket, he got me into Duffel's little office and shut the door. He then took down my shorts and started to suck my cock."

"Paul…don't be stupid; he didn't do that!"

"He did, I tell you, I'm not lying…he sucked my cock. He's a homo."

Mr Salmon walked in and we started the lesson. Paul mentioned it again during our lunch break and reminded me of the shower session the previous autumn.

"He's a homo, I tell you…remember the shower in November; holding us against the tap?"

"Yeah, but that was just fun, Paul…he's not a homo."

"He is!"

Paul would not be convinced otherwise and his persistence did make me wonder if there was any truth in what he said. I also remembered Michael Soall telling me to be watchful with Mr Miller; *kiddie fiddler*, he had said.

This was my first experience of flying…and I loved it! The school had arranged for a school trip during the summer holidays, for the first and second years, to Dinant, in Belgium and we flew from Heathrow to Brussels. I was growing at a fast rate and towered above most of my year; and my voice had finally broken. There was a fairground and we all ventured into the various stalls and side shows, though the more serious rides were too expensive for more than one ride. A few of us stood outside the *Ghost Train* as Mr Miller got on.

"Room for one, if you want?"

"Me, sir, me, sir…" we all shouted, with our hands up. Mr Miller selected me and off we went. Once inside the tunnel, he put his arm around me.

"Scared, Ian?"

I wasn't but told him that I was and he hugged me tightly. I did not like this contact at all, but said nothing. They train slowly climbed up to another level and we approached a door that led back outside to the viewing public. It dawned upon me as the door opened, that he withdrew his arm as we waved to my classmates down below. Once again, he put his arm around me as we returned through another door and back into the dark. After that, I became wary of him as he had made physical contact with me and it had made me feel uncomfortable.

I awoke suddenly, aware that someone was beside me. It was Mr Miller. We were staying in some kind of boarding school that was vacant for the summer break and all the 'rooms' were composed of individual cubicles, sharing a common ceiling. It was the last morning and, though the light was shining through my window, I knew it was early. I felt his hand inside my pyjamas and resting on my penis.

"Have you had a nice holiday, Ian?"

"Yes, sir…thank you."

"That's a nice willy."

And with that, he started stroking my penis, which I found repugnant. He pulled back the sheets and told me to get out of bed. It hadn't occurred to me, but I realised he was whispering, probably so he didn't wake the others.

"Let's go to the toilet and finish off…"

"I'm tired, sir, and want to go back to bed."

I obviously spoke too loudly and he pushed his fingers to his lips.

"Shh, ok…ok, back you go."

And he left. Then all the memories came flooding in…he was a *homo*, as Paul had said…and a *kiddie fiddler*, as Mikey Soall had said; and yet, I didn't think to report it…I was too young to really appreciate what had just happened. Though I was an adolescent, I was still a naive kid emotionally and, as far as I was concerned, what had occurred was normal in the adult world; after all, I had been subjected to minor corporal punishment from Miss Rogers's plastic ruler and smacked repeatedly with a slipper in front of the class by Mr Hopkirk; it's just what teachers did…it was normal, even though I didn't like it.

After returning to school for the new term as a second-year student, I didn't see Mr Miller and found out sometime later that he was no longer at our school. Whether he had been dismissed, or moved on to pastures new to try his paedophilic practices elsewhere, I never knew. I became aware of another teacher, Mr Bates, commonly known by us pupils as *Basher Bates*. Rumour had it that he kept a cane up his sleeve and, I must say, he did walk with a very stiff arm. However, his reputation preceded him and he always looked fierce, never smiling; no one messed with *Basher*. Though it didn't occur until several years later, after I had left school, I was told that the head sports master, Mr Pat Duffel, had been sacked for kissing and embracing a sixteen-year-old girl in the very office that Paul had been molested. It appears that the abuse of children may not just have been confined to the Catholic and other religious sects of this era; it may have been more rampant than will ever be known.

I had always loved cycling and one Christmas in 1962, my parents bought me a *Blue Streak* bicycle. Whenever I could, I would go somewhere for a ride and often would haunt the lanes of Hertfordshire, sometimes venturing as far as Hatfield during school summer holidays. I did not like to backtrack and would try and find complete circuits, if possible. It was September and with the nights drawing in, I was somewhat restricted during a school-week with routes that would please me. Though the road was an unmade, pot-holed, mud track, I knew that eventually it would join the tarmacadamed road at Bullsmore Lane, leading to Enfield Chase, and from there I could cycle down the A10 and back home to Goff's Lane. With no homework one evening and the sun as enticing as ever, I jumped onto my bike and began the trip, which I felt that I could complete within a couple of hours, bringing me home just before dark. I cycled up Dark Lane and at the top end of Bury Green started the more precarious route, trying to avoid the pot-holes, but was determined not to stop and walk. I knew the route that I had taken several times previously with friends, but felt confident on my bike. I passed the track where a few years ago I had seen the police scouring the wood and rode on, before arriving at *Temple Bar*.

This time, I wasn't afraid, even though alone. However, I did not like this spot, though I knew of no logical reason why this should be. Time was going to be short to get home before dark and I knew that I would still make it, so I stopped outside the gates and dismounted. I rested my bike against some bracken and ran my fingers over the rough and gnarled wood. Knowing a little about the story of *Temple Bar*, I began to appreciate its significance to our own history, but still for the life of me was unable to understand why it was here, hidden in the woods, covered in bracken, ivy and all kinds of creepers. I rested my face against the solid, wooden gates and then it happened! As though being drawn into the very experiences of the doors themselves, I was transported into the world of those barbaric times and heard the groans of the headless corpses as their heads were plunged into the spikes, whilst the jeers of the mob celebrated another traitor's fate. I was petrified and, looking up, could swear that I almost saw the spiked head in its agonised death throes looking down. I grabbed my bike from the bracken and rode like I had never ridden before, passing through the pot-holes, regardless of the outcome...I just had to leave this wood. Then, there in the distance, was the safe, tarmacadamed road of Bullsmore Lane. It was the last time that I ever visited *Temple Bar*.

Chapter 19

I had just left school; it was 1965 and I had entered the world of adults, as I started to serve my five-year apprenticeship as a trainee chemist. It was too early to have lost contact with my old school friends, and even though our paths had started to diverge, I had arranged to meet up with them one September evening by the swings in the playing fields opposite Cheshunt Great House. There were four of us; Dennis Spooner, Louis Deadman, David Basford and me. David had grown a beard, that didn't seem to match the colour of his hair and, as I had been unaccustomed to him with hair on his face, in my opinion, didn't suit him.

"What's this!"

"Facial hair-something you don't seem to be able to grow!"

The sniggers started

"It's more like a lavatory brush."

David smiled as the rest of us roared with laughter.

"Hey, Dave…my toilet's blocked; you wouldn't come around and clean it out, would you?"

"Bollocks!"

David laughed along with us, even though I sensed that he may have been a bit hurt by our playful comments.

"Let's see you grow one then!"

"Nah, my toilet's good, thanks, Dave…and the girls seem to prefer the smooth skin. Smoke?"

I handed around the cigarettes and we drew on them as we idled away the September evening lolling about on the swings. In the distance, some 300 yards away, Cheshunt Great House faced us.

"Fancy a stroll?"

"Yeah, where too?"

"Up there," I said pointing ahead.

We meandered up to Goff's Lane, just as a 242-bus passed on its way to South Mimms. Crossing over, we came to the fence preventing further progress.

"You been in there, before?"

"Nah...You?"

"Yeah, long time ago?"

"How d'you get in, then?"

"Follow the brook to the end of the field; there's a hole in the fence there."

We followed Louis and, sure enough, the fence appeared to be broken and we walked over to Cheshunt Great House. Though this was a heritage site and, probably, the most important in Cheshunt, it represented an ugly building, that had no appeal at all to us teenagers. We had absolutely no concept of its historical worth; it was just an...ugly building.

"You know this place is haunted, don't you?"

"Haunted...rubbish! You've been reading too many spooky stories, Louis; just trying to scare us, that's all."

"Nah, it's true. Been told. Last century, they found two skeletons in the cellar...you can check for yourself."

"Ok, but haunted...that's a bit far-fetched."

"I didn't make it up, you know; this house has a reputation for being haunted..."

"Haunted by who, then?"

"By ghosts, of course; who else haunts places?"

"How did you get in then, Louis?"

"Broken window round the back."

We walked around the back and, after some fumbling, found a small broken pane.

"You couldn't have got in there, Louis; far too small."

"They must have repaired it-it wasn't this window."

But the pane was loose and though hardly touching it, it gave way and came out into Louis's hand. The window latch was now accessible and we climbed in. The inside seemed to have been neglected and sections of plaster had broken from the walls. There was no evidence of the grandeur that this house once boasted. We walked into a massive, deserted room, in which the were no furnishings, nor furniture, save for some old chairs and a wooden table. Without any reason, the house had an eerie feel about it and felt quite cool, despite the warmth from outside.

"Come on, let's go…there's nothing here."

"No…I want to explore; let's go upstairs and look at the playing fields from there."

"Ok."

Access to the staircase was at the far end, in another adjoining room. The stairs were sturdy and solid and made of a dark wood. As we climbed, Dennis held me back.

"What's that?"

"What?"

"Ha, ha, ha…"

"Oh, very funny, let Louis get us all on edge and then you jump on the band waggon!"

"No…listen; everyone, listen!"

We all held our breath and remained quiet, listening as intently as we could. It could not be denied, there was the unmistakeable sound of voices upstairs; they were faint, but nevertheless audible…almost like children's voices. Louis's pep talk, and Dennis's antics had got me on edge and I could tell that David wasn't relaxed either. Our minds had been influenced of spectral happenings by our very presence in this house and I wanted to leave.

"Come on, let's go…"

"Scared of ghosts, Ian?"

The snide remark hurt, but the truth be known, I was scared…and I wanted to leave. Louis continued to climb the stairs and then there was an almighty crash. Suddenly, twelve-years after I first saw him, there he was running down the stairs.

"Fire, fire…get out, get out!"

The torso and legs ran past me and disappeared at the bottom of the stairs. I ran like mad with the others joining me as fast as they could; even Louis seemed perturbed now. Almost diving through the open window and into the field outside, the others followed suit, as the sun was dipping below the trees in the distance.

"What was that?"

"Just a bang, but I'd rather not find out…after all, we're not supposed to be here; we are trespassing."

"No not that…those legs running down the stairs."

"What legs?"

"Yeah, what legs, Ian? Are you spooked up, or summat?"

"The legs…legs, did you not see them…they ran past you Louis and you Dennis!"

David looked on worried, but both Louis and Dennis looked at each other and then at me as though I had fabricated the whole façade.

"Louis, no more talk of hauntings and ghosts, look what you've done to Ian! He's spooked and you've sent his imagination into worlds of fantasy. Ian, there are no ghosts and no phantom legs, it was just the crash upstairs…probably those kids that we heard, that's all."

I was still trembling as I made my way home, having left the others to go back to their homes, as well. But I knew what would happen; the forewarning had been told.

I watched Cheshunt Great House burn down from my bedroom window, with crowds of people outside as the sound of the fire engines raced passed my house. The flames leapt into the night sky and cracked loudly as they consumed whatever would continue to fuel them. The next morning, I went to work and though the flames were now absent, the smell of damp, burnt wood reminded me of my experience over eleven-years ago, when the phantom legs had forewarned me of the impending fire taking place at 20A Lordship Road.

Addendum
Cardinal Thomas Wolsey

The son of an Ipswich butcher, he obtained his degree at Oxford University at the age of only fifteen. Whether it was from the inspiration of the proceedings, or merely his own ego, he loved the pomp and ceremony associated with grand events. After his ordination, he eventually became chaplain to King Henry VII, before his meteoric rise in status as Henry VIII's Lord Chancellor and chief minister.

Wolsey was popular with the populace and this ruffled somewhat Henry's vanity. With his successes in diplomacy and performing those duties too tedious for the young king, Wolsey must have felt that he had a free hand in the running of the kingdom, to the point that a portion of the history of England is due to the influence, or even direct involvement, of Thomas Wolsey. Having been close to Henry VII beforehand and being Henry VIII's confidant for nearly twenty years, Wolsey must have felt that he was untouchable and probably started to take the king for granted. At one time, there were mutterings within the court circle whether it was Henry or Wolsey who ran the country. Perhaps, his proximity to the king, together with his arrogance, became the initiators in his fall from grace, as those close to the king, used every opportunity to seed suspicion into Henry's mind as to the genuine motives of the king's advisor.

Wolsey always had divided loyalties between the king and the pope. This conflict of interests was somewhat akin to that of Thomas à Becket and Henry II, over 350 years earlier, both cases ending in the early demise of the holy men. Wolsey was a staunch Catholic, being created as both Archbishop of York (1514) and then as a cardinal in 1515 by Pope Leo X. He accrued vast wealth which he unashamedly and lavishly displayed. This, together with his well-earned position as Henry's advisor, earned him resentment within the nobility of the land. This resentment ultimately led to his downfall, as those aggrieved voices created doubt in the paranoid mind of Henry as to the loyalty of his Chancellor, after his failure to secure an annulment of his marriage to Catherine of Aragon. *Hell, hath no fury like a woman scorned* was true of Anne Boleyn, who had never forgiven Wolsey for his refusal to allow the marriage between her and Henry Percy. Poisoning the mind of Henry that it was really Wolsey and not the pope that had prevented the annulment, the king finally succumbed to the ideas that Wolsey's involvement with Rome took precedence over his loyalty to the king. Finally accused of *praemunire*, effectively reducing the position of the king as head of State to be subservient to the pope and, hence, Rome, the fate of Wolsey was sealed.

Wolsey, towards the end of his life, was obese. Too much ostentatious entertaining had altered the peasant boy into that of a fat and unhealthy man. His death then, and even now, remains an enigma. Knowing that he faced imminent execution, his depression must have antagonised an already insalubrious body to the point of exacerbating whatever maladies he was, unknowingly, infested with. As an extremely religious man, suicide was out of the question. However, murder was not and rumours spread throughout French circles that his death had been orchestrated by, probably, Henry. During his stay in Sheffield Castle under the care of the 4th Earl of Shrewsbury, his otherwise hidden malaises either surfaced naturally, or were quickened by the hand of an unknown third party. Henry, must have been concerned as to what revelations his former chancellor would publicly voice and his death prior to trial would have suited the Tudor king. Though the symptoms displayed by Wolsey shortly before his death have suggested that he died of natural causes, mediaeval potions and natural toxins long lost in the annals of history, may have been equally responsible. Whatever the cause, his pre-trial death was a blessing for both himself and Henry.

Richard Cromwell, Lord Protector of England, Scotland and Ireland

An uncanny resemblance to the stained-glass window at 20A Lordship Road

Despite becoming the most powerful man in the commonwealth, a large part of his life remains a mystery. He was a reluctant leader and during his twenties, never expected to succeed his father, being the third son of Oliver Cromwell. With the death of his two older brothers, the reign of power became his by default, though whether he was nominated by his father to assume the role of Lord Protector also remains a controversial subject, as no written document to that effect exists; some believing that Oliver Cromwell wished for his son-in-law, Charles Fleetwood, to be more suitable for the position. Richard assumed the position of Lord Protector, though almost certainly more by persuasive forces keen to feather their own nests, rather than his own reluctant commitment to the role.

Historically, his family name was well-established and his less aggressive personality would have made him an ideal candidate for those who felt that they could manipulate his decisions to suit their own ends. However, with the army reluctant to accept his authority and a belligerent parliament unwilling to conform to a dictatorship, his term in office was guaranteed to be limited. Had Charles Fleetwood assumed the role of Lord Protector, as has been suggested, then the Republic of Great Britain may have changed the course of global history.

With the restoration of the monarchy, Richard made haste for the continent, never to see his wife and family again. He remained incognito, travelling under various pseudonyms, *John Clarke* being the one that he was associated with mainly. Upon his return to England in 1680, he had befriended a wealthy merchant, Thomas Pengelly, whilst in exile and resided with him, his wife, Rachel and their son, Thomas, both in Finchley and in Cheshunt. It has not been recorded whether Thomas Pengelly ever knew Richard's true identity and it also seems somewhat strange that he would encourage him to share his home with himself and his wife, as a single man, especially as he was absent frequently. Whether there was some kind of familial arrangement, one can only speculate but malicious gossip suggested that young Thomas Pengelly was, in fact, Richard's son. *Pengelly House* at Churchgate in Cheshunt, has been quoted as the residence of Richard Cromwell, but this is unlikely, as Pengelly House was not built until the eighteenth century, after Cromwell's death. It is almost certain that his residence in Cheshunt was at the Parsonage, in Churchgate.

20A Lordship Road

The street party on 2 June 1953, celebrating the coronation of queen Elizabeth II. I am at the 'T' section of the table, next to two girls. This is Lordship Road, a cul-de-sac. Behind us, where the cameraman is, is *The Lordship* wooded ground leading on to the playing fields, which are set in front of Cheshunt Great House. To the left of the table, as we see it, is St Mary's church. The last house on the right of the picture is 20A. Notice that this house is not only taller than all the others, but it is at right angles to them and the road.

My birth house today. I am stood in front of the original door depicting the stained-glass image of Oliver Cromwell, exactly as I remember it. The door has now been moved from the porch entrance to the back. The house numbering has now been changed; 20A is number 23 and 20B is number 25.

Cheshunt Great House After the Fire

The Cheshunt and Waltham Weekly Telegraph

Hertfordshire Archives and Local studies

Built in the fifteenth century, the house was reputed to have been owned by Cardinal Wolsey. It was originally shaped in a quadrangle and had over 40 rooms, including a magnificent banqueting hall. In the 1750s, it was remodelled and encased in red brick. For most of the nineteenth century, it was owned by freemasons. Later, part of it became a museum and visitors were shown the vaulted cellars where some skeletons were found in the 1880s. The stories of ghosts, murders, secret tunnels and bloodstains were legendary.

Author's note: Even immediately after the fire, local rumour was rife that the historical significance of Cheshunt Great House prevented property speculators from using the land for development and that local children had been used to create the damage that ultimately sealed the fate of this heritage site.

Temple Bar at Theobalds Park, Cheshunt

Temple Bar in its magnificence, but not as I remember it covered in overhanging branches, creepers and ivy

In 1976, the Temple Bar Trust was established with the intention of returning the Bar to the Capital. The trustees are drawn from members of the Corporation of London together with others involved in the preservation of the nation's architectural heritage.

In the December meeting of the Court of Common Council 2001, the Corporation of London agreed to fund the return of Temple Bar to the City of London. At a cost of just over £3.0m—funded by the Corporation along with donations from the Temple Bar Trust and several Livery Companies.

In 2003, work began to move Temple Bar back to its new home in the City of London, next to St Paul's Cathedral. Late 2004, the move and restoration were completed.

A Final Irony

In a final irony, the manor of Theobalds, being the place that King Charles I decided upon, and drew up his plans for, the Civil War before riding north to Nottingham (thus incurring the involvement of Oliver Cromwell), ownership then passed, in the late eighteenth century, to one *Oliver Cromwell*, great-grandson of his more famous namesake.

St Mary's Church

Hertfordshire Archives & Local Studies

It is recorded in the Domesday Book, in 1086, that Cheshunt had a priest, and a church is mentioned in documents dating back to at least the twelfth century. In 1331, a chapter of the Augustinian canons was held at "Cheshunt Church," apparently because the abbot of Waltham Abbey at the time was "rebellious."

The present church was built between 1418 and 1448, while Nicholas Dixon was the rector. Although it isn't recorded why the rebuilding took place, it's possible that the church, like many others, had fallen into neglect during the chaos following the Black Death. It may have been at this time that the dedication was changed from St John, the Baptist, which appears in some early documents, to St Mary, the Virgin.

There are many monuments and family vaults, both inside the church and in the churchyard surrounding it, including one for the *Cromwell Family of Cheshunt Park*, descendants of the Lord Protector, as well as memorials to various local families, including the Dewhursts, the Russells, the Dacres the Meux and the Dodsons. The church also contains a memorial to Nicholas Dixon.

Unmarked Tomb at St Mary's Church, Churchgate, Cheshunt

A quote from the current incumbent, Reverend Eugene (January 2021):
There are a number of tombs in the churchyard where the names are not visible
There is a monument on the south side of the churchyard, towards the west end,
without a name
I have also found the brass, which is protected under a rug

If I can be of any further help, please do not hesitate to get in touch
With all good wishes,
Rev Eugene